THE ISLE OF ENNISKERRY

THE ISLE OF ENNISKERRY

Peter Culling

The Book Guild
Sussex, England

First published in Great Britain in 2004 by
The Book Guild Ltd
25 High Street
Lewes, East Sussex
BN7 2LU

Typesetting in Palatino by
Acorn Bookwork, Salisbury, Wiltshire

Printed in Great Britain by
Antony Rowe Ltd, Chippenham, Wiltshire

A catalogue record for this book is available from
The British Library.

ISBN 1 85776 886 8

1

It was one of those sticky, hot, mid-summer days in central London when pollution levels were rising. Three of my colleagues and I had gathered, hoping to spend half an hour or so in a pub near to our workplaces to relax and catch up with each other's news. We found the establishment crowded with a group of city delegates from a nearby convention who were spilling in increasing numbers towards the bar. It was busier than we had bargained for. Nigel had already skilfully negotiated the noisy scramble near the bar where the group members were clearly identified by the triangular sweat patches on their white shirt backs. He now made his way towards us, deftly placing four pints of lager on the table without spilling a drop. We waited for his first grumble.

'You know, it's a pity that we don't work nearer the country. I would prefer a more peaceful watering hole than this.'

'And how do you think you would keep tabs on all that is happening in your office here while you're gadding about in the country?' Ron was quick to ask.

'I suppose you're right,' Nigel replied before he sat down, 'but there must be a better life than this, you know. Sometimes I feel like chucking the whole lot in.'

'Great idea, and what would you do for the old "filthy lucre"?' Ron asked, thinking that it was not a great idea at all.

'OK, I know, I don't think I would have the guts to leave without setting myself up with a new career, and

I'm probably too old to be thinking of that now. I suppose you're right, I'll have to keep my nose to the grindstone and grin and bear it all.'

'You miserable old sod, you don't know how lucky you are,' Graham chipped in. 'Lovely wife and family, big house and all the perks you get from that cushy job, but I know what you mean, I could do with a break myself. You know, get out of the rat race and all that.'

'What we need,' Nigel continued, 'is to win the jackpot on the lottery.'

'We would certainly all like that but I've got a feeling that you wouldn't know how to handle that sort of money even if you did,' Ron stated.

'You bet I would,' Nigel quickly replied with a hint of annoyance, feeling that Ron would put down anything he said, but then Ron issued a further challenge.

'OK then, what would you do with, say, the odd couple of million if it landed in your pocket?'

'Well, I'd buy a brand new top-of-the-range Mercedes and a big house in the country and I'd live the life of a Lord,' Nigel replied.

'You could get your top-of-the-range car and top-of-the-range house with just half a million, but apart from the rest of the money, what would you actually do?' Ron enquired again.

'Well, I'd see the family were not short of a penny and all that.'

'Yes, I know you would. We probably all want to do that. What I mean is, what would you do with your time? Look at the telly, and watch the grass grow? What would you *do*?' Ron persisted.

'I wouldn't need to do anything, would I, with all that money?'

'That's pitiful,' Ron snapped back. 'You might as well continue at work.'

'I'd give up work, that's for sure,' Graham volunteered.

'And how about you, what would you actually do with your new-found freedom?' Ron repeated, seeing that Graham was happy to join in on the same theme and thinking there must be more to owning a fortune than Nigel had offered.

'I'd buy a home in the south of Spain and sit in the sun all day.'

'So, you wouldn't do anything either, that is, other than burn yourself to a cinder.'

'That's right,' Graham said in complete agreement as he sat back, imagining the sun on his face, and took a long swig from his pint.

Ron, now a touch frustrated and a little disappointed, turned to me and asked, 'You're sitting there keeping very quiet, Jim – you haven't told us how you would handle a whole load of money.'

'No,' I replied hesitantly, 'that's because I *have* just won the lottery.'

They all burst out laughing, naturally, all completely disbelieving.

'What, all of ten quid, I suppose, just like I did last year,' one of them tentatively ventured.

'No,' I volunteered quietly, 'something over five million.'

Three pairs of eyes stood out from their sockets, three jaws sagged slightly, giving a rather strange and comical shape to their mouths. For a long moment there was a stunned silence. Oblivious to the raucous chatter in the background, they were all having difficulty in knowing if I was pulling their legs.

Then Ron whispered, 'You're joking.' When I replied that I was not, he leaned forward and conspiratorially said, 'OK, sir, Your Highness, what are you actually going to do with all that dosh?'

'I'm going to buy an island.' I replied calmly, and he,

incredulous, repeated, 'You're going to buy an island?'

'Yes, I'm going to buy an island. It's on the market for about four million and I've put in an offer.'

'But what in heaven's name are you going to do with an island? Where is it? In the Caribbean? By the way, a small point perhaps, but having bought your island, what then? What will you do with it? Sit on it like Graham and soak up the sun all day?'

'It's off the west coast of Scotland. I want to set up a sort of commune, where people like you can do something completely different, where they can work the land or engage in other activities, but be free of bureaucracy and get satisfaction from working for themselves in a healthy environment.'

'Not very sunny there, I should say;' Graham observed.

'Sunny days can be important but they are not on the top of my list,' I answered.

'You're crazy,' Ron said. 'An island maybe, but off Scotland?'

'You've asked a lot of questions but haven't offered your ideas yet. I would be interested in what you would do.' I countered.

'Well, I wish you well, you lucky bugger,' Graham said, 'At least it's the best idea any of us have come up with. But how, in heaven's name, could you come in here and just sit quietly and not go jumping and screaming all over the place? By the way, it must be your round.'

'I did get a bit over the top when I first found out, but after that I started trying to work things out and I found I was getting more serious about wanting to use it wisely. But you're right, it is my round. Would you like to change the order to something stronger perhaps?'

As I walked away to the bar I heard someone say, 'If I was in his shoes I'd need something very much stronger. How could he keep so calm like that?'

4

2

I had never been much of a gambler but, on the spur of the moment, having regularly seen people in the local newsagent filling in their National Lottery forms, I thought I would have a go. It took me a little while to get the idea of filling in the form and I had to scrap the first attempt. I made the little marks quite randomly and paid my five quid to the cashier. That night as I tuned in to the TV, the realisation that my chances were millions to one did not stop me excitedly wondering if I would be a winner. The numbers flashed on to the screen, I looked from paper to TV, then back to the paper, then back again to the TV. I could not believe it, I had not even selected one correct number. Over the following weeks I made a few further half-hearted attempts, but each time I expected to be a loser. On one attempt something cropped up at work and I did not even bother to check the results.

Then, on one memorable day, some two months after my first attempt, I was nonchalantly sitting in front of the TV checking the numbers. As they rolled into that colourful device they use for the selection I realised for once that I had ticked more than one as correct. I was saying out loudly to myself, slowly at first, 'Yes,' and then 'Yes,' again. Then, as the adrenalin began to flow, I became confused as to whether I had ticked one incorrectly because in my increasing excitement I had looked at the same number twice. I questioned whether it was in the third or the fourth line. My eyes were darting backwards and forwards and I realised that I had been shouting, 'Yes,' rather often. I was not sure how many I had got right and as I began to re-check what I had written, the programme ended and I was left bereft of the full list of correct numbers. I was desperate to see them again and again.

It was a strange situation. I thought that I must have won something but I was not sure. In the confusion, my mind was telling me that most, if not all, the numbers in one line were correct. I needed to see those numbers again, but how could I get hold of them? Should I ring someone? No, I thought, that would not be a good idea; the results must be shown again on some other channel. I grabbed the *TV Times* and rapidly ripped through the pages as I frantically tried to find the right place. Yes, there was another TV channel showing them one hour later. Thank goodness. I will never know what happened during that hour other than that I kept looking at the lottery form, becoming more and more confused as to whether my markings indicated anything meaningful or not. When I finally saw the results again I composed myself and wrote them down separately on another piece of paper. I was not going to get into that state again.

The final check confirmed it. I had all the results in one line correct. I sat on the settee exhausted. What should I do now? I read the back of the form and learnt that I would have to make a claim, and did this the following day.

Rightly or wrongly, I decided not to say anything to anyone. I needed more time, much more time, to think this through.

Later, I learnt that it was believed that there were two winners, sharing approximately ten million pounds, and my reeling mind took another leap into the unknown.

I had never craved wealth. I had a good job and income,

my house was paid for, I had savings to cover the usual emergencies. I took holidays abroad each year. I had a pleasant social circle of friends and I was in good health. What else could one wish for? I didn't really want for anything.

Or did I? Perhaps I was not being completely honest with myself. I thought back over the past and realised that after Anne had died in that fateful accident, life had never been so completely fulfilling. I missed her terribly. Perhaps it was time to move on. Perhaps now that I was going to be awarded wealth to a degree I had never imagined, life would not be the same. I should use the money wisely and seek something worthwhile that I could do for society.

What can you buy for five million pounds? Like most of my friends in the pub, I had imagined the usual material things, but as soon as one has rejected the fast car, the big house, the travel-the-world type of activities, the mind has to become much more concentrated. Yes, there would be all the charities begging for help, there were all the poor and starving people in the world. I found that I was asking myself what would a true man of God and a strong faith do. Would he give it all away to those in need? Where, when one was rewarded in this way, did one begin and where should it end, if indeed it should end at all?

I remembered once reading a quotation from a book called *Small is Beautiful* by E.F. Schumacher. I walked over to my bookcase and looked it up. It went like this:

Give a man a fish, and you are helping him a little bit for a very short while; teach him the art of fishing, and he can help himself all his life. On a higher level: supply him with fishing tackle; this will cost you a good deal of money, and the result remains doubtful;

7

but even if fruitful, the man's continuing livelihood will still be dependent upon you for replacements. But teach him to make his own fishing tackle and you have helped him to become not only self-supporting, but also self-reliant and independent.

I hope this does not make me sound too pretentious, but this isolated thought set me searching my mind again about how my windfall could be put to its best use. Struggle as I did with my thoughts, I could not put anything meaningful for me together straight away. Then one night, as I strove to stop my mind racing round all the possibilities open to me so that I could get some essential sleep, I recalled some of the pleasant holidays I had had in the past in Scotland. I remembered that I had recently read about an island off the west coast of Scotland that was up for sale. Something clicked in my brain as the asking price came to me. It was about four million pounds. I did not get the sleep that I was longing for that night. The more I thought about that island, the more I became convinced that this could be what I was looking for.

More and more questions, all without answers, kept piling up in my mind. Where had I seen the island advertised? Had it already been sold? Was the island inhabited? Where was it situated?

Then, some ideas gradually started slotting into place. If I had an island, surely I could do something useful with it. At least I now had a path to follow.

Now, remembering back to that hot and sleepless night, I knew instinctively that it had been the decisive moment when I had convinced myself that it was the right thing to be doing, irrespective of the undoubted risks and uncertainties with which I would be confronted.

In the colder start at the dawn of the new day I showered and quickly felt fresh enough to 'spill the beans' to my family and friends to let them know of my good fortune. I would then face the task of tracking down the advert and start on some of the other investigations that I had, during the night, set myself for the new venture.

3

My parents moved from London to Yorkshire when I was but a toddler and it is this county that I most remember with affection. It was there that the early influential parts of my life were formed. By the time I had completed my formal education I was looking for adventure and had spent some of my later teenage years travelling abroad. The experience gained on these journeys proved useful in getting employment in a number of jobs on my return.

As a result of the shifting location of my father's work, my parents moved back to the south-east of England and, when I landed a more permanent job in the health service, I also resettled in the south-east, living not far away from them in Kent.

Most of my social life had revolved around a few long-term school friends, family connections and some acquaintances from work. I am not a particularly gregarious person by nature but I would have been greatly saddened by any reduction in those social contacts that I had formed. I couldn't imagine my life leading to a situation where I was not making or receiving requests for parties, dinner arrangements, evenings out or suggestions for group holidays.

I had developed an early interest in jazz and, for a short time, played saxophone or trombone in a local band. It was nothing very professional but it was great fun and we did a few performances at local pubs. Anne attended one of these gigs and we got talking. It was, as they say, love at first sight. We had so much in common and, from then on, spent as much time as possible in each other's company. She was bright, enthusiastic and full of the joys of spring. I felt the same and she said I made her happy. I proposed and she accepted. We married but were not able to arrange a honeymoon straight away as we both had commitments at work, but several months later we found the time to have a short holiday in Cornwall. We stayed at a five-star hotel and were fortunate with a brilliantly sunny week. Most days were spent down on the beach, delighting in our newly found pastime of swimming. On the last day before we were due to return, Anne challenged me to dive from the rocks to a deep, clear pool below. We raced towards it and she reached the edge before me and dived. I heard the splash and then the cry for help. When I looked down I saw her spread-eagled above a submerged jagged edge of rock. There was blood mixing into the green water of the pool. I clambered down with some difficulty and lifted her out of the water. She was virtually unconscious but, mercifully, still breathing. There was an ugly gash on her head and she was moaning incoherently. I carried her up to a path where a few cars were parked and someone phoned for an ambulance. I went with her to the hospital, where she was rushed into accident and emergency. They tried for four hours to revive her and save her life, but it was not to be. She died that evening from a massive haemorrhage on the brain. I was devastated.

Following that time, I experienced a continued mixture of emotions. From a previous peak of happiness on meeting and marrying Anne to her sudden death less than a year later, I had only just started to try and get my life together again. Now I had won this large fortune. It could not compensate in any way for the loss, but life was certainly moving in very odd ways for me. I had travelled so quickly from peak to trough and now to another peak with totally different concepts. I wondered what I had done to warrant such a roller-coaster ride.

Over the last few months, my life had been filled with all sorts of invitations. Several of my friends continued to include me in their dinner parties but, although I was appreciative, I saw them as being designed to help me through this disastrous period and I believed that they would inevitably tail off. The worst occasions were always threesomes, with unspoken difficulties for both parties when the extra, unfilled space at the table was a constant reminder to everyone of the loss. I soon got to the stage where I was so aware of these things that I returned more and more to the comfort of my family and very close friends while resolving not to allow my widower status to become a burden to me. I suppose I had, to some extent, retreated as if into a shell. Invitations continued to come but my enthusiasm had not been there to respond positively.

After Anne's death both my mother and father and Anne's parents had pulled together marvellously well, giving each other, and me, much support at a very difficult time for us all. We all remained good friends. My father had always been an important influence upon my life. It was not that we always agreed or held similar views on everything, that would be far from the truth, but he had the quality of always being able to accommodate an opposing view or argument with tolerance and he was able to logically move a discussion forward to the benefit of both parties. My recent time had been spent more and more with him and my mother. My first call would unquestionably be to see them and hear what they had to say.

I found my mother in the kitchen. As we kissed I noticed my father working on a new summerhouse near the bottom of the garden.

'Mum, dry your hands quickly and come with me out into the garden to see Dad. I've got some good news for you both to hear together.'

'What's the urgency?'

'You'll see. Come on.'

'Hallo Jim, you're just in time to give me a hand with this length of timber. I need it lifted up to the roof.'

'Jim says he's got some good news for us,' my mother said, trying to get his attention.

'Great. What's that?'

'I've just won some money on the lottery.'

'Well, that's good news. Just help lift it over that beam for me will you.'

'It's rather a lot of money.'

'The more the better, I suppose? There's one more beam like that and then I'm finished. What will you buy with it?'

'What do you suggest? It's over five million.'

'What! You're joking.'

'No, no, it's no joke.' I had his full attention now. My mother was speechless. Father abandoned the beam and walked towards the house.

'Well now, we'd better go back inside, we seem to have something to talk about here.'

Once in the comfort of the lounge, my mother produced tea and cakes while I outlined my idea for a new community on a Scottish island.

'I suppose most people winning a fortune like this would buy a larger and better house and live a more expensive lifestyle, but I want to do something different from that. What do you think?'

My father leaned forward and said, 'Most times when I've heard of people winning large sums of money I felt rather sorry for them, because many of them would be unable to handle the total experience in a sensible way. I

13

have actually asked some friends what they would do with this sort of money if it came their way. It is, at first, quite difficult to grasp even the numbers, and understand how many a million actually is. I think your idea is as sound as any I've heard. Is there a Scottish island available for you to buy?'

'I don't know yet. I thought I saw one advertised recently in the paper but I still have to find out. What do you think I should do with the money, Mum?'

'I think you should replace that old carpet in your front room. I noticed it was getting a bit threadbare when I was round last week.' We laughed together.

'Thanks Mum, I might just get round to that now.'

'Seriously, I think you should do exactly what you think best,' she continued. 'We certainly have had some wonderful times in Scotland, haven't we?'

'I feel that I need to set myself on an entirely new course, something that will be a challenge and help me move out of this widower complex that is enveloping me. At forty-two years old there has to be a positive future.'

'You just get to it and find out all you can. If you need any help, just ask. We'll do all we can. I think it's a great idea.'

4

It was not difficult to find out who the agents for the sale of the island were. Just a couple of calls and I had the number and then the address in Edinburgh. A short telephone conversation quickly established that the island, named Enniskerry, was indeed still available for purchase. I was addressed as 'Sir' rather more often than I was used to and a meeting was arranged.

I journeyed north the next day and a young secretary showed me into a luxurious, deeply carpeted office where everything had been discreetly and perfectly arranged, as one would expect from a firm that dealt in properties for sale with those all-important seven digits. The 'Sirs' continued for a while but, mercifully, reduced in frequency as a conversation got under way. I soon realised that this was covering only the preliminaries; I had not as yet reached the inner sanctum of this establishment. A gentleman emerged to shake my hand. His appearance was sudden but not intrusive. I noticed his refined Scottish accent as he welcomed my presence and offered tea or coffee. He was probably older than he looked but I find I am rather a poor judge of people's ages. He placed on the desk before him a large colourful brochure and said that, as far as he was aware, it contained virtually all the essential details relating to the island.

Gradually, he edged out of me something of my background, who I was and how I was in a position to consider this particular property. I think he sensed quite early that I was not used to dealing in purchases of this magnitude. I did not feel at a disadvantage but I needed to know that he was a person that I could trust, and so I talked around rather than about the subject of the actual purchase for some time, gradually getting to know him better as an individual as opposed to the estate agent that he was. At the same time, I gave him some more indications of my lack of experience. The most expensive thing I had bought was my own house, which several years ago, only cost about seventy thousand pounds. Although inflation had now increased this figure considerably, I was now considering something around four million pounds. Fortunately, I gathered that it was not a normal sale for him, he was quite used to selling properties up to and above this value, but they tended to be luxury mansions and even castles – he had never yet sold an island. I suppose, from his point of view, the actual deal would not be vastly different to his previous sales but he seemed personally involved and interested to the extent that I believed it was in some way special for him. He had obviously done much research, and I wanted to avail myself of every possible detail that I could extract.

I learned that there had been two other prospective purchasers but they had been unable to make an offer to the satisfaction of the vendor even though the agent had given considerable time, effort and persuasion to conclude the deal. It would seem that my offer should be equal to or above theirs but also of some importance were my intentions with regard to how I intended to manage the island. Although I sensed that the price was by far the overriding factor, my objectives would also rate highly.

The agent told me that the previous owner had made his fortune in the tailoring business in Hong Kong and had hoped to make a profit as a result of developing the forestry potential of the island. However, his business interests in the Far East had demanded more of his time and he had decided to sell after a relatively short period of ownership. There had been a series of absentee landlords for much of the time before his period of ownership and this had contributed to the increasing despair of his tenants and their declining standard of life. The agent felt that although the owner had good intentions regarding his tenants and the island's well being as a whole, he was unable to bring any of his ideas to fruition. Hence his interest in the intentions of any new owner to bring some of the benefits to the island which he was unable to achieve.

I established that the island was administered as one of the Western Isles and was within the district of Argyll and Bute. It could be reached by way of the peninsula of Kintyre but there was no regular ferry service, which of course was not surprising, given that the island was now uninhabited.

'Many of the smaller islands, particularly in the Outer Hebrides, are uninhabited,' said the agent. 'Depopulation was exacerbated in the nineteenth century by the Highland clearances when the landowners forcibly evicted the crofters from their lands in order to convert them into extensive sheep farms. In addition, there was a continued depopulation of many of the smaller islands in the twentieth century, primarily because of the lack of economic opportunities.' He went on to explain that rural depopulation was felt particularly severely on the islands off the western coast, and continued today, reflecting the marginal nature of hill farming in general and the attraction of better employment opportunities in Inverness and the oil-related industries of the west shore of the Moray Firth and Aberdeen areas. Enniskerry was the latest casualty of this process.

Crofting had been the traditional mainstay of the

economy. The typical croft, a small rented farm, could be just a few acres with a handful of sheep, a cow, and enough crops to supplement the diet and provide a small income. On Enniskerry the standard of living had declined, and when the ferry company withdrew its regular service the council had little option other than step in and take the remaining few off to the mainland as an act of compassion. This had occurred just over a year ago and the island had remained unpopulated since then, the current owner never having been in regular residence in recent times.

'The main lodge on Enniskerry,' the agent continued, 'known locally as the Laird's house, consists of some sixteen large rooms on two floors. It stands in a quite extensive garden stocked with herbaceous plants, mature pine and palm trees, together with rhododendrons and azaleas. There is also a walled garden with a greenhouse, although this is in a poor state of repair, and fifty acres of woodland. There are about twenty crofts and houses, about half of them habitable, the other half needing refurbishment. And there are numerous other outbuildings, barns, sheds and derelict homesteads. The island is a natural habitat for pheasant and other game birds, three freshwater lochs stock various varieties of fish and there are salmon fishing rights around the island. The eastern shoreline has three magnificent beaches and four safe anchorages. I think that should give you an idea of your intended purchase,' the agent concluded. 'Is there anything you are not clear about?'

There were many other questions and we continued our discussion, now on a much more informal basis. 'Do you know,' he said, 'when I last spoke to the Laird of Enniskerry, he explained that Lairds of the past and present have, in general, had a very bad press in regard to the history of the Western Isles. So often they used their power unfairly and the crofters' life was hard and without adequate rewards.'

He told me a story about a crofter who questioned his Laird concerning the rightful ownership of his Hebridean island.

'The Laird had purchased the island, some years before, and had signed an agreement of sale on the dotted line. It was totally legal. But the crofter wanted to know, did the Laird have the historical right to own the land? The crofter believed that the indigenous Scots were the rightful owners long before the Laird was even born, let alone just a year or so ago when he had paid out money for the island. Furthermore, the Laird was not even of Scottish descent.

'He continued to reason that a person could buy and own a house, a plot of land, even an island, but thankfully, he couldn't buy an area of the sky above or the air that is there to breathe. Real ownership was something quite different. "Who owns England? Who owns America?" he asked, his voice rising to make the point.

'The Laird did not have an immediate satisfactory answer, but he understood the crofter's basic message, that we are all here momentarily, in a sense on trust, and in that judgement he saw that he could not own the island, the land belonged to those who had lived on the island before or even to everyone now. In effect the Laird had, by virtue of his monetary power, plundered the land on which he stood. The onslaught did not, and perhaps it was not intended to, encourage him to give up any of his land or wealth, but it did cause him some time of inward reflection on the status of ownership.'

The agent leaned back in his chair. 'This is not to put you off the purchase, I hasten to add, but I thought it might give a flavour of how the crofting population of the isles can think about their landlords.'

'It certainly does,' I replied.' 'I'll keep these comments in mind, but perhaps you'll agree that I will be somewhat insulated because I won't be lording it over anyone. My fellow islanders will all be volunteers.'

'That's true,' he said. 'Can I offer you another drink?' I accepted his offer and we continued with our discussion. I was learning fast.

5

It took several weeks to conclude the purchase. There had been no further contact from the previously interested parties, but I learned that two others from abroad had made enquiries. However, neither had proceeded further. It was of course, essential that I arranged a visit to the island before I signed the contract, and I made the arrangements immediately.

It was not a pleasant day that I chose. The rain fell incessantly during the journey north. I stayed at an unexceptional bed and breakfast, and spent the next day looking round the town in the drizzle and arranging for a boat to take me across to the island first thing the following morning. My reason for wishing to go to this uninhabited island, now up for sale, must have been obvious, but the boatman's prime need was to convey to me that given the poor weather there was no guarantee that we would actually complete the crossing. Even if he did succeed in making the landing, then the length of time he would be prepared to stay there would be governed totally by the weather and tides. 'It could,' he said, 'be for less than half an hour.'

As it happened we did get away in the early morning. There was a blustering wind with huge, dark, rain clouds scudding across a grey sky. Nevertheless my boatman was not discouraged and even predicted the day should improve. It would have been too much to assume that he would not be curious as to the purpose of my visit and, by way of a number of innocent general comments from

21

him, I found myself telling him my reason for wanting to see the island. He was politely non-committal but I felt it was my first opportunity to get valuable information of the type I would not get from any estate agent. I enquired gently how he felt about the island being evacuated. As we strained against the strong headwind I noticed his weather-beaten face line with what seemed to me to be an effort to choose the right words to express his sorrow.

'It was always a hard life, you know,' he said. 'There was not much fresh food apart from the birds during the last years. But the islanders didn't want to leave. It was the bairn, you see. They were down to the last child, poor lass. She was having no formal education, and what with the increasing sickness and that, it was deemed that it would be cruel to let them stay. But you know, it's ironic, they are just as sick now, living on the mainland, as they ever were. Being isolated for their lifetime, they've no resistance to infection.'

We stared silently ahead into the mist; the island was not visible.

'Could people still live there?' I enquired.

'Well, I suppose they could, but there's not many about here that would want to. It would need a miracle now to see it happen and there's not many miracles here these days.'

'There's water on the island?' I asked.

'Aye, there's good fresh water on the island, and plenty around and up there above us as you can see, and there's an electric cable from the mainland just below where we are now. Would you be wanting to live there then?'

It was not an intrusive question; it flowed from a natural interest in his world.

'Maybe,' I volunteered. 'What would people think?' I added. He paused. It was a long pause. The diesel engine throbbed, and the rhythm was unchanging.

'I think they would believe that you were off your head and that you had too much money to waste. They would wonder what sort of a person you could be, to sit out there all day with nothing to do.'

I wondered how much I should reveal about my intentions. It was too early, of course, but I felt an empathy with him and confessed.

'No, I'm not a recluse or a bird-watching "twitcher" or someone like that, I'm thinking of re-establishing life here with anyone who is prepared to take the risk with me. A new community in a new age.'

There was another long silence as he grappled with conflicting emotions. Previous Lairds on several of the other western islands had not been popular with the locals and now a new owner such as I, and a southerner at that, would undoubtedly have extra hurdles to mount. We sighted land quite close and within minutes, as we approached the jetty, two seals dozing on the cold rocks were disturbed by our passing. They stared at us for a moment, annoyed at the intrusion, and shuffled lazily before sliding into the sea. Then there was the grating sound of the boat meeting the inclined gravel of the island beach.

'The weather is improving.' he said, 'so you will have a good few hours. Would you like to be alone or have company?'

'I would be very pleased if you could show me around, I have a lot to learn.'

We trudged up the hill and were soon approaching a long line of cottages in various states of repair.

'As you can see,' he said, 'this is the old high street. It's not that long ago that it was de-populated and so most of the crofts are structurally good but some are in a pretty poor state inside. Best preserved is the Laird's house up there on the hill.'

The grass around the crofts was a brilliant fresh green and I could see that same green extending up the hill towards a cliff top. He pointed out some ancient narrow strips of cultivated land that lay abandoned nearby.

'They are known as lazybeds,' he volunteered.

'Why lazybeds?' I asked.

'It's an old name. They may be so called because only part of the land was used as crop bearing, the other part being given over to the drainage ditches.'

'How about animals?' I asked.

'It's not bad grazing and the island has had sheep in the past. Some islanders had their own cow for milk, but that was a long while ago. Rabbits were plentiful at one time but they seem to have almost disappeared now.'

We rested on a grassy bank. I removed some food and drink from my rucksack and offered it to the boatman. He took it thankfully. We noticed the sun breaking through, causing shafts of sunlight to illuminate the calm silver sea around. It was a wonderful experience.

'You like it then?' His steady voice broke through into my mind and its ramblings.

'Yes, yes, I think I do.' I did know something of Scotland from previous holidays. But this was different, it could not be regarded as anything like a holiday, it could be my future. The view was vast, the colours were continually changing, the air was pure, and the silence was unique. The moment seemed like the dawning of a new era, but I did not express it like this to him.

'Perhaps it could work, perhaps with the right people, the right attitude, the right amount of good hard work, a fair allowance of good fortune, perhaps it could work.'

'Aye,' he said softly. 'You will need a lot of all that.'

I noticed that there was no further suggestion that I was 'off my head' and was further encouraged.

'Will you show me the water source?' I asked.

As we walked further up the hill past the spring and a placid lake the overall size of the island became more apparent to me. Blue sky was now visible and the panoramic view through 360 degrees revealed the whole island and the mainland shimmering in the distance. I felt 'on top of the world' and it was not just visual.

We trudged on over the grassy hill to a point where we could view the almost sheer drop of the cliffs to a beach several hundred feet below. Sea birds wheeled around screeching in their quest to find food and space on the narrow ledges. He identified the various species for me and I resolved to become more acquainted with them in the future.

It was late afternoon when we cast off and returned to the mainland. It had been an informative day for me and I could now focus on finding the answers to tangible tasks. I thanked my guide, to whom I paid my dues with a generous tip, feeling already that he was more a friend, someone who had the interests of the island in his heart. As we parted I said, 'I'll hope to see you again.'

'Aye,' he said with a grin. 'I'll put a good word in for you. You'll need that as an Englishman, and a good deal more!'

6

WANTED
Self-motivated persons required to live
and work as part of a newly created
community on a Scottish island.
Applicants should be of good physical
fitness and be able to offer skills related to
the on-going well-being of the community.
Commitment by contract for one year.
Salary – Nil.
Benefits immeasurable.
If you are interested please ring
Jim Henderson on 0208 837 3398
to arrange an interview.

I placed this advert in one of the national newspapers immediately after I returned from the island in early October. I was gaining confidence as a result of my visit. I felt that the idea was feasible and there was no reason why it could not be brought to fruition. This next stage, to select the people who would accompany me, was crucial to the whole scheme, but I was uncertain of the sort of people that might respond to such an advertisement. I was concerned about the possibility of cranks applying. But perhaps most of all I feared that no one would show interest at all and my idea would founder at the first fence.

It was my intention to make selections with a view to occupation in the early spring of the following year to ensure that the worst of the winter weather had passed and that time was available to work on those houses that needed repairs to make them secure for the following winter.

I just did not know what the response was likely to be. Would I have so few replies that the whole idea would just not be practically viable, or would I be overwhelmed and have to sift through the applications and disappoint people even though they possessed much needed skills and enthusiasm?

Two whole days went by and the early twinges of doubt were getting to me. I feared that it would be the first situation that was going to be my problem and my downfall and that my idea would become 'pie in the sky'.

Then, just as I was preparing for bed one evening, the 'phone rang and a hesitant voice said, 'About the advert.'

'Yes' I said.

'I could be interested in this Scottish island opportunity, but I need a lot more information.'

'Yes of course you do,' I replied. 'In fact I also need to know quite a bit about you. I can answer some questions now but a face-to-face meeting will probably be the best way to proceed.'

'I'm a builder by trade but I feel that I need to take a bit of a risk and do something a bit different.'

'That's fine, the renovation of old buildings is just what we will be engaged upon right from the start. Why don't you come round for a chat sometime?'

'I'm off work all this weekend.'

'How about tomorrow morning about eleven o'clock? Oh, and what's your name?'

'That's OK, My name's Bob. My wife and three children would like to come along as well. Where do you live?'

And so the process started. Bob arrived with his wife and three children, and I gave them a rather long description of the sort of thing I had in mind. I explained that the objective was to build a community that would develop into a thriving and satisfying way of life for those who had the right attitudes to the task. I mentioned that he was in fact the first to reply to my advert and so it was very early days in terms of being able to say when and how the idea would get off the ground. I was interested not only in what he could offer in practical terms but how they and their children might react to the totally different way of life. Apparently they all enjoyed the outdoor life and when I showed them some of the photographs I had taken on my recent visit they were suitably impressed.

Bob was a short, muscular individual with fair hair just recovering from a complete shaving. A small circular tattoo decorated his left arm. He spoke with a deep sing-song voice that held one's attention as he expressed his surprise that he was the first to apply, and he seemed initially worried that he would not yet be part of a larger team. Susan explained that she had pledged that, whatever he decided, she would go along with him. Their oldest girl. Jane, was not enthusiastic, having just met a new boyfriend, but Sarah, the younger daughter, was keen for a change to something unknown. Their son Paul was unconcerned, but he thought a change would be good for them all. I explained that I hoped that children would form an important part of island life and that we would have a teacher or teachers apply so that their education would not suffer.

By the end of several cups of coffee we agreed that it was too early to make a definite decision, I would keep him informed as we hoped that other applicants would soon be forthcoming. I felt that he and his family would make valuable members of a community. As they prepared to leave, the phone rang. It was another enquiry about the island. I motioned them to sit down again for a while and they waited, pleased to discover as I put the phone down that I had been able to make another appointment for a young lad named James to visit me that very next afternoon.

James, aged 21, was single and unemployed. He did not look particularly fit or well fed. He was clean-shaven but small nicks to his chin suggested that it was a hurried event before setting out to meet me. He sat awkwardly and fidgeted, alternately rubbing his hands together and then tapping his fingers on the side of the chair. In a somewhat reticent manner he told me that he had average GCSE results and had taken on a number of part-time jobs. He felt that his less than exciting CV, which he passed across to me, was as a result of the break-up of his parents' marriage and the suicide of an older brother. Quite understandably, he thought my advertisement was like a light at the end of a long dark tunnel, which he had been struggling through for the last five years. He had done some decorating work and helped an uncle with some DIY jobs. He felt he could turn his hand to any practical tasks that were asked of him. He seemed a kind-hearted lad, not a leader but genuine in his attitude to the unknown. He told me he had just filled in an application to join the police force and he asked what he should do in the event that he was offered an interview. I said he should take the interview if it was offered but the option to come to the island would still be open to him. It was for him to decide. But it might be possible for me to offer him some preliminary work prior to our departure if he was interested. His eyes seemed to light up at the thought of some immediate employment. I said that he should let me know within the week whether he was likely to be interested.

*　*　*

The next person to arrange to see me was an attractive young girl named Lynda who had long, blonde hair that she kept brushing across her forehead to keep it away from her eyes. She immediately came over as a strong, extrovert character. In reply to my usual questions about her previous employment, I learned that she was a model. She admitted to posing topless once for page 3 of the *Sun* but said she would not do it again. She was single, 21 and looking for new challenges. I took her through the general requirements and skills that would encourage me to take people to the island and said that posing topless or modelling had just not been at the head of my list of necessary accomplishments. We laughed and I asked if she could offer any other skills.

She thought for a while and then smiling, replied, 'Well, I did milk a cow once, and I kept rabbits and a goldfish as a young girl.'

'Great.' I said, wondering if this interview was heading for the rocks. 'We will certainly have at least one cow on the island. You could be a dairy maid or even help the fisherman!' Having noticed her well-manicured fingernails and the care she had obviously taken about her appearance, I said that I could not see her maintaining the same standards of perfection on a windswept Scottish island. We both saw the incredulity of our imagined picture of the two extremes. She had an infectious laugh and sought to reassure me that she did have another side to her character.

'At interviews, I always get the topless thing out of the way first. If I don't, it's sure to crop up later to my disadvantage. As far as modelling is concerned, it isn't something I'm wedded to for the future. I really do think I have the ability to change my lifestyle. Anyway, I have three brothers and my father taught me all the practical things like woodwork and auto engineering too, and I even played football. I'm quite fit and I've done the Duke of Edinburgh Gold Award. I have also been a member of the crew for an Atlantic crossing and I am just about to gain my black belt in karate. I suppose I'm a bit of a tomboy really.'

'Well, that might just balance the scales,' I said, now quite impressed. After further discussion about her family situation and her attitude to the more primitive existence on the island, I thought she would adapt well to the change.

She asked several questions about the location of the island, how many people were expected to live there and what tasks would have to be undertaken and by whom. I told her as much as I could, adding that I was still at an early stage of interviewing people. She thanked me and said she would feel privileged to come if she were invited.

Although I had several enquiries that did not lead anywhere, things were now moving along at a faster pace and within days there were at least half a dozen enquiries pending, including some from people unable to get to my house in Kent for a while, but I was encouraged because each person that I had so far interviewed met with my approval. I was confident about my ability to judge character correctly but wondered if I should become more circumspect. Then, one evening, I received a visit that set me thinking in a direction that I had not up to that time considered.

Giles arrived in an expensive chauffeur-driven car. He was a big, round-faced, confident, well-groomed and well-dressed executive type of person with a slightly sallow complexion, which suggested he was not a man for the outdoor life. He had a quick-fire method of speaking that implied that he was used to giving orders rather than

31

taking them. My first impression was that he must be living with constant nervous tension and responsibilities, which marked him as a prime candidate for stress-related problems.

'I'll come straight to the point,' he said. 'I understand that you have bought this island and you want to make it work as a fully fledged island economy. I would like to be part of that venture.'

'You mentioned a proposition on the phone.'

'Yes. Something, as I said, that I feel you can't refuse.'

'I'm intrigued. What is it?'

'Money. Money to the tune of a million pounds.'

I was completely taken aback. Now I should keep calm or I would become stressed. There must be a catch, I thought.

'That's a huge sum of money to offer. I don't want to appear rude, but what's in it for you?'

'I consider myself to be an entrepreneur. I've done a bit of homework on this scheme and I think it could work and be a good investment. I believe that you have some good ideas but I also think you may not have thought the scheme through thoroughly or correctly. Without a heavy cash input as part of the investment at the outset of the project, it is doomed to wallow in the doldrums soon after it starts and suffer a prolonged decay over the early years. With my investment I would hope that the island economy would get off to a much more healthy start without financial worries. Those otherwise inherent worries would be relieved and in the longer term it should prosper and we would both reap the rewards.'

His remarks hit me like a kick in the stomach. There was no doubt that I had concerns about the lack of cash in the early stages but in my enthusiasm had not confronted those thoughts head-on. But that was not the only problem. In my now apparent naivety, I had thought we could get by without a huge additional investment to start. In fact I had even considered that maybe we would not need to exchange money on the island. I collected my thoughts and tried to express a suitable reply.

'You are right, but only up to a point. I have given myself some guiding principals that I believe are essential to the successful outcome of this venture. It is not only dependent upon money, even though you may think it is. One important aspect to me is that everyone contributes to the economy of the island to the best of his or her ability. That contribution is given free and is not reclaimable. I believe that it is best that all members of the island community are full-time residents and that their offer of work is carried out during their stay as a part of the whole package. If I read you correctly, you will have several if not many interests elsewhere other than this particular island and that you would hope to, as it were, benefit from afar. It is a fact that other small islands have been blighted in the recent past by absentee landlords who have directly contributed to their own island's demise. To be totally frank with you, in the last few minutes you have opened my eyes wider than they have ever been since I embarked upon this island project and for that I thank you wholeheartedly. However, I could not accept your generous offer unless it was a totally uncon-ditional gift to the island economy and you became a member of the island community. It may interest you to know that I intend the island to be run democratically with a freely elected council of six members all taken from the community. If I accepted your offer and you agreed to live on the island, it is possible that you could be elected to that council and have a direct input on the way in which money is used, but of course I cannot guarantee that. You see, I want a total commitment to the island from each person, certainly during the first year, whether his actual effort is by way of labour or finance. I intend to devise an arrangement whereby a certain proportion of the profits from a person's work will be given to the island economy and the rest will, shall we say, be that persons own to keep on a private enterprise basis. If you could agree to that, I should be delighted to accept your offer. Hoping that I am not going to offend you, I would suggest, guessing at your hectic lifestyle, you could benefit greatly from a period on this unpolluted and beautiful Western isle where you would not always be confined to aeroplanes and meetings in smoke-filled rooms, eating and drinking too much fine wine and good food. You would become a healthy man and, dare I say it, your life span would be extended by at least ten years'.

He sat for a while, uncharacteristically, I thought, soberly twitching at his moustache; a smile fleetingly passed his lips.

'You create an almost impossible situation for me. I cannot conceive that I could give up my present life-style and interests. I'm tempted to say that you would be an idiot if you did not snap up my offer but I do have a sneaking regard for your ideals. I will think about it and I'll be in touch shortly. But you yourself, should also think long and hard again about the repercussions for your potential extended island family and the responsibilities that you would bear if all that you hold dear goes down the pan. You are about to become famous as the person who gave up the offer of a million pounds for that simple ideal of yours – do you think you can live with that refusal in the future?'

With that he rose. The discussion over, we parted with a quick shake of hands, and I was indeed left with my thoughts.

* * *

Just two weeks after returning home from my first visit to the island I received a letter from Scotland. It read:

To Mr Henderson

We have the informations that our island may be returned to us by the Lord himself. If it be in your wisdom to allow us to return to our home we will help with the dailies as best we can. So help us God.

Yours truly

Jock and Morag McInch

How could I resist such a request? I carried out a little research before I replied to their letter, learning that Jock and Morag were husband and wife. They were both 55 years old and, as the letter suggested, they had lived on Enniskerry for the whole of their lives. I did not enquire after their health, as it seemed to me that to have two of the original inhabitants back on the island was a prize that must be accepted without question. I did not need to interview such a couple, although I resolved to call and meet them when I next visited Scotland.

I did call and see Jock and his wife Morag. They lived in a simple council property, clean but with few obvious possessions of their own. They both greeted me almost as a long-lost saviour, with a kindness that was rooted in a God-fearing belief in the Almighty. Jock had a long grey beard and did not seem to get around very easily. I felt he looked almost 20 years older than his actual age. Morag, a kindly grey-haired, diminutive and softly spoken woman, offered me a cup of tea, and together they told me about life on the island. As they spoke I felt humbled.

'It was hard for everybody, you know – the cold weather, the lack of any variety in the food, the dampness and of course the reducing number of our friends. But in many ways it is worse now, as we have no resistance to all the ills of the mainland. People here have been good to us but we think we would be better back on the island. We have always had the faith that God will choose our path for us. Are you really going to invite us back?'

'Yes, you are invited back – we will all benefit by your presence and I hope to see you there early next spring, if not before.'

Angus had phoned saying that he was a fisherman who lived on the west coast of Scotland near to Enniskerry and was therefore familiar with the waters around the island. He too was interested in becoming a resident, so after I left Jock and Morag I made my way to the sea front, where I was confronted with a tall weather-beaten fisherman of about 40 years of age. I felt reliability and confidence exude from him immediately we shook hands.

'Well Angus, I gave you an idea on the phone of what I was up to. Why do you want to do this?' He replied in a deep voice showing straight away that his mind was made up. He had rightly assumed that his services would be needed and there was never a question or uncertainty about anything I could raise. He had decided what he wanted, and that was that.'

'Fishing is not what it was,' he continued, 'what with quotas, rules, regulations and most of our fish being caught by foreigners. I was looking for something different, but I love the sea and these western isles and the thought that my efforts could still benefit people nearer home appealed to me. By the way, I'm bringing that fishing boat over there with me,' pointing to one in the harbour, 'I own it. Come aboard and have a wee dram.'

I went aboard and we drank and talked well into the night. He told me about his youth, his love of the sea, his feelings for the islands and their inhabitants. Slowly, I gained an insight into an islanders' mind and it was most rewarding. He did not need to ask many questions, he knew the island better than I did and he had the broad skeleton of what I wanted to do. To be frank, that was about as much as I had.

Bespectacled, dark-haired Belinda, came to see me wearing a frown and looking rather nervous. In answer to my opening question she replied.

'To be honest, I'm not sure why I'm here. I'm at a stage of my life where I have to decide what to do next. I've completed my course of study at the Royal School of Music and I feel I should branch out and see and do something completely different for a while. I've not experienced much of the outdoor life, but I hope I could fit in with whatever I have to do. I know I'm not selling myself at this interview, but I don't want to mislead you or be misled myself.'

I warmed to the way the girl was expressing herself.

'I am pleased that you are not, as you say, "selling yourself". I'd like you to think that you are talking with me as a friend. This is not an interview. Look at it as a chat between us to enable us both to come to the best end result.' She nodded in agreement.

'Life on the island could be hard, and I can't tell you whether it's the right choice for you or not. What I can tell you is that your musical skills will be invaluable to us. It's my hope that the school will have a music teacher, and it's probable that a regular ceilidh will be held for the community. But I haven't asked you which instrument you play?'

'Oh, it's the cello, but I am familiar with most stringed instruments.'

'Tell me,' I asked, 'about your family and friends. Will you not miss them?'

'My father has always had to be away at sea for long periods, but I will miss my mother a lot and she will miss me. We talked over your advertisement for hours and hours. She was all the time encouraging me to phone you. I think in her heart she would like me to stay nearer to her. As far as friends go, I suppose I'm a bit of a loner; I've had to spend most of my free time practising. But that is part of the reason I responded to your advert – I don't want to stay in this groove.'

I showed her some photographs of the island, being careful to point out the misty as well as the sunlit ones. She looked at each one very carefully, soaking up all that I had to say.

'It looks beautiful. I've never been to Scotland but it looks a bit like Canada, where I once spent a week on a concert tour.'

'I'd like to try and convince you to come,' I said, 'but I also need to express that I think it will be quite unlike anything you have experienced before. The good news is that we will all be learning together, it will be like a new family situation for us all.'

As she left she was smiling as if a load had been removed from her shoulders. I hoped she would decide to come.

It occurred to me that I had interviewed mostly single people so far; perhaps the married couples had more responsibilities and more things to talk over with each other before they could show interest.

It was against all my expectations when Charles phoned, saying that he was a veterinary surgeon. Knowing that we would put great store into the care of our animals, I had predicted that lack of veterinary care on the island would be a significant cost factor against us. Charles was aged 55, divorced and recently retired, and he had experience with farm as well as domestic animals. His reasons for wishing to live on the island were not easy to extract from him. He was experiencing the first weeks of retirement and looking for an activity. He had visited the Western Isles for a holiday many years ago but most of his life had been spent in London and the Home Counties.

As the responses appeared to be tailing off, I realised I must re-advertise in other national newspapers, including the middle-class broadsheets as well as the more popular daily papers. So far I felt pleased with the results, and decided to arrange a general meeting with those who had so far shown interest in joining me on the island.

7

'As most of you will know, my name is Jim Henderson and I am now the owner of the Scottish island named Enniskerry. I welcome you all to this, the first meeting of the proposed Enniskerry Island Community, and I am sure you will take this first opportunity to get to know each other. We will become neighbours, each bringing with us our share of individual assets, difficulties and responsibilities. Now, we are entering upon additional and wider shared responsibilities with a much larger group.

'You, I hope, will join me, not as tenants, but more in the way of an extended family on Enniskerry, living as a community and working together to build a stable, efficient and enjoyable life together. It will not be easy. There are prophets of doom – you may have heard some of them giving vent to many reasons for their belief that we are destined to failure. Not least of these is the historical fact that many of the small inhabited islands off the west coast of Scotland have failed due to the population decreasing to a point where continuance is not viable. This has usually occurred soon after the number of children drops to low single figures. But we must not be despondent for we have the potential for several children to start life with us on the island. I'm very positive that it can be a success, but this will depend as much on you as on me.

'Let me talk now about commitment. As you will be aware from my advertisement, my basic proposals include the need for a safety net of continuity. Applicants will be asked to sign a simple contract committing them to live on the island for one year, working together with the other members so as to provide the basis for a stable and lasting community that can survive into the future.

'I want this enterprise to be as democratic as possible but I have a simple choice to make. Should I allow the inevitable uncertainty of people arriving and departing at their will or should I strive to proceed in a more orderly fashion?

'This contract is my way of getting those of you who think as I do, to agree that we are embarking upon something more durable than an annual holiday, and sign a simple form to that effect. In order to show that future islanders do in fact have a commitment to the island's profitability, they should be able to show it to me in some easily recognisable way, each according to his or her means. For some, this may just be their word, for others it may be a more substantial offer.

'Before I talk more about this matter I will re-state what many of you already know: I envisage, after we are all adequately housed and the necessary farming and other services are in place, that islanders could eventually revert to other private methods of income. A certain proportion of their profits (yet to be agreed) would be allocated to an island fund, their remaining profit being theirs to use as they wish. Some, who commit themselves and their family to island life, may wish to keep their options open. For instance, if they own property back on the mainland, they may wish to rent it out during their absence in case they decide to return at some later stage. Others will probably sell up, lock stock and barrel, and commit themselves totally.

'We will start with next to nothing. We have to feed ourselves, construct accommodation and improve our situation from the day we arrive on the island. It will not be possible for you to make the crossing, step off the boat and wait on the landing stage or look around and ask, "What shall I do now?" or "Who is going to feed me?" Everyone will be responsible for themselves as individuals or as families until we can establish communal food supplies. Although some accommodation will be available straight away, you should, unless you have been given an allocation before, come with adequate tents and bring sufficient food to last each person in your family for at least one or two weeks.

'We shall be taking emergency supplies of foodstuffs for ourselves and hay and feed for the animals. There is fresh water on the island but work will still be necessary to pipe it to the various locations. There are many more aspects to reveal to you but I would now like to open the meeting to comments and questions, I'm sure there will be many, but first can I have a feel of your immediate reaction to the question of commitment by way of a contract.'

'Yes, Angus? By the way, thanks for coming all the way down south.'

'I would just like to say that it is only fair and right that you should have some evidence that people will support you for the first year. Any contribution should be a matter between you and the person giving it, otherwise it could result in unpleasantness and unworthy comparisons as to who has given or not given of their best.'

'Thanks Angus. Charles?'

'You say you want us to operate in a democratic system but it seems your first action will not be at all democratic.'

'What in your view is undemocratic, Charles?'

'Well, the need to get into contracts between us. One does not need this degree of control.'

'I have thought long and hard about this. I do not see my request for you to sign a simple contract as undemocratic. I do not demand that you come to this island. I ask you to come, but on the written understanding that you would stay for at least the first year. A person without a recognisable commitment is a risk to us all, over and above the actual risk of the basic idea. Do you see this to be a problem for you, Charles?

'Yes, I think it would be. How would you deal under the terms of this contract with someone who had legitimate call back to the mainland for, say, the death of a close relative or someone in need of urgent medical attention? Would they have broken the contract?'

'No, of course not. I think you misunderstand my values and intentions. There would never be a situation where I could hold anyone against his or her will. The way I see it is a bit like a marriage: people pledge themselves to each other in good faith. This it what we will be doing and we all hope that it will not end in divorce. And, on the point about medical attention on the mainland, we will be at the mercy of weather and tides. Individuals should consider their own needs for insurance cover.

'Before we go on, there are about twenty-two potential members here tonight. Can I have a show of hands on the commitment issue?'

Eighteen voted in favour of everybody giving a commitment, and four voted against.

'Thank you. Are there any other questions? Yes, Lynda?'

'How will things actually be organised on the island?'

'A useful question. Before we leave for the island I will appoint some individuals who I think will have the qualities for a specific organisational role. For instance, one person will be responsible for land, agriculture, food etc. Another will be responsible for building, engineering, supplies and maintenance etc. A third will take on education, personal queries and other matters. These three will form the nucleus of a committee of six people plus myself, and I will have the casting vote if required. The committee will also consist of a secretary and a treasurer and one other person. Any member can be voted off the committee if there are more votes cast for a new member than for the existing one. These votes can be taken at any time after the first three months.'

'Belinda?'

'So we can't democratically vote you off?' There was a ripple of laughter through the room.

'You're quick off the mark, Belinda. The answer is no, you might want to vote me off before we've even started. This is, I believe, to be my one small compromise with democracy.'

'One last question. Angus?'

'How many people do you want to start this enterprise and how many applications have you received to date?'

'My feeling is that about forty including the children might be about right. I have to be mindful of the number of dwellings existing and those which stand a reasonable chance of being completed before the winter. As of now, sixty-three have shown interest, but I suspect that no more than forty-five are serious at this stage. You may like to know, however, that I have had a request from a husband and wife who lived on the island until recently and now wish to return. Thank you all very much, I will be in touch with you all shortly.'

A few evenings later, Bob and Susan and their daughter Jane, who I had met on my first interview, called round again for a chat about her future education.

'Jim, sorry we were unable to be at the meeting. As you know, Jane is seventeen and looking forward to going to university. Susan and I wondered how she stands regarding the one-year commitment to the island.'

'Don't worry, it has no legal standing. It's just my way

of getting people to think of a longer term and not just coming for a holiday. Jane, there are no restrictions to hold you on the island. We're going to try to do everything we can to give you as good an education here as you could get on the mainland, and we will encourage you to get to the university of your choice. I have always envisaged that people will leave the island, but my task is to try and make the time that they do spend there memorable, and that they look back on it as their home. There is the option of study through the Open University but I really hope that you and other youngsters will explore the world beyond the island's shores.'

8

At last, not a married couple but partners. Bill had travelled widely and had had numerous jobs but said carpentry occupied most of his time at the present. He had met Helen in Australia, and they now owned a detached property in Kent. Bill appeared to be a very strong person, and Helen said she believed he could lift a horse, and was very humorous. They both fired question after question at me, at first mainly about their role, what was expected of them and their young children and how they could all integrate. This was followed by more searching questions about how the affairs of the island would be handled. This was particularly helpful to me too, as I could consolidate plans that I had and get an immediate feedback. Then Bill raised another matter that had troubled them.

'Jim, I thought we should let you know that our son Richard – who's five – has been diagnosed as being hyperactive. He is causing us some problems and I wouldn't want it to cause anyone else difficulties.'

'If you can both cope with him, I'm sure others can make allowances.'

'I think the main difficulty would be his effect upon others at school. We've been told that hyperactive children find it hard to sit still at their desks and concentrate on lessons, also they may misbehave and be disruptive. They also have difficulty making or keeping friends and some are more aggressive than other children but we've only noticed a little of this yet. He's only five.'

'Thanks for telling me. I'm sure we will cope, and surely he will benefit from the small class size. There will be more chance of one-to-one tuition.'

'That's true. So you'll take us then?'

'Of course, you are all welcome.'

Another single person, no matter, this time a student named Brenda, 18 years old, who said she would like to come to the island as her 'gap' year between grammar school and going to university. I enquired whether she would definitely part with us at the end of the year that she would commit herself to and, sensibly she said she did not know.

I asked her what she would study at university and she replied that she was interested in genetics and perhaps it would be in some area associated in this field. In answer to the question did she think a year on the island would help in any way, she replied that most of her peer group went off abroad, usually with a fairly open mind about what they would do during the year. Generally it was just to see the world and have a good time. This would be something a bit different.

Several applicants used this word 'different.' It would appear that the type of person I was attracting gave value to something that was not the usual 'run of the mill' type of thing.

I did not think I would invite Brenda to come as a fill-in for time before university. I judged that the likelihood of her wanting to continue life on the island at the expense of her university education was remote, and although I had no guarantee that any one of those that I had so far met would be with me in the years beyond the first, I did feel that with most of them it would be a real possibility. In Brenda's case I felt that there was a real probability that

47

she would not. It seemed to me that the 'gap' year offered something that was very close to being a holiday and I did not want at this stage anyone coming only for that reason.

It was so pleasing to get another application from a qualified professional. Philip, at 44 years of age, was an experienced and qualified solicitor. He was single and prepared at this important stage in his life to give up a chance for advancement in law to spend time on a lone Scottish island. Having explained the whole scheme to him, I realised that I needed his services at once and offered to engage him for a fee to deal with additional matters relating to the purchase of the island and give advice on my intended contract with the new islanders. He said that he would do all this *gratis* if I would give him the opportunity to become a new islander. It was agreed on the spot and we set out for an evening meal at a local hotel where we were able to talk everything through in some greater detail.

I was looking forward to meeting Denise. A university graduate, currently working as personal assistant to a director in the Department of Education, she had, in her efficient manner, previously sent on her CV for me to peruse although I had not asked for it. It showed quite clearly that she had great organisational abilities and impressive references. She was far too highly qualified for the job I had in mind for her.

When we met, I put it to her that this surely was a retrograde career move. She agreed.

'I've been lucky, I've put a lot of time into study and work, and highly paid jobs have fallen into place. It sounds trite but now I believe that money isn't everything. If you can use me on this island, and civilization does not fall apart in the rest of the world for the next year or so, I will be able to get another job if and when I return.'

'The biggest challenge I can give you on the island would be as a Manager responsible for the education and social care of all the islanders, also the distribution of food etc. where necessary during the early months. Your immediate tasks would be to organise the efficient management of the school and leisure facilities for children and adults, liaise with teachers and helpers that I will appoint shortly, organise a collective kitchen/canteen to commence operation from the day we arrive on the island and seek volunteers from islanders for kitchen staff. Needless to say, it must be carried out with the maximum degree of delicacy, bearing in mind that everyone on the island will be a volunteer to the task to which you may ask of them. This therefore also requires the minimum number of rules and, particularly in the case of the teachers, paperwork. Does this appeal to you?'

'That's fantastic,' she said. 'I would welcome the challenge and I have to confess I had no idea that such an interesting job could be available.

A call that I had hoped for. Gerry was a farmer from 'God's own country', as my previous home county has been called. He and his wife Doris have two children: Patrick, aged 22, who worked with his father, and Theresa, 19, who was currently working in their local tourist office.

'It was my daughter Theresa who first saw your advert. I think she would like to tell you the reasons why we decided to apply,' he told me when we met.

'The moment I saw the advert I became excited and

wished I could ring you straightaway. Pat and I talked about the opportunity together and although we were of the same mind, we knew that Mum and Dad could not sustain the farm as it is at present without Pat's help. Then a few days later, the subject of the advert cropped up again. To our surprise Dad said that he had also seen it and said, "Suppose we all go? I could probably rent it out". He thought a move would provide a welcome change for all of us. And so here we all are.'

I asked Doris if the family had ganged up on her.

'Oh no,' she said. 'Gerry and I have always been of the same mind and whatever we have done we have done together. But if we could not do this I would seek to convince him that Pat and Theresa should have the chance to go'

Theresa's eyes moistened and I realised that they were a very close-knit family. They would all certainly be on the final list that was for sure. In fact, Gerry seemed to be the person to fill the second managerial position, responsible for all the agricultural aspects on the island, so I put my request to him.

'I dunno. It sounds a bit too grand for me. I thought we were going to some little Scottish island. Now it feels that I'm going off to Brussels talking about the European farm policies.'

'No, no, Gerry. This is far more important than Europe. Will you at least come and talk with me?'

'Aye, aye then, I'll come. Will I have to wear a suit? If so I'll have to buy one.'

'No again, Gerry, it won't be what you look like, it'll be whether you can cope with all those townies. See you tomorrow then, and perhaps Patrick, would you come along too? If your father agrees, I think I may have a job for you as well.'

* * *

When we met again the following day I outlined some of the things I would want them to do.

'Gerry, the most obvious thing I would like you to arrange first, is to list, and obtain before we get to the island, all the livestock and farming materials, including fencing etc. that will be required in order to set up a viable island farm. I have an information pack that will be of some help, but I intend to go with you and the other managers to the island in the very near future to assess the whole situation. It will be your choice as to how many sheep, cows, pigs, chickens or even canaries we take. Also, I have this idea that we should investigate the possibilities of starting a fish farm. They are all the go around Scotland at present, and I would like you, Pat, to take this on and find out everything you can about fish farms and what we will need to set one up. I would also like you to become more acquainted with fishing and shell fishing in general. Can I suggest you have a word and work with Angus on this? He has been fishing around these islands for a long time.'

I pointed out to Gerry that I wanted him to be responsible to the islanders through the island council and said that I would give him a guide as to his budget allowance in due course. I saw him raise his eyebrows and he cut in.

'Now look here Jim, I think I can do all you have asked of me about the farming, but I'm not keen on dealing with the money, ordering and all that sort of thing.'

'That's OK, Gerry, don't worry, I'll find someone who will do all your ordering. You say what you will want and he or she will get the prices, keep all the records, do all the arithmetic, type it all up and give it to you to look over. If it's all OK, we go ahead and get it ordered.'

'Well, that's a bit of a relief' he said wiping his brow.

*   *   *

51

Edith, a simple homeowner, (her words), sat comfortably relaxed and over a cup of tea she gave me a potted history of her life. She was perhaps about sixty, with a kindly face, but her hair was greying and there was sadness in her voice that spoke of hardships along the way.

'It was just on the spur of the moment. I read the advert and thought how enterprising that someone in this day and age would think of revitalising an island that I knew as a child. You know, I was born on a nearby Scottish island but I moved to Delhi when I was quite young with my mother and father, who was in the Diplomatic Service. When they both died prematurely, I was left virtually stranded in India, but I eventually begged and hitched my way back to England. I would like to come to your island. I have nothing to lose and only a little to offer, but I am capable of hard work.'

She convinced me. It was the mix of people of different ages bringing varied experiences and outlooks upon life that would make for success on the island.

Dafydd, who, not surprisingly, was from Wales, was totally committed even before I gave any indication that he and his wife would be selected. Both he and Gwyneth had been looking for a complete change in their way of life. They had reasoned that with a young family, now was the time to break out. They felt that my advert was made for them. Dafydd was a butcher by trade, voluble and confident in his manner, Gwyneth was just as enthusiastic, and their two children, Alison and Mark, were a delight and well behaved.

'Not many people like the butchering part of the animals they eat and, at least in the towns, generally ignore that it happens,' commented Dafydd. 'They enjoy the meat on their plate but often don't know or want to know how it gets there. It's my guess you won't get many offers to do this essential work, even if you get farmers applying. If I'm wrong I'll eat my apron and still offer you my strength and willingness to do any job I am capable of. Gwyneth is good with her hands; she makes all of the children's clothes and most of her own. She's actually quite a good mechanic too; she can strip down a car engine and put it together again. I know there won't be any cars on the island but there will be engines. Alison is already being taught to cook and Mark always wants to make thing tidy, so you will take us, won't you?'

It was more of a statement than a question but I had to admit he was offering many useful attributes and agreed that I was sure he would be there and, yes, there would be several engines in tractors and the like on the island.

John, a 34-year-old engineer, was generally enthusiastic about flying and gliding during his spare time, and he had met his wife Alice at the gliding club. She had been a secretary, and they had two sons, Jonathan, and Trevor.

In many ways he was over qualified for the role of Manager of Engineering, as the engineering needs of the island would seem to be minimal. But I was becoming aware that the electricity supply might not meet our requirements and we might have to generate our own. The challenge for John would be in how he would adapt his knowledge to new areas.

John had received a thoroughly sound mechanical training at Rolls Royce, but I needed to know that he could cope with the electrical services and, more importantly, whether he had experience of involving others with his work. His reply was satisfying.

'About my experience of being responsible for staff, I'm afraid that is a bit limited. We all worked as part of a team with different specialities but I can tell you that I have been a local councillor for the last year or so and that has brought me into contact with many different people of varying political persuasions and of different personal characteristics. I have tried, and it has been very trying at times,' he quipped, 'to get on with everybody in the town and it has been largely successful. I have also had to attend several meetings with the general public which does rather tend to concentrate the mind.'

I indicated that I would be happy for them to join us on the island and asked him to do some research about generation and wind power. I liked his manner and, as with everyone I interviewed, I relied very much on 'gut instinct'. It is something that is usually evident soon after meeting a person. Somehow you 'know' if there is an affinity or, conversely, if there are inhibitions or areas of less than total open honesty between you. My initial feelings had usually proved to be a reliable guide in the past.

At last, against the odds, I had an enquiry from a doctor by the name of Matthew. He was married to Ruth, who had been a nurse but was now at home looking after their young children, Andrew and Nicola.

Matthew was enthusiastic about the prospect of living on the island and anxious to move on from his present situation as a London GP. It turned out that he did not get on with his other practice doctors. At first I was a little worried about this and I asked Ruth if she had the same difficulties. She confirmed that they were an odd bunch at the surgery; and it could possibly be that nearly all the partners tended to be heavy on the drink whereas they were both teetotal.

I told them that I was pleased that they wanted to come to the island, and added that an early task would be for him to make an appraisal of medical needs for an occupancy of say 50. They should give me the bill and then assemble the necessary medicines and equipment for a year, before departure. I assumed that Ruth would be able to resume her previous role as a nurse if the requirement was there.

I had now concluded another eight successful interviews in this session, and rejected four applicants. So far I had recruited seven couples, and eleven single people. There were thirteen men, twelve women and about a dozen children, of whom six were between the ages of 4 and 11 and four were between the ages of 11 to 16. It seemed a good general mix overall.

The number of applications had now tailed off, so I repeated my advertisement for the third and last time.

9

Having now appointed the three Managers, it was essential that they, with several others who would have work to do before the actual occupation, visited the island. I gave Denise a list of names and her first job was to contact all those on the list and arrange their train journey, hotel accommodation, the boat trip to and from the island and of course the return trip.

About 25 were able to make the journey, including a few of the older children. As a surprise, Angus offered to meet us up there and to take us across in his fishing boat.

A good atmosphere was apparent on the train journey up and it continued at the hotel in the evening, with everyone getting to know each other and seemingly all getting along rather well. The good spirits were heightened the next day when it dawned fine and Angus was waiting in his fishing boat ready for the trip to the island. It was like a holiday venture, the group enthusiastically discussing the future that was in store for them.

It was a pleasant crossing with a stiff westerly wind to blow away any cobwebs and it was interesting to see how those used to working outside were much more able to appreciate the exposure than those who had office jobs. It was a practical guide as to what type of clothing would need to be part of our wardrobe when we eventually came to stay. Angus, at his first sighting of the island, pointed it out in the distance and we all strained our eyes, only to see it positively some minutes later. Anticipation increased until we were able to step on to *terra firma* and look around, first impressions often being the ones that last in the memory.

As we all tramped to the row of crofts and then on up the rise towards the main lodge the group broke into two, those who wanted to see all they could of the village where they would be living and those who strode ahead to see as much of the whole island as possible in the short time available. The questions began to flow fast and continued to do so for almost the whole time we were there. They were not all directed to me, it was all part of the excitement and infectious need to be part of the enfolding experience. Eventually we arrived at the top of the central hill, meeting those who had gone on ahead, and together we admired the expansive views around. Everyone was ecstatic and I took a minute to remind them that we were lucky, this was one of the all too few summer days and that it was not always as good, they would have to contend with wind, rain, cold and mist, but I hoped that the sunny days and the community spirit would offset these disadvantages.

We made our way down again to the main lodge and noticed on our approach that several, somewhat worn, wicker rocking chairs had been left ready on a covered veranda at the front of the entrance. It seemed rather welcoming and some took the opportunity to rest and have a bite to eat. I had obtained the key to the lodge and invited everyone to come in and have a look round. The large rooms with high ceilings and general space available within the house impressed everyone. There was a certain mustiness about certain parts of the house but several items of furniture were still in place and I felt that we could make use of some of them. There were even some old books in a glass-fronted case. I picked one up and read the title: *The Willow*. I guessed it was the subject dear to the heart of the previous Laird, who, I understood, wished to cover most of the island with these trees. Generally the house gave me comfortable vibes, with its large fireplaces and good-sized windows allowing the light to flood into nearly all the rooms. There was general approval and a few ribald remarks about my position as Laird, and how I would be sitting up there smoking cigars while they toiled, without adequate clothing, as they fought against the elements. The aristocracy were always lording it over the serfs.

Wandering outside, we were surprised to discover what had been a well laid out garden, with overgrown shrubs, a vegetable garden, a rose garden and an apple orchard. Most surprising of all were half a dozen mature palm trees swaying in the breeze. I am not a gardener but I did have thoughts that I would love to bring this garden back to what, it seemed, was a former glory.

As we returned, the questions related more to who would have what accommodation. I could not answer this yet but said that on our return I would soon hold another general meeting, by which time we should have been able to finalise on some of these issues.

We continued on our walk, passing some of the crofts, round to where a beach came into our view. The extensive sweep of shell sand was backed by steep sand dunes covered with marram grass, which rose sharply to the green fields above. But it was the sea that caught all our eyes, for the sun, having found an opening of blue between the rolling cumulus clouds, suddenly illuminated the sea to a brilliant turquoise blue which captivated all of us. We had to stop and watch the transition and interplay of the colours. The white-topped breakers, viewed from above, appeared to move slowly towards the beach to make it a peaceful scene, but we knew only too well that the weather could change in a very short period of time to render the scene totally different. We would, we guessed, talk much about the weather, good or bad.

We all then wandered down to inspect the crofts again. Denise, I noticed, was taking copious notes and I guessed that she would try and accommodate everyone's wishes as far as she could in the allocation of these properties.

10

A colleague who had worked for me on a number of jobs during my previous employment rang up. At first, I thought perhaps it was to arrange a reunion or to invite me round to meet his family again. But apparently he had heard on the grapevine what I was up to and believed that I would welcome his company on the island. He was right, Paddy was one of the most delightful people to know and he was also one of the most practical I had ever met and would turn his hand to almost anything. He wanted to know quite a bit about 'the job', as he called it, and then it was as simple as that. He said, 'Can do,' as if he had heard all that the job entailed and he would just carry it out as indeed he had so many times in the past.

'Hang on a bit,' I said. 'What about the missus, what does she think? And the youngsters? You'll not be on your own this time, you know.'

'Oh, Rene will be OK, she's been to lots of places with me before, as you know. Shaun will definitely come, he's getting stale and needs a bit of fresh air in his lungs, and Colleen will fit into island life. She needs a change of scenery.'

And that seemed to be that. Just like old times. They were a close family and I remembered many happy occasions, and that I had been in their debt for help several times over the years.

'Look,' I said, 'why don't you bring your tribe round for a drink. It's ages since we last met.'

When they arrived I had a shock, for Colleen was cradling a newly born baby.

'Got herself in the family way, ' Rene said after our initial greetings. 'Silly girl,' she added.

'Oh, Mum, you do go on, you know you love 'im to bits.'

'Maybe, but that's more than I do for the father, and more than the father does for him, leaving you and his baby like that. A kid needs two parents.'

'I know but I'll manage, and he'll probably have dozens of new parents on the island. What do you think, Uncle Jim?'

She always called me uncle and it was nice to hear it again. I was with her family at her birth and always had a soft spot for her.

'I'm sure you will manage very well,' I said. 'If you take after your mum and dad, you will.'

'I'm going to name him Jim after you,' she said, smiling at me.

'I'm truly honoured,' I said, feeling quite touched, and added. 'Some other friends of mine named their new arrival Jim after me, but unfortunately it was a sheep dog and it never seemed to do as it was told.

'Shaun, how are you?' I continued.

'I'm OK,' he said confidently, 'Dad says you've got a lot of work for me to do.'

'That's right. Basically we've got nothing as yet that's working. We've got to take everything to this island and put it all together, sort of make a village, and we will need a lot of hands.'

'Sounds great,' he said. 'I've never made a village before.'

'You're not alone.' I replied. 'I don't think even your dad has done that before.'

It was fortunate that Terry, an electrician who had also worked for British Telecom, applied, as I wanted some back-up for John on the electricity side. Terry was married to Kathy, a hairdresser, and they had three school-age children.

They told me that when they saw my advert they remembered being fascinated by a TV programme where a group of people had tried to re-create the life of a community in an Iron Age settlement. I laughed when they said they could imagine some similarities with my scheme and said this could well prove to be the case, but I hoped there would be an increasing number of mod cons to assist us into the future.

They asked a number of sensible questions and I was able to reassure them, before inviting them to join me on the island.

I was not happy with my meeting with Nigel; he came across with a suave manner bordering on the arrogant. He was a City trader. Early in our conversation it was disclosed that he was very wealthy. At 27 he had virtually made all the money he needed, in fact much more than he needed, to retire with a secure lifetime ahead of him to do whatever he pleased. I was somewhat bewildered. It was not just the money: after all, who was I, given my financial gain, to be in a position to make judgements on this account. No, it was more a question of: did he have the capacity for this change, this rapid down-market plunge? My judgement was that he would not be able to stay the course. As I edged the conversation to get behind the bravado, it became more evident that he did not possess any practical skills and, more particularly, he did not present any sign of ambition or desire to do anything with his time or make any comment or suggestions about island life. His philosophy had been from the start to 'make a fast buck', which was the way he put it, not me. In this regard he had indeed been supremely successful, it is true. I could not make out why he asked to see me; perhaps it was some form of curiosity about me and the scheme I was proposing. Did he really want to make an application to come to this far-flung place where his financial trading skills would be completely unnecessary? What would he do? I could not extract from him how he saw himself in this picture. We parted, both agreeing to think about it. I never contacted him or heard from him again.

'A teacher, you're just what we need,' I said. 'But why do you want to come to the island?'

Miranda considered her reply carefully.

'I would like to teach children in an environment where there is an absence of two things which I believe are jeopardising, if not destroying, education: behavioural problems and bureaucracy. The teacher's role is progressively being undermined; certainly it is where I teach in suburban London. Having said that, I don't want to give you the impression that I just want to opt out for those reasons. I still want the challenge of doing a good teaching job but I do not want to be head-on with the aggression of my pupils and all the social problems that exist in society today. Do you know, it's only a few weeks into the new term and I have been kicked, spat at and sworn at by young children six times already. A fellow teacher is actually on sick leave because she was attacked by a boy only nine years old.'

After I had described the lifestyle she could expect on the island, she asked how many children were expected.

'There could be about fifteen, of all ages. It is probable that they would all come under your direct supervision although there may be unqualified help available. Also, you would have to create the school or classroom from scratch yourself, apart from the actual building. If you agree to come I would need a list of your requirements in terms of furniture, books and other materials as soon as possible.'

'How will I know where to draw the line on cost with these requests?'

'You won't know. What I suggest is that you assess what you think is necessary, bearing in mind that everything we do will start at a basic level. The worst-case scenario, although unlikely, is that I would ask you to teach without any of the items on your list. What would your reaction be to that?'

I did not imagine that this would happen but I was interested in what she would make of it.

'I will prepare for that eventuality, I have some books and teaching aids of my own which I would bring anyway.'

This was just what I wanted to hear, not that she would bring some books of her own, but that she was not alarmed at the possibility of starting with next to nothing. I offered her the opportunity to come. She walked out with the biggest natural smile possible, and I thought that the benefits of my decision were happening even before I was living on the island.

I picked up the 'phone.

'My name is Robert. I work as an analyst in the field of Information Technology, experience which I imagine you would have little need for on your island, I suppose you would need skills of a more physical nature.'

'It depends. We will have a need for computer skills above the average and I would like to explore what possibilities there are. Will you come round so that we can discuss things in more detail?'

Robert was at my door bright and early the following morning. Overnight I had thought of one or two matters to ask him. I told him all about my proposals for the island in general terms and then came to the subject of computers.

'Robert, I've given you an idea about how I hope the islanders will respond to the various basic tasks, many of them using working methods which have been proved over the centuries, but I also want to look forward to the future and to that end I want all of the islanders, including of course the children, to have access to the internet. I thought also of the creation of a possible internet café, as I believe they are now called, and although I am not sure of the benefits it may bring, perhaps a website for the island. What do you think, how can you help and, by the way, you do realise that it is necessary to commit yourself to actually living on the island?'

'Yes, I got the picture about living there. I'm enthusiastic and willing to be among a new group of friends. There is an increasing tendency for more people to be able to work quite successfully from their homes rather than commute to and from an office. About your other questions. I've played around with computers since I was a boy and I've built many computers from the basic components for friends, and others for a fee. It is considerably cheaper than purchasing from your local computer store, so I could help in that area. A website is quite easy to set up, I have done several. As to its value for you, it would depend to an extent how much you or your islanders wish to communicate with the rest of the world. I can see possibilities with regard to tourism but that sounds rather against the trend of how you introduced your objectives for the island. Perhaps this would be more for the future but on a low scale. More likely, perhaps, is individual islanders having skills or products that would be of interest to a wider audience. Take for instance, an artist. There would be very little scope for this person to hold exhibitions locally, but the World Wide Web would allow their work to be viewed internationally. An internet café is, of course, just a table with a number of computers all connected to the World Wide Web and available for the use of the public for a fee, but with the added bonus of access to a coffee machine. One point I could mention is that for an island community such as yours, you must surely have had to strike a balance in your mind as to the inward-looking island, can I say "isolationist" attitude, and the modernising "people of the world" view. I'm sure it will be a compromise but modern technology will help you. Communication by e-mail is just one, there's the mobile phone – although reception may be poor or even non-existent – and there is always the poss-ibility of using satellite telephones.'

I asked him, as his first task, to set up the school with the requisite number of computer workstations and intro-duce computer-training classes.

'Eventually, when the islanders become more free from the essential initial works, I would want you to extend these classes to the adults, as it's my intention to introduce free Internet access for everyone. I hope it goes without saying that you would cope with the maintenance and upgrading of the systems when required.'

'Let me know how many units you want and I'll get started right away,' he said with marked enthusiasm.

'I'd rather you made an appraisal of our needs in consultation with Denise. She is in overall charge of education and the like, I think you will find her helpful. She will also have a view on the level of expenditure that can be allocated. I'll give you her number.'

Trying to juggle who was going to do what on the island had not been too difficult so far, for the various jobs had fallen into place as the applications came in, miraculously not duplicating themselves very often. I had not decided who should be asked to help Gerry with his farm accounts, when a full-time secretary named Kate came to see me. She was a young Lancashire lass, already working in a busy office of a wholesale marketing company, but it was the fact that she came from a farming background that convinced me. She had worked on her parents' arable farm until her father died as a result of an accident on the farm some three years ago. I commiserated and asked how her mother was coping. She told me it was hard for her, the farm had been their life but it all had to be sold up.

'But guess what?' she said suddenly, as if we were both family talking together.

'What?' I replied.

'She's met this man and they've gone out together and get on very well, but she's worried that it's so soon after Dad and she wonders what people will think.'

'What do you think?' I ventured, slightly tentative about her involving me in her family matters.

'I think he's lovely,' she said with genuine enthusiasm. 'I keep encouraging her, but she keeps saying it doesn't seem right to get married to Jack when I haven't found anyone yet.'

'If you come to the island with us, you may find some eligible bachelors to speed things along,' I said.

'M'mm are you trying to encourage me?'

'Yes, too sure I am, I've even got a job lined up for you.'

'Oh, what's that?'

'It's to help a farmer with his secretarial work, you know typing, estimates, purchasing orders, invoices, filing, help him keep to a budget, everything.'

'At least you're honest with the job description. When do I meet him?'

'Soon, I expect. I hope you will get on together, he's a foreigner.'

'Really, should that make any difference?'

'It might. He's from Yorkshire, as I am by adoption. His name is Gerry.'

'It seems I shall be outnumbered.'

We laughed as I deliberately repeated that it was such a pity she came from across the border. But, I added, I thought they would get along very well, they would have much in common with the farming.

My bell rang and I opened my front door to find a lanky, spotty-faced youth with long red hair falling over his eyes, grinning at me.

'Are you the guy who's bought an island?' he asked without introduction.

'Yes, why do you want to know?' I replied uncertainly.

'Thought I'd see wot you're like. Might 'ave a go an' come along.'

'What makes you think I would invite you?' I asked.

'You probably won't, what wiv all the money you've got, I aint got nuffin.'

'What do you do?'

'I nick fings.'

'You're a thief?'

'Yep, an' I'm good at it, I've just got into your car an' nicked the parcel off the front seat.'

'What?' I said aghast, not being able to think of anything more sensible to say.

'It's easy wiv them early Fords. Don't worry, I didn't damage the car, and 'ere's the parcel.'

'So your name is Nick and you nick things.'

'Yep, Nick by name, Nick by nature.'

'It's hardly at the top of the list that I'm looking for with the people I want on the island. Can you offer anything more – more, normal, shall we say?'

'Nope. But the way I looks and sees it is like this. I 'eard that what you been tryin' to do is to 'av on this island a cross-section of society, yep? Well, you ain't got no one like me, 'ave you?'

'No, but your way of life isn't something that I want to encourage in you or anyone else.'

'What about givin' people like me a chance to kick the bad 'abits?'

'Why haven't you kicked them up till now?'

'You blokes just don't understand do you? You stand there actin' like God and choosing them that goes through the pearly gates and them that don't. You sit in your nice 'ouse wiv a nice bed. All I've ever 'ad is a grotty squat in a part o'town you'd never put yer nose in, a cardboard box an' some old cloves, an' sometimes they've got nicked.'

'That's an irony. How does it make you feel?'

'Just the same as I feel all the time, knackered, no hope, no way out, bugger 'em all!'

'Did you go to school?'

'Yep, 'til I got chucked out.'

'What did you do?'

'Nuffin. Then Mum and Dad split up, 'e chucked 'er out, then me.'

'Where do you live now?'

'Nowhere, just on the street.'

'Do you do any work?'

'Nope. Well I did at first, a few odd jobs, labourin', bricklayin', and paintin', then I found stealin' a lot easier.'

'I'll tell you what you can do. Come back tomorrow and paint the woodwork on the front of this house. I'll see what sort of job you do and I'll stop you soon after you've started if you've made a mess of it. If it's OK you can carry on and we'll have another talk about giving you a chance.'

'OK, guv, what do yer wan' me t'do 'bout the paint an' fings. Shall I nick 'em?'

I saw the first hint of a positive expression in his eyes and wondered what I was letting myself in for, would I be judged crazy after all?

'No, I shall pay for them.'

''Ow much do I get paid for doin' the job?'

'Nuffin.' I said, getting into the swing of the moment. 'You're on probation.'

'Fought you'd say that,' he said as he walked away. By the way, I've just nicked your car keys off the 'all table, and was goin' to drive your car away. You orter be a lot more careful, there's a lot of crooks round 'ere in this area y'know. 'Ere, catch.'

I awoke the following morning to the crash of breaking glass. My God, I thought, it's that lad, he's come back to break in. I rushed downstairs and found him looking at me through the front room window.

'What the devil are you doing?' I shouted.

'Calm down, guv, this 'ere window pane was cracked. You wouldn't want me to paint round it wivout reglazing it, would you?'

'No, I didn't think you would be so efficient, and you frightened the life out of me.'

'Sorry, guv. I fought I'd get an early start.'

'Where did you sleep last night?'

'In your shed, 'ope you don't mind.'

I turned around to go upstairs and get dressed, still unsure if I was losing it or not.

When I returned to the house later in the day, I saw that Nick had found my ladder and was painting the upstairs window frames, whistling away to himself. My first thought was, my God, I've been a fool again. He's got access to all the upstairs rooms.

'Have you been inside?' I shouted up to him.

'Well, I did get free monfs once for breakin' an' entrin'.'

'Not that, I mean have you been inside the house?'

'Nope,' he said, 'I've decided to trust you from now on.'

You're a cheeky blighter, I thought. But I looked over the painting that he had done and could not find any faults with the standard of work.

He spent the next few days completing the painting and doing various other odd jobs for me. He continued living in my shed and I noticed that he had sorted it all out very tidily.

I was going to either rent or sell the house and I realised that whatever path I chose, I would have to separate those items that I would take to the island from those I would not. I decided that Nick could help me with this, and gave him the job of disposing of some of the things that I would no longer need.

'Some of these fings are worf somfin' on the street, y'know,' Nick observed.

'If you can sell them,' I said, 'you can keep the money as payment for your work here. Just clear the lot.'

During the next few days everything seemed to be going very well, and I came to the conclusion that he would be an asset on the island.

'You can come if you want to,' I said simply.

'Fanks,' he said with a sort of choking effect from his throat. 'I've seen you in a different way since I've been 'ere. You know you said get rid of them fings you don't want? I got free 'undred an 'fifty quid for 'em an' I'm givin' it back to you. 'Ere, it's for the island, y'know.'

I hesitated but I did take the money, it seemed the right thing to do.

'You're a good lad,' I said. 'I've a feeling you might find it a lot easier living there than some of the others.'

The phone rang.

'This is the Nuffield Hospital in Harley Street. We have a patient named Giles here. He wanted me to contact you to ask if you would be able to come along to see him.'

'What's the problem? How is he?'

'He's suffered a heart attack and he's had surgery for a quadruple bypass. He is in the intensive care unit and is comfortable but still very weak.'

'I'll be along. Are there any special hours for visiting?'

'No, you can come any time.'

I walked into the hospital and found Giles in his private room. He looked drained of his previous ebullience. Numerous patches, tubes and wires on his upper body, connected him to monitoring equipment. TV screens gave a colourful yet impersonal indication of his heartbeat, body temperature and breathing with a barely audible monotonous regular beeping

'Sorry to see that you're out of action,' I told him.

'Jim, I'm so glad you could get along so quickly. I'm a bit groggy, but I'll try not to fall asleep on you. I'm sure you guessed when we met that my work has been my life. I made a mess of my marriage and as a result of that I have virtually no close family. This heart attack, so sudden, has made me focus on things to which I have given very little thought before. I've been told by my doctors that, in effect, I have to switch off completely or take the inevitable consequences. I have to delegate most, if not all, of my business interests. To be frank, at first, I could not think what I could do, the future seemed to present me with an immense void. Then I thought back to our conversation and decided, Jim, I would like to come with you to your island and start a new life too.'

'Giles, you will be most welcome.'

'I have also thought about your strictures of acceptance to the island and decided that when I'm a bit fitter there may be one or two areas of my experience where I may be of some value to all those concerned.'

'I'm sure there will, don't concern yourself about those things now, we will find something that suits you between us.' The nurse was making a few discreet hand movements behind Giles so I made my way to leave.

'I'm being urged to leave you to rest. I'll be off, but I'll pop in again shortly.'

'Look after him,' I said to the nurse, unnecessarily.

'We will, he needs a lot of rest and a total switch-off from all his previous dealings,' she replied.

'Bye then, Giles. Get well.'

'Goodbye Jim, and thanks for coming.' Before I had reached the door to leave the room he stopped me.

'Just one more thing before you go, Jim. You didn't mention the subject and I am not surprised – it confirms my regard for you. The money. I've had a word with my bankers and it's in the system. You'll have it by the weekend.'

The meeting with Giles sobered me. Only hours before I had been talking to Nick, who was hoping to rise from the bottom of the pile, and now here was a man at the top who had fallen. In the recent weeks I had indeed met a fascinating cross-section of society. I was so excited at the feeling of being able to draw them together as a group and Nick's words still rang in my ears, 'Well, you ain't got no one like me, 'ave you?' It was only too true.

He had admitted that he was a thief; it was possible that he was also mixed up in drugs. There could be all sorts of other unsavoury areas of his life but there did not seem any other opportunity for him to change for the better. He was underprivileged, with no fixed address, which was the missing key to any government or council based assistance.

Would it be a sham or a fraud if I didn't include someone like him? Probably not, but his comments had troubled me and, dare I say it, I was beginning to see his good points. I was beginning to like him. Was I his only hope? The decision was entirely mine, there was no island council as yet for me to get the feeling of others or put it to any vote. I would have to carry the can if he became a nuisance on the island.

Graham rang and asked with a pronounced stutter if he could come along for an interview. He was a very quiet individual, sporting a black goatee beard. He worked as an assistant librarian in the city library in Belfast. It quickly became apparent that I was faced with a difficult decision, because he was not offering any skills that I could immediately see as being useful.

'Why do you want to live on this island?' I enquired. His reply was considered and controlled but I believe it originated from a deeply felt frustration.

'I w-want to get away from c-c-city life and all that it r-represents, I've had enough of the r-r-riots, the noisy and d-d-dirty streets, the r-r-religious b-bigotry, intolerant b-behaviour, and the l-litter and the g-g-graffiti that is regularly d-daubed on my p-p-p-property. I feel I am now an alien in the p-place that I was b-b-born.'

'I can see you have good reason to leave, but what will you do on the island?

'I aspire to b-b-being an author, I write p-poetry and have had a few minor w-works accepted.'

'That's fine but there is much to do collectively on Enniskerry in order to make this new community function. Everyone needs to contribute in some way.'

'I s-s-suppose that I could m-manage s-some office work or c-c-certain things at the s-school if there was a n-need.'

I was trying to find a good reason to invite him because I did have sympathy with his desire to leave and seek a new life. I wanted to help but was struggling for ideas on this one, until Nick, having met Graham in a local café, asked, 'You goin' to ask 'im to the island then?'

'I'm not sure,' I said 'but I don't think so. I can't see him fitting in.

'Yer know 'e was abused as a kid, don't you? 'Is father beat the 'ell outer 'im until 'e ran away. I fink you orter give 'im a chance, 'e's ad a rough life, an' 'e's worked 'ard to get at what 'e's doin' now.'

'Well, thanks for telling me, perhaps he does deserve a chance.'

I intended that my interview with Ken, a BBC TV producer, was to be my last. He was married to Jenny and had two children.

Ken came with a purpose, and before I could ask him my usual question about why he wanted to go to the island he said, 'I've been mulling the idea of your project around since I first saw the advert and I've done a little homework. Do you mind if I ask you a few initial questions to get some things clear in my mind?'

'Go ahead.'

'The history of this island and of small islands in general

is that the life is not sustainable. Nevertheless, you have the confidence to think you are offering a way of life that is different, based more on the modern technologies rather than relying on methods that in the past have failed?'

'Yes, past history is not encouraging, but I have put in place a number of things which I believe will get the island off to a good start for the first year and, if successful, we can build on that.'

'This is exactly why I have come to see you. I went through a similar process of thought and saw the picture, I believe, much as you have. But I wanted to push those ideas forward beyond that first year. Stop me if you can clearly see you and your island's economy and general situation in the future, say in five years' time.'

'Some of my ideas will, I hope, continue through into those later years. But carry on, I am interested in what you have to say.'

'Am I right in thinking that you wish to operate the island without the use of money and without interchange with the national economy?'

'Yes and no. I am playing, with increasing advice against the idea, of there being no need to use money on the island because each will give according to his or her ability and receive services from others in return. But on your other point, certainly not, I understand fully that the island will have to participate and exchange goods and services. In fact I am continually looking at new ideas that stand a chance of adding support to the island in future years.'

'That is just what I hoped you would say because although I am among those doubtful about the wisdom of operating without money, I feared that my idea would go against your basic principles. But before I go into that, first allow me a little diversion.

'Millions of people have in the past and continue to this

day to listen on their radio to *The Archers* "An Every-Day Story of Country Folk". Peter Mayle wrote a book about Provence and as a result, millions flock there every year. What have become known as soap operas portraying the everyday life of "ordinary" people captivate young people and others for hours every evening on TV.

'I can see by the look on your face that I am worrying you, but please hear me through. What I have in mind is this. We capture on tape and film the whole of your island project from now on as it happens day by day. It will be done sensitively. Your islanders will, in time, ignore that filming is even going on. It will be the story of the creation of your island, the thrills, the excitement, the disappointments of the islanders and their fears and successes. It will gradually create a new cult of interest. Your island will be unique and millions in their own homes throughout the country will follow the day-to-day life regularly. The value of this will be two-fold. There will be the TV rights, of course, but in the future an increasing number of people will want to come to your island and will pay good money to do so. You could expand on the island to accommodate a suitable unobtrusive number of dwellings for specialised island experiences and this would produce a regular income.'

'There is a lot to think about here. I understand and agree with the basic thrust of your proposal, although I'm horrified at the thought of becoming a soap opera. But first I have to ask you, where does your primary interest lay, how would you like to fit into this picture and how do I know that you will not utilise the film for your own personal gain?'

'These are fair questions, I have in the past worked as a freelance cameraman and I am now offering my services to you in order to carry out the filming – *gratis*. I would like to stay on your island working in this way to ensure the future viability of Enniskerry and I've thought of one way in which I can give you a form of guarantee. It is this. I would gather and edit the film on a weekly basis, each of which would represent say one thirty or forty-minute programme. I would, when it had been edited and processed, hand it to you, with a written statement to the effect that it is the only copy. The film would then become yours for safekeeping and you would in fact become the owner of the film. It is possible that we could let this arrangement run for any time up to fifty-two weeks of the first year before offering it out commercially. This would be a decision made either by you or with my advice should you need it. I, too, can proceed with the understanding that we will share between us similar views as to what is financially reasonable in whatever situation prevails. I can also supply numerous references regarding my own background history and to my good character if you wish. Further, I would conform to all the other standards that you would expect from other islanders which I believe includes a commitment to actually live on the island for one year. I do have other work that I would like to fit in during the year but you can be sure that I will pull my weight on the island as well as doing the filming.'

I later asked several people for their views on this matter of filming. There were a few that at first expressed a little reticence, but overall, when I explained the longer-term considerations, everyone understood and said that they could live with it; and that it was my decision anyway.

I agreed to break one of my journeys to Edinburgh to meet Ian and Madge, who were farming near Dumfries in Kirkudbright. Ian was a robust personality, seemingly very fit and confident. He had inherited the family's Scottish farm quite recently on the death of his father and they had been considering selling up since the foot and mouth crisis in 2002. When they saw my advertisement they had come to the conclusion that there would be little to lose and much to gain by relocating to the island.

I explained that we already had one farming family who would concentrate on cattle and dairy farming but there was a further need to deal with arable aspects, and suggested that the best solution might be for them to meet Gerry, Doris and Patrick.

I had learned at an early stage to recognise those who just could not comprehend the principal idea of my advertisement. I was continually amazed that people would ring having clearly not understood what they had read. One or two asked for details of the hotels available, three asked about the quality of the golf courses and fees, one thought I just wanted someone to look after my Scottish property while I was away. A few could not grasp the concept of working but not getting paid. Several wanted to know about what I was doing but had no intention of actually taking part. One thought that I was in some way breaking the rules of the minimum wage act. A couple were abusive and accused me of being one of the landowning rich who were exploiting the poor and labouring classes. One seemed to see the island as a refuge for concealing some illegal activity associated with weapons and the arms trade.

In addition, there were several others who telephoned and either they or I decided during the call that island life was not for them. There were others who seemed sufficiently interested to meet me but were subsequently rejected, proving how necessary it was to meet people face to face. A telephone conversation was simply not sufficient to give anything like an adequate understanding of the person.

11

I decided it was time that the three Managers and I had a chance to get together and to get to know each other better. We four would be spending a lot of time in each other's company and so we needed to be a good team. We met at my own home, breaking the day with a pleasant lunchtime meal at my local pub.

John seemed a stable personality at 34 years of age: he did not jump to quick conclusions. You could feel him weighing the odds and he had a quiet confidence that was reassuring.

Gerry was ten years older than John. Although slow in his speech he was not slow in his mind. He was inclined to let everyone else do the talking, never interrupting a conversation and speaking infrequently until, when he did, it was with a deep voice which commanded attention. He was devoted to his family, and I believed that he would never let anyone down. He had a wicked sense of humour that, for the sensitive, bordered on the harsh and would not be to everyone's taste. Second to his family, Gerry was devoted to his animals, the beasts, he called them. I was sure he was looking forward to stocking the island; it was a new challenge that had come at a good time. I knew he was not keen on the Manager's position but I guessed that he was more worried about the title than the actual work. I was sure I had made a good choice.

Denise was an extrovert, but not overpoweringly so. She was also talkative and always gave additional expression to whatever she was saying by a variety of different hand movements. She had positive ideas on almost everything that came into question and was eager to set things in motion.

I felt I had in these three people the catalyst for the island to move in the right direction. The first thing I wanted was their views on the composition of the island council. I had already proposed that it should be composed of the four of us with the addition of a secretary, a treasurer and one other person, but I had a feeling that the secretary could be underemployed and the treasurer would have little to do.

Denise was the first to comment. 'I think we do need a secretary, even though you want to keep paperwork to the minimum. There will still be agendas, minutes and letters. I suggest you ask Kate to come on the committee and combine her work for Gerry with ours. As for a treasurer, this is more in your hands, you've put up all the money.'

John agreed, adding, 'Can I suggest that Denise and I will also produce our own share of secretarial work, and it may be more efficient to keep it under one roof. And although we could easily operate with a committee of five, seven would give a greater spread and reflection of opinion.'

Gerry agreed with Denise's first point and continued, 'There is a need for a treasurer. There will be many transactions and a lot of money, I imagine, will change hands. You yourself are the best person for this role, it's your money.'

'Thanks.' I replied. 'We will ask Kate to give an even greater effort for her work for the same salary rate of zero! The reason I want a treasurer is because I want the whole affair to be transparent, and to dispel any "kingdom and serf" mentality that is present on other islands. I have in mind to ask Philip, my present solicitor, to do the job, if he is willing. Next, can I have your views on the seventh member of the committee, who is to be drawn from the islanders? I want the committee to comprise of an odd number of people, not in their attitude, I mean in their numbers.'

'Perhaps we are all a bit odd by virtue of being here,' laughed John. 'I think this should be your first referendum vote as we get onto the island. Let everyone get their first vote in.'

Denise then suggested she should bring out the first newsletter, and went on to discuss in some detail the budgets I had proposed and the practicalities of packing and transporting belongings to the island. When it came to the subject of food, John worried that wealthy islanders could provide themselves with additional supplies from the mainland and thereby cause an imbalance in the stability of the island.

'I certainly want to avoid this,' I said. 'We will collectively purchase some essential or specialised foods that we cannot produce ourselves, but I urge you to spread the message – and put it in the newsletter – that islanders should not expect more than a basic diet at first.'

Denise then told us that she had been reading up the history of some of the other islands.

'It does seem that among the islanders in general, one of the factors in their situation that they could not escape from was their system of tied cottages, which could not be purchased or leased. They lacked the satisfaction of owning their own homes. Now I know our situation will be somewhat different but each of our islanders will be in much the same position of not owning their own property. Ownership will I think be a greater incentive for them to continue residence into the future. For the long term perhaps you'll keep open the possibility of islanders being able to purchase their property? I believe this would be a big incentive for anyone wanting a commitment beyond the first year and I understand that they would be entitled to grants and loans for them to improve the buildings.'

'You're right Denise, I am very much in favour of this, I think it's too early to raise this generally at present but I will keep it in mind.'

'I've just had another thought,' Denise continued, 'it's about your generosity in providing all that you are for the first year. It occurred to me that looking at it from our side as it were, some would find it rather difficult not to be paying for their accommodation, heating, water, gas and all those other services that they would normally have paid for in the past. Although one could believe that few would object to being given something for nothing, some may feel indebted and therefore unequal in the sense that they are dependent upon your good-will in these areas. I don't believe that you would want them to feel this way. Should we therefore allow them the ability to show their commitment by way of some form of payment rather than let them harbour the thought that they are totally dependent upon you for these services?'

'Do you know, Denise, I've never thought of it like that. You are absolutely right, but to change the basic idea at this stage and start charging people would introduce a whole range of new problems. The first being that most are not actually earning, certainly not from their work on the island. My immediate reaction is to fall back on my often-stated word "reasonable" and ask for a contribution. Do you think we could introduce a scheme of voluntary payments? What do you think, Gerry?'

'I think this has opened up a "Pandora's box," answered Gerry. 'If as you say correctly, they are not earning and several have sold up their interests on the mainland then they would have to pay from any savings that they possessed. Not everybody will have savings so therefore it's not an option.'

'OK,' I concluded. 'I will have to develop ideas beyond this interim arrangement of voluntary payments and I hope to resolve the matter before the end of our first year on the island.'

I was so glad that these considerations had been pointed out to me. It showed the value of having the right people around to help.

12

I think every person, with the exception of some of the children, that I had so far approved as an island member turned up at my local village hall for the second general meeting. I had asked Denise to arrange the venue for me and produce an agenda along the lines:

1. Introductory talk
2. The Contract
3. Progress to date
4. Buildings, Engineering and Maintenance
5. Agriculture, Fisheries and Food
6. Education, Arts, Crafts, Music
7. Timescales
8. Finance
9. Questions

'Welcome again to those who attended the first meeting and a special greeting to those who are here for the first time. The purpose of tonight's meeting is first to give another opportunity for you to meet with each other, second for me to update you on the progress so far, and to talk more on some specific issues, and for you to ask questions at the conclusion.

'The first somewhat important point is that today I've concluded all of the final details relative to the purchase and setting up of the island. My scheme for a permanent society of selected people to inhabit the island can go ahead. It seems that I inherit the title Laird but I would prefer that you all know me as Jim.

'A second point, which may allay some uncertainty with regard to selection. I have found no reason to reject any person here tonight. You may all assume that you are invited if you wish to take part.

'Several of you enjoyed your first day visiting the island recently and I picked up a number of questions there, for which we can now produce some answers, and I will deal with any further questions at the end.'

'Item two on your agenda. The Contract. At the first meeting the vote was eighteen to four in favour of a commitment between us in the form of a contract. I would like you all, other than children, to sign the contract that was sent with my last letter to each of you, in order to become an islander in this first phase. If you have any objections or comments on the wording, please mention it at the question session at the end of this meeting and I will try and accommodate your views. You will remember it is as follows:

' "I offer to reside on the island of Enniskerry for a minimum period of one year. I also freely offer in reasonable proportions to the Island Community one or more of the following for the same period of one year. My Labour, My Knowledge or Professional Skills, My Material Gains from my past employments, My Word of Commitment. Further, I will not take from the island anything that is not freely given to me by the Island Community.

Signed .... Witnessed by .... Date ....'' '

'Item three. Progress to date. I have now appointed the three primary people who will carry much of the responsibility for the well-being of the island. They are John, who

87

will deal with building, engineering and maintenance. Gerry, who will deal with agriculture, fisheries and food, and Denise, who will deal with education, social care, arts, crafts and music. They will not be allowed to employ anyone but they will ask for volunteers to work with, not for them.

'These people, I will call them Managers, will be responsible to me through an island council of six members made up of the three Managers, a secretary, a treasurer and one other member. As I indicated at the last meeting I have awarded myself the casting vote in the event of a tie dividing the six members and I intend that any one of these six members can be voted off the committee and replaced.

'Progress with potential new islanders is now such that 25 of my interviews have resulted in successful appointments. These have included 11 couples and 14 single people, and about 18 children below the age of 18. These add up to a total number of 54 individuals. It seems a good general mix of social background, age and skills overall. My estimate at the moment is a final figure of the order of 60.

'Item four. John has established that the electricity supply to the island would only cope with our lighting requirements. He will shortly be deciding between individual generators for each family and a more powerful one to cope with the total needs, and we have agreed to consider wind generators at a later date. He has drawn up details about how we get fresh water supplies to each family, but the pipe laying for this can only reasonably commence when we are resident on the island. Apparently there is no major problem with telephone connections but the number of lines out from the island is limited, therefore I ask you to be patient until the system has been improved. Individual crofts are to be heated with bottled gas and arrangements are in hand to provide the heaters and an adequate supply of cylinders. We estimate that we require a minimum of 26 accommodations in total. These will be provided from the 10 crofts that are in a good state of repair, plus another 10 crofts for conversion as soon as possible. In addition, there are 6 rooms in the lodge that can be used for temporary accommodation.

'Item five. Gerry has agreed with Ian that they will operate their farms individually. Ian will bring his 500 sheep to the island but will concentrate mainly on the arable side of farming, and Gerry on the cattle. Even so, they hope that there will be some interchange of labour between them as the need determines, and it was agreed that more assistance will be needed and additional machinery will be required. They were wondering if James would be interested in helping. Gerry's son Pat has progressed with his knowledge of fish farms but his time will be much in demand with Gerry in the first weeks of setting up the farms on the island.

'Item six. Denise has been very busy with the arrangements for our trips up north to the island. Her flat has become a temporary office for our business and is rather bursting at the seams as a result of some early deliveries. If anyone can offer some temporary storage space please have a word with her. She has now met with our teacher, Miranda, and agreed various strategies to cater for all our children. There are many ideas forming for further education as well as social and sporting activities at the school during evenings and weekends.

'Item seven. Timescales. I am now proposing that we should be able to occupy the island during the first week of March next year. It may be possible to arrange a number of visits to the island before then. An advance party will carry out essential work on the crofts. I would be quite happy for any members to arrange visits themselves but would urge that they are flexible about their time. Please be aware that all sailings are dependent on the weather.

'Item eight. I have one comment to make regarding our finances. It has been drawn to my attention that some could find it a difficulty not to be paying for their accommodation and services. You may feel indebted to me and therefore unequal. I am quite happy to continue to provide these things initially. However, anyone who feels they would be happier to make a voluntary contribution can do so to me personally for that specific purpose. Are there any questions?'

'I think the most uncertain element of the contract is the 'Material Gains from my past employments'. Can you expand on what this actually means?' asked Matthew.

'Yes, I can. I have said that I require some reasonable indication that you will commit yourself to our cause for the first year. I will have an informal talk with each of you, so if you are offering, for instance, your physical labour while on the island, I will see this as a reasonable statement of your intentions. In your case, Matthew, you are offering to be our doctor, and that is sufficient. But for those to whom it applies, are you, for instance, going to keep your wealth on hold and allow me to house you, feed you, provide you with heating and allow you access to other services that I can provide, free of any charge? I am not asking you to pay me for these things. I do not want to know about your financial situation, and, if I did know, I could not and would not want to stop you doing whatever you want to do. What I believe would be reasonable is for you to give me an indication during our talk together that you believe in the idea that our island community can support itself with everyone putting in sufficient effort, each according to his means and ability.'

'Will your treasurer provide complete details of income and expenditure for us to see?' asked Charles.

'Yes, six monthly or annual reports will be available.'

'If islanders or others make a donation to you, will this information be available to us?'

'Donations will be listed anonymously in the treasurer's report.'

'Will there be opportunities for our children to go on trips to the mainland?' asked Terry

'My guess is not in the first year. There will be too much happening on the island, but in principle there is no reason why outings should not be arranged in the future.'

'My follow-up questions are, how would you react to a family wanting to take a break or holiday and what are the possibilities for our family members to visit us here on the island?'

'Other than for medical or similar emergency situations, I would be disappointed if you felt you needed a holiday, particularly during the first year. It is not that I want to curtail these undoubted pleasures. My hope is that people would be as enthusiastic as I am about the island, so that it would not be necessary to think in terms of having a vacation. I would like them to think that what we are actually embarked upon what could be regarded as an ongoing holiday. As to the second part of your question, I have no problem about any family members visiting at any time. At first we will not have enough housing for ourselves let alone accommodating extended families, but let's see how things develop.'

Other people asked questions about the makeup of the island council, the possibility of visiting the island before we all finally took up residence there and whether I still had ideas of a 'money-free' island. These questions were easily answered as the Managers and I had anticipated and discussed them at a previous meeting.

13

I decided that it would considerably ease our arrival on the island if I sent an advance party to assess some of the logistics of transporting everything from the mainland. As both Bill and Bob had volunteered to spend a couple of weeks on the island to commence some of the restoration work on the buildings, I thought it would be far better to give them some more support. I asked Paddy if he could spare some time and I knew that James was still unemployed and would be enthusiastic to help. Pat was going to get information for the farmers and said he would stay longer than he had originally planned and would give them a hand. I contacted Angus, who said he would be available with the boat to get some materials across. In all, five of our most suitable members would be together to get things moving.

The Managers had also asked for specific information relating to their tasks as they could not go themselves.

John, wanted information about the state of the underground electric cable from the mainland and its terminations, the possibility or lack of good television reception, the source and position of the springs, what had happened to rubbish disposal in the past, the state of the telephone network and a drawing of the location of all the buildings etc. (I had one photocopied from the estate agent but it was not sufficiently detailed.) He wanted more information on sewerage disposal (if any) from each of the crofis and more detail from Angus on landing stages around the island.

Gerry wanted to know about the state of the land for grazing, the extent and estimate of fencing required to enclose areas for stock and the types of grain if any that the land had supported in the past and would be likely to support in the future.

Denise wanted to find out if there was any existing building available for use as the school, the state of medical care available on the immediate mainland, and any information from the mainland library about Ennis-kerry and its history.

I asked for an up-to-date report on the general state of the Lodge, including the sizes of the rooms, and also that they should locate a suitably large, covered storage site on the mainland, as near to the jetty as possible. I envisaged that we would progressively order materials and store them in this temporary building in preparation for the eventual transfer to the island.

By all accounts, when they returned several weeks later, the exercise was both entertaining and productive. All five related to each other very well and shared a similar good humour. Knowing Paddy I could not imagine it being anything other than a thoroughly entertaining experience. However, they were not idle. By some judicious telephone calls before their departure, much of the building material was available for Angus to transport across to the island for work to commence from day one. Progressively answers to nearly all of the questions asked by the Managers were obtained and duly reported back.

As far as I could gather, they had managed to renovate six of the ten crofts that needed attention. They had all commented on how James had been slow to respond to the rivalry and banter that developed within the group and there were doubts as to whether he would be physically strong enough to help with some of the arduous jobs ahead. In the event, the older men were full of praise for his developing sense of humour and his increasing ability to cope with the hard work that at times entailed continuing outside in spite of unpleasant weather. It must have been a rapid culture shock from being unemployed and living with his parents to suddenly finding himself on a depopulated Scottish island, up at daybreak and working physically hard until nightfall. I understand that evenings approached being riotous, with Paddy telling almost continuous Irish jokes while they all shared a bottle of Scotch before turning in on their camp beds in the first renovated croft. No one found it difficult to sleep but perhaps rising at first light to get the maximum number of daylight hours was a little more tricky.

14

'Good evening everyone and welcome to the third meeting of the Enniskerry Island community. I think every member, including all our children, are assembled here today, with the exception of Jock and Morag as Jock is unwell and understandably doesn't feel up to the long journey south. This will be the last meeting before moving to the island. I hope you will ask any questions to clear up anything that is concerning you.

'First, I would like to give you an update as a result of the experience of our advance party who returned from Enniskerry just a few days ago. The lodge where I will reside has six spare rooms and can house up to twelve people if necessary. As most of you are aware, there are twenty crofts in total. I am pleased to announce that sixteen are now up to habitable standard; the other four will be completed soon after our arrival.

A number of people have volunteered to camp until their crofts are ready. Materials are on site for this purpose and for the construction of two large outbuildings for temporary storage and for a canteen-cum-kitchen. In the meantime two large ex-army tents will be used.

'I would like to draw your attention to the arrangements for deliveries north for onward transfer to the island, which are contained in the folders that have been handed out to all of you. Please read carefully and ensure we have the minimum of hassle on the day.

'You will know that we have now established a large temporary store near to the jetty on the mainland in order to house all communal equipment plus all your individual equipment and belongings. We intend to take delivery of all our requirements into this store progressively up to the eve of our departure to the island and then commence ferrying as much as possible to the island on the day of our occupation.

'Islanders are asked to make their own arrangements for transporting their belongings to the temporary store during the coming weeks and co-ordinate all these delivery arrangements with Denise. We simply cannot risk everybody's belongings arriving on the same day. It is essential that everything is labelled with your Christian name and the number of the croft, room or place allocated to you. We have arranged for a number of large removal vans to be collecting communal requirements from the London and other Midland areas and travelling to our mainland assembly point two days before departure to the island. If you have any difficulty with your own arrangements some space may be available on these removal vans but, in order to avail yourself of this possibility, arrangements must be made via Denise in good time.

'Please note carefully the maximum permitted sizes for crates. If you do not conform to this request, you risk your luggage being left on the mainland for a much longer time. Also you have been given the dimensions of the rooms in your allocated croft, so be careful that your larger items, for instance your bed, table, wardrobe, or cupboards do fit the rooms, if not they may have to be left out in the rain.

'Your own journeys north should be completed by the day before departure to the island. There is no need to co-ordinate these journeys with Denise but please make sure you are there on the day. Hotel accommodation has been booked in your names for the night prior to departure to the island.

'On the day of departure priority will first be given to the transport and erection of the army tents for our storage requirements and kitchen. All families and individuals will be provided with a double-burner bottled gas cooker and a gas heater with gas bottles, two saucepans, a Tilley lamp, a packed lunch and a miscellaneous box containing the minimum of plate, bowl, cup, cutlery, matches and candles etc. for use on the day. Islander's individual possessions will then follow.

'On the day of occupation, transport and deliveries to the island will commence at first light. Angus will provide our own ferry service and will supervise the loading onto his boat. Volunteers will be asked to do the actual manual work of loading and off-loading, perhaps with a rota system. If there is particularly foul weather priority will be given to most essential items.

'Once on the island, belongings will be transported to your individual accommodation by a trailer pulled by a tractor. Again, in the event of poor weather, essential supplies will be taken first. May I suggest that although the temptation will be great to sort out your own belongings in your new home directly they are delivered, please remember that others will not have reached that stage. It would be wonderful if we could all help each other, so as to avoid some, other than the young children of course, being snugly tucked up in bed while others are still toiling in the rain to get their neighbours possessions to them.'

The afternoon session seemed to go well, everyone mixing to exchange their thoughts. The children talked excitedly with each other and before we could believe it we were into the more formal session of questions.

'Nick?'

'Will we 'ave a disco, a pub, a fish and chip shop an' a

bettin' shop, like we got at 'ome?' There was a round of laughter.

'The answer to that is you can have whatever you want provided that a sufficient number of your island colleagues agree. Each request would come before the committee and be voted upon. Sound out Angus and see what he thinks about a fish and chip shop, he might have at least a fifty percent interest in the fish if not the chips. I'm not sure about the betting shop, what with the lack of racehorses and a racecourse on the island, but if you're keen on betting I'll give you £100 to £1 that this island will be a great success.' At that everyone gave great cheers.

'Alison?'

'Will we be able to take pets because we've got a dog and a cat?'

'Yes, you will be able to take your pets but you must understand that we will be effectively living on a farm and so your pets must be controlled and not allowed to worry the sheep. Which brings me to another point for parents to note as well. Resist the temptation to name the animals that are being farmed. It's nice to adopt a fluffy lamb and personalize it by giving it a name but you may then have the responsibility of explaining how your child's most favoured and delightful pet came to be piping hot on a plate in front of them ready for them to eat. Terry, it's your turn.'

'I'm still a bit concerned about this contract. Suppose I want to purchase something solely for my own use from the mainland, and pay for it with my own money, how would this be affected in terms of the contract?'

'The answer to your question lies in the word "reasonable", which is used in the contract. I want the islanders to be free to operate, if possible, in the market economy – free enterprise, if you like. Inevitably there will have to be financial exchanges with the mainland; I will certainly have to involve myself in this way for the needs of the island. In terms of something exclusively for your own benefit or financial gain. I am determined not to act as a God and dictate what any one of you should do or not do. It will be your responsibility to act fairly. If you are seen by your colleagues to be living on this island without making a fair and reasonable contribution to its progress then I would suggest that in fact you would not be an islander.

'I am still considering the possibility of doing away with money completely on the island. You may feel that this is a crackpot idea, but if my ambitions are fulfilled we will eventually be self-sufficient. When you move onto the island, I and many of your colleagues will progressively be providing you with accommodation, food, heating, lighting, education for your children, technical and personal assistance and many other things. Free. Soon we will all owe each other a perceived debt that will only be relieved by us giving freely of our own efforts. I ask you, where would there be a need to exchange actual money? I hope this has gone some way to answer your question. Jonathan, what would you like to say?'

'My dad has just said to me that I might not get any pocket money. Is that right?'

Among some laughter. I replied. 'Jonathan, it's up to your mum and dad whether they give you any pocket money. Think of it like this: Mum and Dad may not yet be earning any money here, and you will not have anything to spend it on even if you were given any. There isn't a shop on the island yet and so there is nothing to buy. Perhaps we will have a shop one day but that needs some thought.

'Andrew?'

'I think we should have a flag for the island.'

'Nicola?'

'Yes, and it should have three colours, yellow for the sun, grey for the mist and green for the green fields.'

'Miranda?' (This was Terry's young daughter.)

'I think it should have a lamb to remind people of all the animals we will have there.'

'All great ideas. You three get together, make a drawing or painting in colour, give it to me and I will get a flag made to be hoisted to the mast on the Lodge from the day we arrive.'

The more formal part of the evening ended and we returned to a number of smaller groups, all in animated discussion, full of expectation and good humour.

During the evening I had a long chat with Miranda, our teacher, about how she felt the school could be best run. I gave her the anticipated number of children with their approximate ages: six children between 5 and 11 and eight children between 11 and 18.

As Mark, Richard, Nicola and Zoe would be five or under, she felt that a playgroup would be more suitable, if one could be formed.

I was pleased that many of her ideas ran in tandem with mine. She had already produced two skeleton timetables for the junior and senior schools. We both felt that the basic structure of the school would be greatly enhanced by having islanders with differing skills and interests combining for a varied input to the lessons. I mentioned Belinda with her musical training, and Lynda, who had many valuable qualities for instructing in physical education. I suggested that perhaps Miranda should also consider Lynda's suitability as an assistant teacher. I added that we were fortunate in having Robert who had volunteered his help and was available for all computer related studies and that perhaps that we should incorporate this into the syllabus, perhaps it was essential anyway.

I learned later that Miranda and Lynda had met, and that they got along well together. Miranda thought she would be ideal as an assistant teacher and Lynda was over the moon to have been considered. Lynda had been given a free hand to organise the entire PE, games and sports during particular periods in the week. Later, I added in the need for adult sports such as badminton, karate and yoga when we were better organised during the evenings.

I was not certain about the school accommodation but envisaged that it would have to be temporary at first, probably in a large army tent of the type that would also be used for our kitchen/canteen. It would be OK in size but would require a suitable solid floor, and, of course, adequate heating and suitable lighting.

Slowly, as the evening progressed, people began to leave and those remaining became less excitable and more constrained in their discussion. I wondered how many would have difficulty in wrenching themselves away from friends, family and loved ones to start on this adventure. I wondered if any would have real regrets. I wondered if the pressures would begin to show in some after the first month or so. I wondered many things but I considered that I had carried the scheme through to this stage without any major disasters and I remained firm in my belief that the project, as a whole, was sound and that only good could come from it, for each of my new friends and for myself.

15

The move onto the island was arranged so that everybody, except Jock and Morag, had stayed overnight in a hotel. The only other local was Angus, who had a house on the mainland not far from our departure point. Before dawn he was at the quayside with his fishing boat suitably stripped of all fishing gear. All other able-bodied islanders were ready to commence the colossal task of loading. Each of the crates in the store had been carefully labelled with the owner's name and croft number. Together with the various items of farm equipment and machinery, there seemed a massive quantity of belongings. It was to take several sailings over a number of days.

The long-awaited day dawned with a weak, pale yellow sun and a thin layer of cloud but there were signs that it could improve. The dark sea lapped at the seaweed-covered jetty walls within the harbour and Angus's boat, *Island Queen*, rocked slowly and comfortably as the first heavy weight of the farm tractor was lowered into position by crane.

No one single person had been suggested to take control of the selection and loading process, but Denise was ensconced inside the store and dealing with a multitude of questions before selecting the order in which crates were loaded onto a forklift truck. Paddy seemed naturally to fill the position of foreman at the jetty and was soon giving directions for the activities in hand.

I saw Nick looking rather awestruck at the loading process.

'Nick! Have you ever driven a tractor before?'

'No, I 'aven't even stole one. Never even seen one of them fings in Lunnon. Wouldn't be much use fer joy-ridin'.'

'Time to learn and start your job for the day. Make sure that you are on the first sailing and when you get to the island take charge of the tractor. Your job will be to transfer everyone's belongings from the jetty to their croft. Hitch that trailer on. You'll get some help to load and unload, but take at least one of the owners with you each time to help you unload at the croft and get it all to the right place. Then get back ready for the next load. If it rains, cover everything up with the tarpaulin. I suspect it will take you all day and maybe tomorrow as well.'

Things developed with a holiday-like atmosphere prevailing, I went with the first sailing and, together with several others was able to watch the grey clouds dissipate and give way to a brighter sun. Two seals watched us depart, just their heads with bristling moustaches visible above the water. There was a strongish breeze once we had left the sheltering confines of the harbour and for most of us who had come from the south it felt as if it was blowing away the cobwebs from our minds. The diesel engine chugged away, the bow creating curving waves from the now deep-green sea. Some looked back over our wake to the receding mainland where our small group were still working to sort things out. They gradually diminished in size until they were no longer visible. Anticipation of what was to come affected most of us as Angus kept us informed of the various landmarks and other islands that we were passing. We were lucky that the light was so good. Ken, who had also been up at first light, was aboard and filming the whole event.

Naturally, Angus was able to point out the first sighting of Enniskerry in the far distance and we all strained our eyes to be sure that we could really see it. Then as we approached nearer we were able to distinguish the dark grey outline among others, rising from the silver horizon. A broad ray of sunshine angled diagonally to highlight the higher reaches of the central hill. Soon Angus said he could see one of the beaches and, some minutes later, each one of us confirmed that we also had seen it. Now more colours were becoming visible and we could make out the brown and the green of the landscape rising to the highest point and then a thin, vertical, bright silver band, a water-fall falling from a cliff face towards the beach. The excite-ment was mounting, and before long, we had reached our destination and were tying up at the jetty.

'Jim,' Angus called, 'I think you should disembark first and lead us onto your island.'

'Thanks Angus, it certainly is a momentous occasion for me. I welcome you all to Enniskerry and I hope you will be very happy here.'

The tractor that we were anxious to get to work was not off-loaded first, so I suggested that anyone, apart from those who were helping with unloading, who would like to, should walk up the hill to explore this part of the island and see the crofts that would be their homes for the foreseeable future.

Nick, in his enthusiasm to get on with his tractor-driving job, jumped off the boat, slipped and nearly fell into the sea.

'Fuckin' 'ell,' he exclaimed as he struggled to gain a handhold.

'Language, Nick. Not everyone likes it,' I warned.

'Sorry,' he said 'I just fort I was a gonner, I can't swim, y'no.'

'OK, but watch it. Next time you'll get pushed back in to teach you not to swear like that.'

As soon as the tractor was off, Nick was in his element.

He found out how to fix the trailer on and was waiting for his first load.

'Nick, while you're waiting, drive up to that junction over there and reverse into it and then drive back. It may not be as easy as it seems.'

He drove up, made two or three attempts at reversing and came back. He looked slightly crestfallen, thinking I might not give him the driving job after all.

'Weren't very good, was it?'

'That's OK for a first attempt,' I replied. 'Have another go. You'll soon get used to it.'

Then the first crates came off, belonging to Bill and his family. As Bill was working at the unloading and had already become familiar with his croft as a member of the advance party he suggested that Helen and the children should go with the tractor and trailer. James would go along with them to help unload. Helen said if their belongings were left outside as near as possible to the croft, they would sort things out themselves. They all climbed on to the trailer and we heard cheers of delight from the children as they bumped along waving as they departed up the hill.

Work continued throughout the day and by lunchtime a more efficient routine had been established and everything was proceeding like clockwork.

Some of us stopped at the same time to consume our packed lunches. We chose a spot away from the bustle of the work at the jetty and watched as Angus departed to commence his third delivery from the mainland. We sat on a grass-covered slope looking out over blue green sea. All was peaceful, not a sound could be heard except for those created by our team sorting out the various belongings of the group. Most of us could not contain ourselves, trying to express in words how we felt about the beauty of the environment that we now found ourselves part of.

105

The view exceeded in its expanse and colour what several had ever experienced in their lifetime A few said they had never been anywhere so peaceful. Some of the children's view of their new environment did not extend to the beauty of the far horizons but they did not miss the expansive yellow beach sweeping round the headland and the colourful flowers at their feet.

Before long, Nick returned to say he was ready for the next journey so we returned to the jetty to continue with the sorting and loading.

More of the islanders progressively joined us with each sailing through the afternoon and, being lucky with the fine weather, good progress continued to be made. As the sun approached a lower point in the late afternoon, I asked that the message should be given to all that we should down tools and meet up at the Lodge. I wanted everyone to attend to witness the raising of our flag on the Lodge.

'Some of you may remember that at our last general meeting three of our youngest members, Andrew, Nicola and Miranda suggested that we should have a flag for the island. Thanks to them we have now had that flag made. I think the lamb at the centre is a most appropriate symbol for it signifies, as of today, the rebirth of this island of Enniskerry. We will have a short fanfare of trumpets from members of our fledgling band and the flag will be raised on this new mast to fly continuously from the Lodge. It will help us to remember, as if we could ever forget, that if you want something good to happen here on your island, you can make it happen even if you are only four years old.'

We all returned to meet Angus and the last delivery of the day. Everyone was getting quite tired by then but some expressed the view that it was a different kind of tiredness from that of the city. It was a healthy feeling that had the satisfaction of a worthwhile effort. We paused to see the age-old spectacle of the large orb of the sun slowly changing from orange to red, from circular to elliptical, from light to twilight. Age-old, but new, infinitely repeated yet never the same. Flimsy clouds adorned the vicinity of the sun like a gossamer garment, their colours also changing, white to pale yellow to orange to red to purple. Some had never seen such a sight.

16

Like everyone else, I took delivery of my belongings into the Lodge and gradually made efforts to sort things out. I had allocated myself two good-sized rooms and this allowed some of the other rooms to be used by those who, as yet, had no permanent accommodation prepared for them, and for storage of those items that needed a greater degree of protection from the elements. There were sufficient rooms for anyone who needed to take one for themselves, but as they were quite large, James and Nick decided to share one room while Kate and Lynda shared another. Robert and Edith took a room each to themselves. The other less comfortable rooms were taken up with spare furniture that would not fit into some of the crofts, because although people had measured for sufficient space, sometimes it was not possible to manoeuvre the items through narrow doors and awkward turns.

After a good, although short, night's sleep I awoke to look, from my bed, out of my window to a completely new vista that I knew would greet me successively on every future morning. The green fields, scattered crofts and old stone walls would maybe change little other than by the nuances of varied light cast upon them by the rising sun, but the expanse of sea and sky, today dramatically enhanced by great scudding clouds being blown across from west to east, would be the panorama which each day would be a new and exciting canvas on which the artist would never repeat the same scene in exactly the same way. I mused on the contrast between this and my previous home. Even there, I thought I was fortunate to be able to look over some Green Belt land, but I now saw that my outlook had been restricted. There I more or less had to go out to look up to see the sky, here it was all encompassing and so much more interesting.

Although all the deliveries from the mainland store to the island were completed, the setting-up process on the island continued both for individual and collective needs. It did not end for quite a long time. At first some islanders experienced a conflict of needs between getting their personal accommodation ship-shape and carrying out work for the island's general needs. However, this only lasted for the first week and then people were asking where their services would be best used.

The two large tents had been erected above pre-prepared concrete bases and on the second week we had sufficient numbers offering to assist in getting the kitchen-cum-canteen organised to see real progress. Prime movers in this task were Madge, Edith and Rene, who all got on well together and soon developed a good working relationship. Their first task was to store the foodstuffs with some sense of order. Terry, the electrician, had to do some quick work to get the freezers working, and frequent calls to various men went out for the assembling and fitting of cupboards and worktops and the provision of cooking hotplates and ovens in one half of the tent. It was a very difficult working environment at first but the female trio did marvels to get the first meal available after a few days of hectic preparation. Tables and chairs were quickly set up in the other half of the tent and the canteen was declared open.

The kitchen operated on a self-service basis and as many of the islanders had been managing so far on small camping-type burners in their homes, they were keen to try and test their first meal in the canteen. The trio excelled themselves, producing a thick soup to start and following this with a meat and vegetable stew that received the thumbs-up from all present. The sweet of apple pie was delicious. All in all, a great success. Morag joined the team later and they were absolutely delighted to hear that she actually enjoyed washing up – a great asset to any kitchen operation.

The other army tent was allocated for general storage and was already half full. An attempt had been made to keep some order but there was a need to reorganise everything. It occurred to me that it could be a job for Jock. I asked if he now felt better in heath and he said that just getting back onto the island had had a beneficial effect. I told him that we had a need for a storekeeper and suggested that he might like to help, assuring him that it would not involve any heavy lifting. It would, in the first place, be a case of noting where everything was and putting those things into some order so that they could be found in the future.

In the early weeks as much time as possible was devoted to outside activities whenever the weather allowed. The two main areas of need were for the farm and for building work, and all available offers of labour were seized upon for extensive fencing for the animals and continuing building work for the unfinished crofts. There was also a great need to build the school and kitchen-cum-canteen to replace the army tents but this would have to take second place to the need to house everyone and get the farm ready to accept the animals.

The main farming contingent was made up of Gerry, Patrick, Ian and Angus, when he was not out fishing. The core group of people engaged in purely building work were Bob, James, Bill and Dafydd who, although our butcher, had little if any butchering to do in the early days.

Our teacher Miranda, with Lynda, succeeded in getting the school operational in the third week in the spare half of the army storage tent. They called upon any person who was able to help them set up cupboards to hold the equipment. At least they were close to the store to rummage about and find other items that they needed. In the first instance they had to borrow tables and chairs from the canteen, which proved inconvenient, but at least their lunch break coincided with meal times in the canteen.

At the end of the first month the fencing of the farmland had reached the stage when the first animals could be brought onto the island. All the work on the individual crofts had been completed and work was to start on the larger buildings to replace the army tents. The school was now open during normal school hours and was divided into junior and senior areas, Lynda enjoying her new task of helping with the juniors.

Life revolved at certain times of the day around one of the two common water supplies in the village. As the pressure on labour became a little less, John was able to recruit the help of Paddy to dig trenches in order to get piped water to all. Paddy had already gained a reputation as a 'Jack of all trades' and could be relied upon to tackle any of the seemingly insurmountable problems that occurred from time to time, whether joinery work, an engineering problem or some difficulty on the farm. His son Shaun would always be found with him, when he was not at school, helping with whatever task was being tackled at the time.

Both cattle and sheep were eventually transferred from each of Gerry's and Ian's farms to stock the island. Gerry was more generally inclined to favour the large beasts and transferred all his Highland cattle, the long, shaggy hair enabling them to more easily survive the cold weather. He also brought some Hereford beef cattle to the island, whereas Ian supplied some Holstein, Friesian and Ayrshire for dairy purposes and also managed all the sheep which were mainly Scottish black-faced ewes.

17

I decided to visit each island home to see how my fellow islanders were faring. My 'home visits' developed into being usually during the evenings, as it was then that I would find the whole family together. So much of the work outside needed all the daylight hours available. The first thing on my mind was to see how Jock and Morag were readapting. I found them warm and snug in their croft listening to the radio. Jock made a move to turn the radio off but I suggested that we could listen to the end of the programme and we sat quietly absorbed for a few minutes. They had one of the Tilley lamps set low, giving muted shadows on the newly painted walls. There was a little shrine in the corner with a flickering candle.

'It all looks quite comfortable,' I said, 'how are you managing?'

'It really is home from home, we canna believe we're back again. We were so sad when we had to leave the island and now we canna stop looking around to reassure ourselves that it's true, we're back.'

'You were somewhat unwell when I saw you last, how are you now?'

'We're both much better, thank you, we both seemed to recover after the first few hours on the island,' Morag replied.

'Health is important,' Jock added, 'but I think we are better in the mind too.'

Morag turned to me and with tears in her eyes said, 'Thank you, we both thank you and thank the good Lord for allowing us back to the same croft. It is so much brighter than when we were here before, it hadn't been painted for years and certainly not in these bright colours.'

'We are glad to have you here,' I said. 'For us you are a link with the past and, in time, I would like you to tell me more about your lives here and something of the history of Enniskerry.'

'There's nothing much to tell,' she said, 'it seemed as though nothing happened from day to day, even week to week. It's a job to think of the time as in any way interesting. It was more of an existence, biding the Lord's time.'

'In your letter to me, I remember that you, Morag, offered to help, and I've heard that you are assisting in the canteen kitchen.'

'I love it,' she replied. 'It's the companionship. They are all so happy and chatty, the day is often at an end before I realise I have started. It was all so very quiet here before.'

'And you're a storekeeper, Jock?'

'Aye, I said I would help but I am not sure I'll be up to it. My only skill was catching birds and working about the croft growing vegetables.'

'I hope you will enjoy doing all sorts of new things, Jock. First you must get some vegetables sown and growing round your croft again as soon as possible.'

I wished them goodnight, satisfied that their health had improved.

Over the subsequent weeks I continued to see each person in his or her new abode. At first I favoured families with children so that I could remember the children in the family environment of their home.

My next appointment was with Terry, Kathy and their three children, Allan, Sally and Miranda.

'You're doing a great job with our telephones, Terry, but how does it compare with working for BT and the electrical work at your last job?'

'My work, whether it is on the telephones or on electrical jobs is not vastly different, but the locations are as if in another world. Most of my previous work has either been in London or the Midlands, almost always in built-up areas of the cities. This is more uplifting. Even when I'm working inside I look out, and whether there is rain or sun my eyes are transfixed by the weather.'

Kathy added, 'I feel the same, whenever I take the kids down to the beach I feel so lucky. Here, we have on our doorstep every day what we previously saved up for the whole year to have on just two weeks' holiday. The beaches seem to go on for miles and more often than not we are the only people there.'

'How are we getting on regarding TV reception, Terry?'

'I'm getting dishes up for everyone at present, which are satisfactory but we may be looking for some permanent aerial for the island eventually.'

I looked towards the children, who were at the table playing some board game.

'How about you three? Have you any regrets about being here?'

'No, it's great, it's like being on holiday,' Allan and Sally agreed.

'What about school? You've just started, haven't you?

'I like our teacher,' Sally answered, 'but I wish she didn't have the same name as my sister. She wants us to all call each other by our Christian names. It seems odd now when I have to speak to one of them.'

'You'll have to blame me for that,' I said, 'I wanted

everyone on the island to know each other by their Christian names. Miranda, how about you?'

'I thought the best thing so far was when you put our flag up on the day we arrived and you mentioned the lamb, which was my idea. Will it always be up there?

'Yes, it's our official island flag and it will always be up there. If the wind ever blows it down we will put it straight back up as soon as we can.'

My next visit was to Bill and Helen.

'Our paths haven't crossed for a while, where have you been hiding?'

'Oh, I've been about helping with the building work,' Bill replied, 'I saw you from the top of a roof the other day but the wind was so strong and blowing in the wrong direction you didn't hear me call out.'

'How are the youngsters, Helen? They seem quite contented.'

'Yes, Zoe is on the bottle now and seems to thrive on each feeding, I was so pleased that we have such a good supply of everything we need and know that we are not likely to run out, and Doctor Matt has been very helpful.'

'I've had a word with some of the mothers and they nearly all say that we should form a group to share looking after the younger children, a sort of crèche.'

'And what about Richard, is he settling in at school?'

'He seems very happy and Miranda is very understanding of his needs.'

'You don't regret coming, do you? It's so much different to Kent, isn't it?

'No, we will be quite happy here, it's a good healthy life and I know we may have to deal with some long dark days in the winter; but you only have to have a fine spell occasionally to remind you how beautiful it can be.

'It reminds me a bit of some places that we visited during the one year we spent in Australia, something to do with the wide open spaces, I think.'

As I left them, I bumped into Nick, and asked him how he was getting along with Gerry on the farm.

'Oh 'e's all right, 'e's got an 'erd of them 'ighland cattle, yer know. I said to 'im yesterday, miserable buggers, ain't they, wiv all that brown 'air 'anging all over their eyes. An' d'yer know what 'e said to me, 'e said, "I thought I had one extra one yesterday when you walked 'em through the gate." I thought 'e were a right cheeky bugger. But I like that sort o' 'umour, 'e's all right.'

'Well, now you've had a bit of experience with Gerry and his farming, I want you to get to know something of the sea. Go and have a chat with Angus, tell him I sent you and say that you want to know how to catch crabs and lobsters. Tell him also that you would like him to teach you first how to make all your own equipment from scratch, for instance the crab and lobster creels, so that you don't have to use his.'

'I'm not keen on goin' out to sea, yer know. All that water gives me the willies.'

'You won't have to go out to sea to get the hang of making the creels,' I said, 'but if he does offer to take you out, give it a go, just for the experience. You never know, you might like it.'

'Didn't care much for the journey out 'ere. I felt rotten an' they all said I looked a bit green.'

I was eager to see Bob and Susan, as their three children were older, ranging from 12 to 17. I remembered that Jane had been uneasy about the fact that she had just met a new boyfriend and I asked her about him.

'I still like him and we said we would write to each other, and maybe one day he would come out and join us. But I am OK here, I quite like Shaun now. He's good fun and we talk a lot at school.'

'That's good. Any problems, Susan?'

'Only the same one that I've always had. Bob spends all his time working on other people's houses and forgets that he's got ours here!'

'What's the most urgent thing you need to be done?'

'Well, the roof is leaking into our bedroom, straight onto my side of the bed.'

'Where are you working this week, Bob?'

'Funnily enough, I'll be up at your Lodge tomorrow. Paddy's asked me to help him with a job on the drains.'

'Well, I shall now take my first autocratic decision as Laird of this island and order you to fix the roof of your own house as from daybreak tomorrow.'

'OK, I give in. I was going to say that the weather is set fine for a couple of days so it's not urgent, but I'll do it tomorrow.'

'I think that's the only time anybody has made him change his mind. We certainly are into a new era now,' laughed Susan.

'Did you work before you had the children, Susan?'

'Yes, after I left school I did a degree in fashion but I could not find a job, so I took on freelance work from a local furnishing business. I used to make curtains, and re-cover furniture, and eventually I learned to re-upholster. Then I got into supplying designs for whole rooms and making them a reality.'

'It sounds interesting work. Perhaps you could help when we start thinking of creative evening classes in the line of arts, crafts, weaving and spinning, that sort of thing.'

* * *

As I walked around the island I would see the islanders getting on with the work of establishing themselves but it was very evident that a lot of building work was going on by individual teams working on common tasks. In the early weeks there was a great emphasis on building and it was a great pleasure for me to see progressive construction work taking place on the three large buildings the store, the canteen and the school. The first two were relatively simple in their oblong design but the school was intended to include two classrooms, library, sports hall, computer room and lecture room, which was a much more complicated task.

When I moved up beyond the village activities, I saw new, extensive well-made fences for enclosing the farm animals. The line extended in some places up to the cliff edges, where it would prevent the valuable animals approaching precipitous drops. It reminded me that there were many other dangerous places for children, particularly on the shoreline and near the caves, where the water levels rose dramatically with each tide. Although one would not wish to restrict their adventurous spirits too much, I thought perhaps I should warn the parents of the dangers at the next opportunity.

I had a good knowledge of John because he was one of our Managers and I had already spent quite a lot of time in his company. I had not, however, had the opportunity to spend time with his wife, Alice, and their two boys. Knowing that John and Alice had met as a result of their interest in gliding, I asked if they had continued flying until they opted to come to the island.

'We kept it going for a few years,' Alice replied. 'Then it became rather spasmodic after we had the boys, and it still is. We've taken the boys a couple of times, but they've also had some tuition at a nearby sailing club and they are probably more keen to do that now.'

Just then the boys came into the room and Jonathan said, 'Hallo Jim, we were just going to ask Dad what the chances were of us continuing our sailing now that we are here on the island? Now you're here, perhaps I'll ask you.'

'I'm sure that it should be possible in the future. What type of craft were you using before?'

'It was one of the smallest, called a Wayfarer, and we only had about half a dozen lessons.'

'A Wayfarer should not be difficult to obtain, but why not look into the possibility of making your own? I think they should be available in kit form.'

Trevor looked very excited at the idea. 'That sounds great. Can we do that? When can we get started, Dad?'

'I've got a lot of more important jobs to do on the island that will keep me busy until winter, and there's the question of space. It will take up room that we haven't got at the croft, but I'm as keen to make our own as you are. I tell you what, why don't you find out who you can send off to for the details? Mind you, sailing on these waters here is a bit different to sailing on the inland lake. It can be very dangerous here,' said John.

I just had another idea and suggested, 'Maybe we would be able to introduce the idea around to others and make it an island project at one of the evening classes, then we could do something about the problem of space. Jonathan and Trevor will you ask around at school and see how many of the others are interested. We might even be able to start a sailing club here.'

Ian was using a tractor to plough an area of land and, seeing me, he stopped to have a chat. He was anxious to give me details of his proposals for growing certain crops and explained that what he really wanted to try out was a semi-circular enclosure like the biomes at the Eden Project in Cornwall. He felt the shape would be ideal for the strong winds that we would experience, ensuring that the horizontal force of the wind would tend to push the pod downwards rather than away. He asked if I would agree to him looking into it further, and I said that I would be very interested.

His wife Madge was apparently feeling a bit off colour at the moment, so I said that I would call down to see her on the way back.

I also took time out one day to stroll around the extremities of the island in order to get to know its every aspect. Once out of the village and past the farms, the track gradually became less obvious and was no more than a disused sheep path. One was then freely able to explore the grass and heather covered higher ground. From the highest point I could have a full 360-degree panorama that revealed the whole island and its relationship with the ocean and other Hebridean islands. It was a good day and Ireland was visible to the west. I sat on a patch of soft heather to absorb the magnificence of what lay before me. There was a light breeze and the silence was palpable. The vast ocean had only one sign of movement due to the efforts of man. It was the almost imperceptible progress of a MacBraynes ferryboat plying its course towards Oban on the mainland. It would have been hardly visible if it were not for the long wake of its path stretched out across the shimmering sea.

This was the first moment I had actually stopped to think about the events that had led to me sitting near the summit of what was now my island. So much had happened, and so much had been accomplished over the months, that there had not been a spare moment. My mind and body had been totally committed to the one objective. In a sense that objective had now been achieved but I realised that I had arrived at what was in fact only just the beginning. I would now be embarking upon the second stage, which was to consolidate on my good fortune to ensure the future for my fellow islanders and myself.

I marvelled at how fortunate I had been to meet and to enlist so many people with skills that had enabled us to get off to such a flourishing start. I was fascinated by the numerous abilities that were available within the group and I was intrigued by their different individual character-istics. Everything and everybody seemed to get along so well, and I wondered if my optimism and their support and enthusiasm would hold into the months and years ahead.

I rose and walked over to where the grassland gave way to the western cliffs rising to several hundred feet above the sea. My musing was interrupted as I disturbed some gulls whose alarm call suddenly set up a more intensive noisy screaming from other seagoing birds on the cliff edges ahead of me. I continued skirting round the headland, passing some thousands of screaming kitti-wakes and guillemots that were circling above me or perched on the inaccessible ledges below.

Continuing on my circular walk, I made my way downhill past one of our natural lochs and then across some boggy ground to find myself beside a bubbling stream. Thick patches of green watercress were growing along its path. Lower down I found some evidence of peat-cutting which had possibly been carried out as far back as the nineteenth century. Then a profusion of wild flowers were beneath my feet, before a vast sandy beach came into view. As I made those few steps to the shingle I noticed the high-water mark defined by the colourful band of seaweed stretching into the distance. I felt thrilled as my eyes rose to see the vista of this sweeping bay of perhaps a mile long. It was of pristine sand backed by marram grass and untrodden by human feet, I guessed, for many years. It was a unique experience. I took off my shoes and made for the sea, disturbing some gulls on the way as I reached the water's edge, where I paddled along the swirling, frothy incoming tide. A wind had risen to give the hint of a white edge to the incoming rollers. I turned to face outward to the sea and sucked in the cold, fresh ocean air. I could easily live with this. I knew from my previous holiday visits to Scotland that one would expect to experience rain, mist and cold winter weather, but I knew also that just one fine day, such as this, during those holidays was enough to forgive the rest. That was how it was on this day. If I could just experience this freedom once in a while, that alone would be enough to satisfy me beyond any call to the sunnier Mediterranean climate.

I continued my walk around the coastline, stepping among and over rocks covered with the black lichen of the splash zone where the winter storms lashed. Half a dozen brown Atlantic seals slid indignantly from some outlying rocks into the water and then swam away, their heads bobbing and then disappearing as they dived into their natural environment below the surface. A series of caves were visible in the rock faces above the shingle but I resisted the urge to investigate them and turned inland to follow a river flowing between hard grey rocks and soft green grass. It seemed clear and fresh enough to drink, so I leaned over a now sun-warmed rock, scooped my hands and drank deeply, the most refreshing drink it seemed for ages, then I splashed it over my face. Delightful.

I climbed for about ten minutes and arrived at a pleasant level plateau set in a valley where there were a number of ruined buildings. Several, no more than heaps of scattered stone, indicated a previous settlement. Some parts of the meadow near the river were rather spongy and flag irises had taken root, giving the suggestion of gardens for the old crofts. The higher land would make excellent grazing but the sight of the remains of this village reminded me of something I had heard about crofting: that it was not a livelihood – it was an existence.

I was approaching Ian's farm again and Madge was hanging out the washing.

'It's a good day for drying, Madge.'

'Yes,' she said, 'the last time I put my washing out it was blowing a gale and I nearly lost everything.'

'Ian said you were a bit under the weather.'

Madge seemed a little surprised 'Och, it's just a bit of a headache,' she said, dismissing the idea.

'Have you heard about young Michael and his parrot?'

'No. What's happened?'

'Well, he's been teaching it to say "Hallo" as people come in and "Goodbye" as they go out and now it's flown off and it's lost. The laugh is that he's been telling everybody he had just been successful in getting it to say "Goodbye," and then it just flew off without saying anything!'

One day, Ken called in at the Lodge to talk about the ongoing filming of events on the island.

'Jim, can I agree with you that we should bring forward the release date for the film series? We now have nearly thirty episodes ready in the can and I think the time has come to consider releasing them.'

'I see no reason why not. But what is your thinking? Why do you want to bring it forward?

'Basically it's the time gap between the event and the showing. If we were to get the go-ahead, the series could start in the new year, and even then the early episodes would be at least nine months after the event. I would not want that period to increase, or it might be regarded as old hat. Also many of the interesting events have naturally occurred in the early period.'

'So if we go ahead, what's next?'

'I have everything filmed from your first meetings back on the mainland but now I would like to do an introductory first episode with you. It would cover your initial lottery win, the purchase of the island, your first visits and early impressions, everything basically to reinforce those things I missed in the early stages.'

'Let's go ahead then. I'll bring it up at the next council meeting.'

'Great, I'll put things in motion directly you get the OK.'

'Now, we said that we needed to discuss further the question of tourism on the island as a result of the film. We may as well do that now. How do you see things developing?'

Ken sat back and explained. 'Beyond the first year, I see the film as an introduction for people to want to visit the island as paying guests. We would offer them a unique experience to involve themselves with the day-to-day activities of the islanders. We would offer them accommodation in a typical croft with meals supplied. They would, if they contributed positively in some way to the general activities, be filmed as part of what we do with the islanders. The attraction would be their appearance on TV as part of the on-going series of *An Every Week Story of Island Folk.*

'I've made a note of some of the other ideas that we could offer. If Angus could be persuaded, and I am sure he would be co-operative, we could provide loch and sea fishing trips. Visitors could be shown how to make their own creel and catch their own crabs and lobsters, or a chance to sail on a round the island tour by boat. There could be bird-watching outings – they are very popular these days – and there are over three hundred species here. We could organise walking tours and even offer seal-watching outings. How about "make your own whisky with Jock", who, I believe, has admitted to an illicit still. I've heard that some are thinking of taking up crafts, such as spinning, weaving, patchwork and tapestry. Some visitors would like to take part, I'm sure.

'For the younger visitors we could offer feeding the pet lambs or horse riding. There could be karate lessons from Lynda, five-a-side football and five-a-side handball when they could join the islands two teams. What about caving, abseiling and rock climbing?

'And there are so many other areas to look at. For instance, there could be an insight into island farming with a talk and some practical involvement. Also anyone who felt so inclined could offer a talk to the children on a subject of the visitor's choice. This talk could also be filmed on request. At least one concert per week by the island's orchestra or band could be open to visitors, and I'm sure they would be queuing to take part in our regular Friday evening ceilidh.

'I'm sure people would want to meet the islanders in their homes or at their work, and certain things could be on sale at the yet to be opened shop, for example videos of past episodes of our own *An Every Week Story of Island Folk*. I could go on,' enthused Ken.

'That's an impressive list and we have quite an incentive to go ahead with it. Of course it can't all happen at once, but we must look to an income for the future,' I answered.

'I think a principle would have to be that if visitors involved themselves with activities together with the islanders, there would be a good chance that they would be caught on the regular filming that takes place every day, and could become part of the national series on BBC TV. If they stood by just watching and doing their own filming and taking their own photographs, then there would be a very good chance that we would not catch them on film and they would therefore not be included in that week's episode.

'You, Jim, would have to say how you see the pricing. I would be inclined to set it rather high. Remember this would be an experience not available or equalled anywhere else.'

'It's still a long way off. We still have to build tourist accommodation and the film still has to be shown and time allowed for interest in it to grow. However, I want it to go ahead and, as I say, I will bring it up at the next council meeting. As a thought on price, I would want to strike a satisfactory balance and not rely just on the wealthy section of society.'

18

'Hi Alice.'

'Hallo Ken. Are you going to point that camera at me again?'

'No, I just wanted a word with you this time. Have you ever used a movie camera yourself?'

'I've been with a lot of people that have, but no, I've always been on the receiving end.'

'On my journeys filming the various things that happen around the island, people have said that they find you very friendly towards them and I wondered if you would join me and help with the filming.'

'But I don't have any experience of being behind a camera.'

'It shouldn't be a problem, I'd teach you how to use one.'

'I'd be only too happy to help if you think I could be useful.'

'It's not just the practical business of using a camera, it is also that the camera man or woman has to have an empathy with their subjects. People have to be at ease when the camera points at them. That's why I've asked you. I think you could move between everyone with a camera and they would trust you. Also you may be able to move more unobtrusively into places that would be more difficult for me.'

'Like into the ladies' toilet?'

'Not quite like that. I was thinking more of it being an extra pair of hands, you know, two cameras in different locations.'

'How would it all work then?'

'Well, the general principle is that I film on a regular daily basis anything and everything that I notice that could be of interest for an episode of that week. Sometimes I concentrate on a particular subject, person or family. For instance, yesterday I was caught up with another delivery of the farm animals coming onto the island. That took up most of the day and I could have done with some help. And there is often more than one event worthy of getting onto film happening at the same time in different places.'

'How long will it take for me to learn?'

'Not long to get the general idea. So much is automatic on the cameras these days. You need a steady hand, steady movement and an eye for the composition of what you see in the viewfinder. Of course, you also have to be in the right place at the right time.'

'When can we start?'

'We can start now, if you're willing.'

'Right, let's go then. I see you have the camera with you, are you ever without it?'

'I try not to be, but I'll start you with a smaller one like this. I'll spend half an hour with you showing you a few things and then you can take the camera and play with it until you get more used to it and then we'll have another chat. Everything we take gets downloaded onto the computer, edited and the best bits taken for the final showing. The good news is that we can record on this camera and then re-record again and again so we don't have to worry about wasting film.'

'Hallo again. How did you get on with the camcorder?'

'OK I think. I took it home and looked some things up in the instruction book first and then I took it into the infants school yesterday for Lynda's afternoon session there. The kids were a bit self-conscious at first but they soon got used to it after they had a glimpse of the recording.'

'Let me have a look. Yes, it's quite good, I like the sequence where they are splashing around with the water experiments. I see that you had the sound on as well. They are not at all self-conscious there are they? Everything is quite natural, so we can use that. Consider it as your first successful assignment. You see, that is exactly what I need, I can't so easily burst into the school lesson and yet it is an essential part of what goes on here. You've been a great help.'

'You're very encouraging, and it is quite an enjoyable occupation. Can I come round with you this morning and see how you do things?'

'Yes, I was going to suggest that myself. I have two things to do today. I thought I would pop up to the farm where there are some newborn lambs and then I'd like to interview Jock to see if there is any truth in the rumour that he has a whisky still. Jim told me that you worked in publishing. Didn't you get involved with pictures then?'

'Yes, I did in terms of selection and what would be a suitable layout, but of course I didn't come into contact with the camera side of the process, or sound.'

'No, but your experience will help regarding the composition of the movie even though it is a somewhat different concept.'

'Do you want to get shots of an actual birth of a lamb?'

'Possibly, although I did get some pictures last night in the barn. It seems they often give birth at the most inconvenient times, but a daytime birth would be helpful.'

'I hope so, I've never seen one.'

'A high proportion so far have been twins. It seems that is quite normal.'

They met up with Gerry.

'Did you eventually get some sleep last night?' Ken asked.

'Only a little. I'm just going up and around to see if there are any lambs left abandoned. Would you like to have a look with me?'

'Yes indeed. Alice here is helping me with the filming, so it will be a chance for her to practise.'

'Why would a sheep abandon its lamb?' Alice enquired as they strode up the hill.

'It happens, Alice, not often but sometimes. For some reason it just will not take milk from the mother. In some cases, if a sick lamb is one of twins, we can take it away from its mother, leaving the healthy lamb with her. A mother will always bring up a single lamb better than twins. If another sheep has produced a dead lamb it is possible to use the skin from it to put over the sick lamb or one that has been abandoned and the mother of the dead lamb will suckle it and foster it as if it were her own.'

'Can you feed them with the bottle?'

'Oh yes, but then they tend to become dependent upon you. Farmers don't always have the time, you know.'

They had a long scout around the field but there were no stray newly born lambs to deal with, or sheep requiring immediate help.

'I'm sure you're pleased that there are no sheep in need of attention today but I'm a little disappointed. I've never seen a birth.'

'Tell you what, there will almost certainly be another lambing this evening. If you would like, I'll give you a ring when one is due and you can come round and see.'

'Thank you very much Gerry, I really would like that.'

They made their way round to Jock's place, intending to try and find out whether he really was producing whisky. He was tending some plants in his garden.

'Jock, how are you today? Is everything growing well?'

'Aye, it's a good soil here and the warm weather helps.'

'It seems you have vegetables as well as flowers.'

'Aye, I have many more varieties now that Ian is supplying me.'

'Will you be self-sufficient?'

'Aye, certainly in the season, there should even be a surplus.'

'So you're OK for food. How about drink? Alice and I were told that you may be making whisky here. We wondered how you are progressing.'

'Ah, well now, I'm not sure about that. Are you sure you heard right?'

'Is it illegal?'

'It could be, I don't think anyone makes it here.'

'So you couldn't offer us a little drink then, if we asked you nicely?'

'Of course I can, any time, come inside. Morag and I would be glad for you to have a wee dram with us.'

Jock offered them a glass of whisky from a nearby bottle. They talked around many things concerned with the island during their earlier days but avoided the matter of the still. After about an hour Alice could not restrain herself any more.

'Jock, you're very kind but you didn't make this, did you?'

'No, but it's a very good whisky.'

'It certainly is but it wasn't made here, was it?'

'Nobody makes it here,' he repeated.

'Jock. Alice and I know that nobody else makes it here, but we think you may know how to do it. Do you know how to make it?'

'Ah, well now, it's not that easy, you know?'

'I guess not. What do you have to do?'

'You'll need a simple closed container in which you can

heat up the liquid and another vessel to receive the condensate. That's the easy part.'

'I don't need these things, Jock, because I'm not going to make any but do you have them?'

'I did have some old bits and pieces around at one time.'

'Could we have a look at them sometime?'

'It's all of a jumble out there in the shed at present, I'll get them out another time.'

As they departed, Alice commented that although he was not forthcoming in admitting anything, she believed he was experimenting with a still if not actually using one.

'You know, he surely wouldn't use the word "condensate" unless he had some good understanding of the process.'

'I think he believes that even though it must be on a very small scale, he is nevertheless engaged in some unlawful trade.'

'I agree. I think it was the cameras – he was frightened that his activities would all be revealed to his disadvantage.'

'Yes, he's lovely really, and so genuine, I think he'll come round to letting us see the apparatus and give more detail eventually, but he needs to be sure that it's safe.'

'Sure, these things take time. With some luck we may even be able to use the cameras eventually.'

19

As I had hoped, people were quick to set up new relationships. With a relatively small island few matters of interest and even those of little significance, could be kept entirely undisclosed. Many thrived on knowing the minutiae of every happening. It was not to be criticised; this was our home and, like in any family home, everyone knew what was going on.

'Colleen, I'm James. I was with your dad on the advance party that came to the island.'

'Yes, he told me about you. He said you worked hard.'

'It *was* very hard work but the evening get-together was fantastic. Your dad was always telling jokes and we laughed most of the nights away.'

'He's always been good fun. He makes everybody laugh and people tell me he is a good organiser.'

'He certainly put a lot of work in beforehand to ensure that we all knew what to do when we got here, but he didn't tell me you had a baby.'

'He hasn't quite got used to the idea yet, it was all a bit of a surprise.'

'You're here on your own, then?'

'Yes, well apart from Mum, Dad and my brother Shaun, and of course baby Jim.'

'His dad didn't want to come, then?'

'No chance. He left the country soon after he knew I

was pregnant. How about you, did you give up a job to come here?'

'In a way I did. I'd just been offered a job with the police force but opted for this instead.'

'I wonder how it will turn out for us all. It's one thing while there is so much to do but it may be different when it all settles down.'

'I feel confident that it will work out all right, I don't think it depends so much on the work we're doing, I believe it depends more on the people, as Jim senior says, it's down to commitment and how we get along with each other.'

'Do you think you could still be here in ten years' time?'

'You can't say, can you? My situation was that I was desperate for something different from the usual, I saw that I could make a new start out here, perhaps make new friends and start afresh.'

'Have you met and made any new friends yet?'

'Well, I've met you and little Jim, haven't I? And I'm meeting people all the time as the work goes on. If it's their own croft that we are working on they keep popping round, and others are always curious about what is going on. I suppose that after those early few weeks everybody has now met everybody else and so we will all become friends really, but I expect it will settle down to a smaller circle for each of us. What about you, you're not going to school, are you? Will you be happy here?'

'I can't see very far into the future but I'm very happy here now. I wanted to spend as much time as I could with baby Jim, I couldn't do that with school as well. It's a good place to bring him up and, like you, I wanted a change. Mum and Dad were very supportive but I was getting a bit fed up with the constant lectures about children being born out of wedlock, particularly when we went back to our family in Ireland.'

'Are you Catholic then?'

'I was brought up as Catholic but I am not a practising believer. With all the troubles in Ireland it really turned me against religion in general.'

'Have you had a look around the island yet?'

'Not really, just around the village, you know. I can't get very far with the baby.'

'We'll have to put that right. You can't stay here and not know what's around. Tell you what, I've got a rucksack. We'll try and adapt it so that I can carry Jim on my back and then I'll show you round. You'll love it.'

Kate wandered down to the harbour to find Angus. She'd been helping with the farm accounts for Gerry when Philip called in wanting to know if she had asked Angus for his expenses. She had tried once before without any success and wasn't keen to keep badgering him. Nevertheless she thought she would have one last try.

As she caught sight of the *Island Queen* moored at the harbour she thought how much happier she felt now than when she had been working in the busy office in Lancashire. She felt quite light-hearted; the rest of the afternoon was hers to do as she liked.

As she walked nearer the harbour she spotted Angus on the deck of the boat carrying a tin of paint.

'Hi Angus, can I come aboard?'

'Aye, of course – how can I help you?'

'I'm needing your expenses claim, the treasurer wants to get up to date with his accounts.'

'You know, Kate, I'm not keen charging anyone, I'm not used to doing any paperwork. I've no need to claim anything, really I haven't.'

'I know, you haven't claimed a single penny, but it must have cost a fortune for all the diesel you used ferrying backwards and forwards for days on end. You have been doing it constantly over recent weeks and there's all the wear and tear on the boat. Surely there are maintenance costs as well?'

'But I enjoyed doing it. It's my contribution.'

'Tell me, what are you doing this afternoon?'

'Well, I was going to spend a little time painting the rails on the boat.'

'Can I give you a hand? While we do the painting, you could tell me how you go about things, where and how you get the fuel and I'll put it all down on paper and give it in for you?'

'You're welcome to help me with the painting, but I'll not be telling you what it has all cost.'

'It's not me, Angus, it's the committee who want to know. I'm sure they will all be very thankful to you for your generosity. I'd like to help with your painting anyway. I prefer to be out of doors whenever possible.'

'Right, let's get to work then.'

After the main activity of the lunchtime meal and the washing-up, Edith, Madge and Rene would regularly sit with their own snacks and chat away for an hour or so. Edith was more of a quiet individual but Madge and Rene, being more outgoing, soon had her talking.

'So, tell us about yourself,' Rene suggested. 'Were you born on Skye and did you always live there?' The two women were soon captivated.

'Well yes, I was born on the Isle of Skye and, as a very young girl, I was taken to India with my mother and father, who was in the Diplomatic Service. It was just before the riots in 1947. We lived at first in Lahore, the capital city of the Punjab, but eventually it was decided that we should move to Delhi. It was a distance of some three hundred miles, a train journey that had for some time been recognised as a dangerous undertaking lasting several days. Trains had been the target for pillage and murder but we did not have a choice for my father's work was paramount. So we set off.

'Lahore was in a state of turmoil, with many of the Moslems fleeing to Pakistan, while we joined the Hindus who were escaping to Delhi. I had been in Lahore long enough to mix with some of the Indian children and had a good knowledge of the language. I had become used to the hot and humid weather, the smells and the close proximity of people, but I had never experienced anything so unpleasant as that journey. It was stifling in the extreme, with overcrowded conditions and the smell of urine a constant companion.

'Suddenly we stopped. It might have been a station but as we juddered to a halt there was the terrific noise of shouting and gunfire. My father looked out of the open window and saw an angry mob bearing down on the train. He must have known that our lives were in danger. He quickly closed the window, ensured that the door was jammed shut and shouted for everyone to keep calm. There followed more gunfire and a banging and crashing at the carriage door. My mother bundled me under the seat and several passengers sat above me; many were also standing. I could not see much but I could hear the crying and wailing of those around. The door burst open and an enraged Indian wielding a huge knife forced himself into the carriage. Peeping though the array of legs in front of me, I heard and saw bodies sinking to the floor and the colour red. I lay still. The panic and noise continued for ages. My eyes were screwed tight but, after a while, I could hear shouting from the distance and all within the carriage became quiet. It was a deathly silence, but interspersed with low moans, groans and the odd cry for help.

138

'I lay rigidly still for a long time before I opened my eyes and, with some difficulty, climbed out over my mother's body. She was covered in blood. I slipped over and past several other blood-soaked bodies. My father lay at an awkward angle near the door, two horrible gashes across his head, and one still oozing blood. I knew everyone in the carriage was dead, and I sensed that I must leave them and get away as quickly as I could.

'I jumped down to the ground, wrenching my arm as I released my hold on the carriage door. I ran, walked and stumbled away from the nightmare scene of carnage. No one stopped me and I did not stop until I felt I was safe. Night fell and I dropped into a ditch and slept the night through beside a field of maize.

'When I awoke I did not know what to do. For two whole days I wandered aimlessly, then as I walked towards a road the thought came to me that we had been heading for Delhi and somewhere there, perhaps, I could find someone to help me. I did not know how far it was or how I could get there.

'When I saw an Indian driving a bullock cart along the dusty road I asked him how far it was to Delhi. I gathered it was a very long way. He looked me over and saw my poor and dishevelled state, and asked if I was hungry. I was, and he gave me a few scraps which I was glad to stuff into my mouth. "You should come with me," he said, "my brother Sanjay works the land and will give you shelter for the night." I went with him and his brother and his wife showed me somewhere I could sleep and fed me the next day.'

'My goodness, how terrible, and you so young. Did you ever get to Delhi?' Madge enquired.

'Yes but not directly. I virtually became a slave around their home. Sanjay's wife, Roop, was not too bad but she had a violent temper and worked me very hard. Later they got me working at one of the lowest jobs there could be, a sweeper on the dusty tracks nearby. It earned just a few rupees each day that I had to hand over to the family to pay for my keep. As I grew older one of the younger brothers, Rajiv, began to abuse me. At first he would hit me if I did not do what he wanted but later he took me out to the fields and raped me. It was not the only time. I became so scared when he told me he would kill me if I ever told anyone.

'It was some years before I was able to turn my mind to what I could do for myself. It was beginning to dawn on me that although I lived and acted as an Indian, I was in fact different. My skin had, over the years, tanned to such an extent that although I did not look totally Indian I would not easily be recognised as English either. My thoughts were that I should try to reach Delhi. That was where my mother and father were taking me before they were killed. Perhaps I could find where we were going to live and find someone there who could help.

'While sweeping I also resorted to some begging. It was the instinct to survive. I would target the few more prosperous-looking Indians and gained a few additional rupees that I hid at a secret place away from the family. I noticed children on their way to and from school and the sight of them jogged my mind to the fact that I had one asset above everybody I knew in India. It was that I could speak English. I mulled this over and over for weeks on end and then suggested to Sanjay and his wife Roop that if I could teach English at the school I could earn them more money. They immediately showed interest and did not dismiss the idea. The thought of any additional money was too great for them to ignore.

'It was perhaps six months later when Sanjay and Roop told me that they had arranged for me to teach English at the school for two mornings each week and that I was to

140

give all my earnings to them. Petrified to confront them, I argued that unless they allowed me some of the money for myself I would not do it. There was a great argument, but I felt if I persisted I would get my way, reasoning that although they could beat me, they could not risk not having the extra money for themselves. It was agreed, and although they took the lion's share of my earnings, I hoarded the little money that came my way, telling them that I used it to buy drinks and extra food from the vendors who regularly plied the track.

'One day I decided that the time had come to carry out my plan. I would have to run away from these people and find my way to Delhi. I chose a day when a full week's money from the school was paid to me and this, together with my other hidden savings, was pocketed and I just walked away. I guessed that I would not be missed until the following day. I had never mentioned any desire to go to Delhi, so the family would not know in which direction I was heading. I walked for two days off the roads until I was able to find a busy road and a bus that was heading to the capital. But after a stifling journey, on arrival in the big city I was at a loss to know what to do next. I slept rough for two nights and then found a corner between two rickety buildings in a shanty town amid a cluster of mud-built, red, rusty, corrugated, iron-roofed shacks. My questions to any likely person about where diplomats could be living had been too vague and the responses were a series of blank faces. Nobody really knew what I was talking about and most regarded me as a crank.

'I decided my approach to the problem had been quite wrong and I should therefore change my tactics. My best plan would be to seek out English-speaking people who might know about these things. I went to the great Red Fort, where I found that tourists would be either arriving or waiting for a return journey to their hotel in air-conditioned coaches. Sometimes I found them just wandering around the city. Generally people were very wary of me. I did not know how pitiful, unkempt and objectionable I might have appeared, and I had not once seen my image in a mirror. However, I did not despair, I realised that it would take time and my persistence would eventually lead to something.'

'We're fascinated,' said Rene. 'Have a breather and let me make you a cup of tea. We had no idea about your past. Are you happy to carry on talking?'

'Yes of course, if you're really interested.'

'Of course we are. What happened next?'

'Well, I approached a couple who did not hurry to get away. Realising that I was not actually begging, they asked me to repeat what I had said. I told them that I was trying to find the area in Delhi where diplomats lived. They didn't know the place but they said I should ask at the police station or go to the British High Commission.

'I wasn't keen on the police station because I thought I might be sent back to where I had just run away from. However their mention of the British High Commission really focused my mind. I asked several tourists for directions and at last someone was able to give me clear directions.

'It was evening when I arrived and the building was closed. Tired out, but not despondent, I returned to my shack for the night. Back at the High Commission in the morning, I could not, at first, make anyone understand what I wanted. It was not until a fair-haired young man came over and asked if he could help that I sensed I could make progress. I told him that no one would let me in. He like others thought I was Indian and asked, "Why do you want the British High Commission?" We sat on the pavement and I related the story of how I came to be in Delhi. "Oh my God, you're a non-person," he gasped

142

when I had finished. "You do need help. Let's see what I can do. By the way, what's your name?" "Edith," I answered, "Edith Curtis." "Well, my name is Gary. Now keep with me."

'We walked up to the gate and inside we joined a queue which moved slowly forward until we came to a desk. Gary explained my situation to the clerk. The details took rather a long to time to record and were complicated because I had no means of identification. Gary decided to become more insistent and demanded to meet with another official.

'It was an enormous building, the biggest I had ever been inside. We were shown into another pleasantly decorated room where cool air was circulating. We were introduced to a very smart and well-dressed man, who asked me to tell my story from the beginning.

'When I had finished he said that he was aware of the attack on the Lahore to Delhi train all those years back. "One hundred and twenty people were butchered on that train," he said. "You were lucky to survive. You should be listed as one of the missing persons even though you were a child at the time. If that is so I will be able to issue you with a passport fairly easily. Come back tomorrow when I may have made some progress.'

'We walked outside into the hot afternoon sun. Gary asked about where I was living and when I told him, he asked if I would prefer to come back to the guesthouse where he was staying – he was travelling overland from Australia, where he had worked on a farm for a year. I took up his offer and was soon enjoying the most wonderful bath with hot water that I could ever remember experiencing. "You look a lot better for that," he said when I returned, "and totally different. But we must go and get some clothes for you, those rags are not going to last another day."

143

'We went out and he paid for everything. I offered to repay him but he would not hear of it. I felt a new person and was so grateful. I slept the deepest sleep I could remember and woke to think how my life was changing. Gary was my lifeline and I realised that I had been very lucky to meet him and for him to then offer his help.

'We returned to the High Commission together and the man with whom we had spoken the day before greeted us with a wide smile and said that everything was in order. All I needed to do was go into another room to have my photograph taken, come back to sign a few forms and he could then issue a passport. It only took half an hour. With my passport, I became a real person with an identity again.'

'So you came home to Skye. Did you have enough money for the air fare?' Madge enquired.

'No, not straight away, it was not quite like that. I travelled overland with Gary. The journey was not without its own excitement. We either hitchhiked or walked all the way. Gary wanted to meet people in their own villages in different countries, and of course you do not meet anyone like that in an aeroplane. It took us almost a year.

'Ironically, our route took us first back to Lahore, where I was tempted to look at the lodging where I had been with my mother and father. It was an imposing house with grounds that had given me great pleasure as a child, where I was allowed to roam as I wished. The garden was now somewhat overgrown and the house had new owners, but I asked Gary to take a photograph of the house and garden as a reminder of my early happy days.

'We moved on and over the Khyber Pass to Afghanistan, Iran, Iraq, Jordan, Syria, Turkey and then from Asia into Europe. I remember so many of the sights, but when on the cross-Channel ferry to England, I first saw clearly the white cliffs of Dover; I was overcome with the pleasure of arriving home. Gary was very understanding and took me to meet his parents in Bristol.

'I applied for an office job with the local council, and gradually made my way in the organisation until I became a secretary. I then moved on to a large international transport company.'

'So you didn't get married, then? We were thinking that a romance would blossom for you with Gary,'' said Rene.

'No, sorry, but we did keep in touch. He married a lovely girl from Lowestoft; but it failed after their children had grown up. We still keep in contact with one another and he never remarried. Now that Robert has fixed me up with a laptop computer we exchange e-mails on a regular basis. In fact, he has suggested that he may even visit me up here.'

'That's wonderful. Wouldn't it be great if you got together again. You would have so many memories to exchange. Well, thanks for telling us your life story. You know, you should write a book about your experiences, it would make an exciting novel for anyone to read.'

'I'll see, I did start writing an autobiography but never got round to continuing with it.'

'You should, now that you have the computer, it will be that much easier,' then remembering that they were supposed to be preparing the evening meal, Madge gathered up the teacups to wash up and said, 'But we'd better check up what we are cooking for tonight, girls, before it's too late.'

Things were now just about settling down from those early days of finding out how to live on the island with everything so new. Some friendships were developing, apart from the obvious close working relationships of the

145

builders, the farmers, the canteen staff and the school. The children all quickly made friends when they started school. Colleen had not been attending regularly as she had the baby and appeared to be all of a tiz-woz when in the company of James, who, in his turn, became rather red-faced and shy when confronted with the suggestion that he had already made a girlfriend. Kate had been asked by Angus to go out on the odd fishing venture in the *Island Queen*, and they seemed to get along very happily in each other's company. Alice had been asked by Ken to assist with the filming and was now often to be found wielding a video camera, her pleasant manner giving her access to almost any situation. It turned out that our solicitor, Philip, played the flute and other wind instruments quite professionally, so at times when he was not busy, he could often be found, unsurprisingly, in the company of Belinda. Giles, although still very weak, was recovering well from his ordeal in hospital and was seen as a jovial uncle to all the children, who often gravitated towards him individually or in a group, knowing that it was likely they would come away with some unusual 'goody'.

20

One Saturday morning, Trevor, Paul, Michael and Kirsty came running up to the Lodge all very excited and all speaking at once.

'We've just come from the cave and we've found a skeleton.'

'It was scary, our torch started going dim.'

'It was right at the back in the dirt and dust.'

'We think it's human.'

'It was all grisly and I nearly trod on it.'

'Hang on, one at a time,' I said. 'I thought you were told to keep away from the caves. They can be dangerous.'

'Dad said it would be all right providing we were all back before the tide turned at eleven o'clock. We went back home, had lunch and he said we should come and tell you,' Michael and Kirsty replied, both talking at the same time.

'How sure are you that it's human?' I asked.

'Well, it's lying full-length on the ground at the back of the cave and it's too big for a sheep, and a cow's skeleton would be a lot bigger.'

'It's just the size of a human and, you know, the arms are at the side, not like an animal.'

'We've seen pictures of skeletons at school. We're sure we're right.'

'OK, I believe you. Ask your dad if he wants to come, and we'll go down first thing in the morning to have a look. You can show us which cave you found it in.'

That evening I called round to see Jock and asked him if

he had any ideas about what the lads had found. He told me that, when he was a boy, his father had told him that there had been a shipwreck in years past, and although several sailors had drowned, one had survived and found his way to the shore. Jock's father told him that the man's mind was affected and he more or less went mad and lived as a recluse. He wondered if it could be that man. Anyway, the following morning, armed with several good torches and Tilley lamps, I set out with Ken, Paddy and the four children, who led us straight to the cave.

It had a large sea entrance but quickly narrowed into a smaller area as we climbed upwards to a crevice that was quite dry. The children pointed, and there, in the dirt, grey-coloured bones were faintly visible. More sand and black soil was scraped away until the form of the skeleton was easily visible in the strong light that we were now able to shine into the depth of the cave. It did indeed give an eerie feeling. There was no doubt, it was definitely human.

'Jock reckons it could be a sailor who was shipwrecked on these rocks many years ago,' I told them.

'Perhaps he brought some treasure from the ship with him,' Paul said hopefully.

'That's called wishful thinking,' I said, 'but you can never be sure, can you?'

'Do you think he was murdered?' asked Kirsty.

'I don't really know,' I said. 'I think the best thing to do is leave everything as it is. I'll ring the police and see what they advise.'

'Wow, that's exciting.'

We returned, and my call to the mainland resulted in the officer saying there would have to be some form of post-mortem, and they would make arrangements to come across the following day. We had a call in the morning to say they were about to depart and would we meet them and take them to the site.

Four men arrived at the jetty and Paddy, the children and I escorted them to the cave. They spent quite a long time in there and eventually came out to inform us that they did not suspect any foul play. Even with the modern technology that was now available it would probably be quite difficult to make a positive identification. They thought they might have to make arrangements to get the remains back to the mainland.

'When you have done your work, can we dig around for treasure?' Michael asked.

The police inspector who seemed to be in charge replied, 'Yes, but you must wait and not touch anything until we have removed the bones.'

After a few further visits and investigations the police carried out their post-mortem examination and I was asked if I would agree to a burial being carried out on the island. It seemed appropriate in the circumstances, so I agreed. In due course it was carried out at an old burial site in the vicinity of the ruined crofts on the site of the old village with just a couple of officials from the coroner's office present.

A few had taken to call this place 'Old Town', and it now seemed a good time to distinguish between this and the village where we all lived, for which the name 'Main Town' was suggested. Only one other suggestion was forthcoming, and that was that we should split the island name into Ennis for the main town and Kerry for the ruined village because it was the one nearer to Ireland. These were the names that became established over time.

In later weeks Miranda asked if there was any more information about the police investigation into the skeleton as the children were asking her from time to time. I told her that there had been no positive identification to any known individual but it had been confirmed that there had been a shipwreck near that part of our coastline, as Jock suggested. The local newspapers had made a big splash about it and they had come up with a number of different stories about this man. I didn't know which, if any of them, to believe but I offered the cuttings to Miranda as she thought that she might be able to make something of the story in the classroom.

One evening, some time after the children had exhausted their search in the cave for treasure, three of the boys excitedly told their parents that they had seen a monster in one of the lochs. This of course was met with some scepticism from each family, but the boys persisted and convinced Bob, John and Paddy to go with them the following morning to check it out.

'So, describe it to us again,' Bob asked them as a party of about ten walked uphill towards the loch.

'It's like a huge black swan, about three times the size of an ordinary swan,' said Paul, 'except that it sits very low in the water so that you can only usually see its neck sticking out.'

'And I suppose it's got two heads,' commented Paddy.

'No, it's got a round head, but not with a beak like a swan. It doesn't dive, it sinks slowly under the water.'

'Well, now we're at the loch everything looks very calm,' John said. 'We should be able to see it if there is anything there.'

'We had to wait ages yesterday, but we saw it twice.'

'Could it be like the Loch Ness Monster?' asked Trevor. 'I've seen pictures of it and this one looked a bit like it.'

'I doubt it,' said Bob. 'I didn't believe in that monster either.'

'I asked Jock, and he believed it could be,' replied

Trevor, 'and they have found things in Loch Ness that they can't explain.'

'This loch is quite deep,' Shaun said. 'I reckon it's true. We should have brought a camera to prove it to everybody.'

'That's fine if you've got a monster to photograph. I haven't seen anything yet,' Paddy commented.

'You have to be patient,' added Trevor. 'It'll come up soon.'

Paddy turned to have a word with John, and as he did so he caught the faintest of grins on Paul's face as he talked to Trevor. He hesitated.

'You little buggers. It's the first of April, isn't it? April Fools Day.'

The boys started chanting, 'April Fool, April Fool, April Fool!' before the men chased them, ducked them in the water and spread liberal quantities of mud on their faces. They didn't mind at all, they laughed, joked and sang, 'April Fools,' all the way back to the village.

The event led to our three lochs being named. Obviously the boys wanted this one to be Loch Ness, but we also named the others Loch Marie and Loch Lyon.

21

There was another quite unexpected occurrence when a strange dinghy, powered by an outboard motor, moored at the jetty and four youths with video cameras strode purposefully up through the village filming. They spread out and, without any of the usual courtesies, walked uninvited into islanders' crofts and started filming and questioning them about their daily activities. The word spread fairly quickly about the intruders and the general consensus was that non-cooperation was the best policy. Our islanders were quite happy with our own filming arrangements and had built up an empathy with Ken and Alice, who now moved among everyone at any time of the day or night without any embarrassment and often hardly being noticed.

When the youths met with this noticeable lack of co-operation they became more aggressive. A scuffle broke out in which Bob, James and Bill were involved. When I became aware of the problem I called on some of the other men as reinforcements and we decided to escort the youths back to their boat and send them packing. Further scuffles continued as we manhandled them back to the jetty, where some of their filming equipment accidentally fell into the sea before they were all pushed back into their dinghy. There was a lot of cursing and swearing and threats that they would return and pay us back for our treatment.

We did discuss how we could respond if their threats to come back were carried out but decided that we could best deal with things as they occurred. However, we agreed to keep a wary eye open for their return and thought that generally non-cooperation was fairly effective with regard to their filming, but the men would assemble if there were any need to eject them from the island again.

Late one afternoon, some two weeks later, they arrived again, and it quickly became apparent that they were up to no good. As before, they moved up along the crofts, this time trashing early crops, daubing paint and spraying insulting slogans on every available surface, but, more seriously, they went into Jock and Morag's home and threatened them with sticks. They did not steal anything but it frightened the couple out of their lives. The intruders then moved on to where Lynda was living and were unpleasant and abusive to her. I think she gave as good as she got, but they were still causing havoc when I heard about the problem. I quickly contacted Angus and asked him to immobilise the intruders' boat down at the jetty. Then I spread the news that I needed volunteers to gather at the Lodge. It seemed that within minutes most of the men were present. As we assembled we noticed that our hay store was ablaze. My advice was to act in two groups, one to tackle the fire, the other to hunt for the youths – I wanted the four youths captured and tied up with their hands behind their backs. It took about half an hour for us to capture the first three but the fourth ran away up the hill and it took a further half an hour for Lynda to find him hiding in some bracken. He was no match for her with her karate skills and when we arrived on the scene he was cowering amongst the heather in submission. We then struggled to drag all four of them down to the canteen, where we tied them up more securely with hands and feet together.

By late evening the fire at the hay store was still raging. The report was that about half our stock had been dragged safely away from the fire but that the rest had to be abandoned because no one could get close enough owing to the intense heat. I had a telephone call from the police on the mainland saying that a coastguard had notified them of a fire. They asked if we required any assistance. I assured them that things were under control but that I would be sending the four culprits back the following morning. Perhaps they would like to interview them on landing. They asked if they had caused any other damage. I detailed what had happened and said I would ring again in the morning. I decided that we should all get to bed and asked for volunteers to arrange a rota to monitor the still burning hay store and to stay guard over our prisoners until morning.

The four individuals, unsurprisingly, spent a miserable and uncomfortable night. The following morning everyone gathered at the canteen to find out what was going to happen next.

I called on Kathy, our self-appointed hairdresser, to come to the canteen with her hairdressing equipment, saying that there was an urgent need for four haircuts to be carried out straight away.

'Now, Paddy and Bob,' I said, 'help me hold this lad still. Kathy, shave his head clean.'

There was much rolling about the ground until Paddy warned him, 'Stop struggling, you, or we may have to break your neck.'

As Kathy set to work Nick muttered, 'Blimey, 'es on the warpath, 'e means business.'

'How close shall I go?' Kathy asked, as the first youth was held in an upright position, her electric shaver whirring.

'Just try and miss the bone,' I replied, as everybody was beginning to see the funny side of things.

She completed the task, seemingly enjoying the experience, and brightly called, 'Next customer please.' The next youth again put up a struggle but was soon submissive under the strong hands of the men.

Before long, four scowling and miserable youths had lost all their hair and much of their aggression but they still angrily kept repeating, 'We'll get you for this.'

I decided to organise some food for them. 'Right, that's a good job done. Now, I want four hot soups from the kitchen and as much food as they can eat.'

Four steaming bowls of soup duly appeared, followed by substantial meals that were eagerly consumed.

'Make the most of it. Eat as much as you can. You'll need all the warmth inside you that you can muster,' I warned them as a plan of action formed in my mind.

'Angus, make sure that they have enough fuel for a trip back to the mainland and that the motor is in good working order, and Paddy, will you untie this one?' Paddy obliged and I then turned to one lad and said. 'Right, you, take your clothes off.'

He looked at me aghast. 'You're joking? I'm not doing that for you or anybody.'

'Take them off or we'll take them off for you.'

Paddy and Patrick moved forward towards the now petrified lad.

'OK, OK,' he said, slowly removing his shirt.

'And the rest.' I said.

He could not believe what was happening. 'You don't mean it?'

'Oh, yes I do,' I replied. 'If you don't get on with it soon, we will do it for you.' Reluctantly he conformed to his intense embarrassment. 'Good. Now Angus, escort this lad to their boat and wait with him while we deal with the others.'

Soon, all four bald-headed intruders were sitting in the

155

dinghy miserably trying to hide their shame from the gathering audience. They now had their legs and wrists untied.

'Right, so you're now free to return to the mainland. It's approaching midday so it's not too cold, but it will be cold enough out there to perhaps make you wish you had never contemplated this adventure. I've had a word with the local police, who are anxious to meet you at the jetty and ask you a few questions. I have also been in touch with the local press to ensure that your arrival will be well documented with pictures in the papers. You will be watched from here and from the mainland, so don't try for any other location – and don't come back here again or we won't be so kind to you next time. Start the engine.'

The engine started and, watched I believe, by almost every islander, they slowly made their way out to sea on the correct course. Too slow and their time out in the elements would be longer, too fast and the wind chill would drop the temperature by a few degrees. They soon appeared smaller and smaller as they moved into the distance. Nick was heard to mutter again, 'Blimey, that's the way to teach 'em a lesson.'

We all turned to disperse, everyone chattering about the events of last evening and this morning, most saying that they could not have believed that island life could be so exciting.

A few days later we had sight of the local mainland newspaper complete with a large photograph of the miserable naked youths walking up the slipway. The full story was printed under the headline: ARSONISTS GET FREE HAIRCUTS ON ENNISKERRY.

The loss of the hay and the damage to the barn itself was a problem but not a disaster. Morag and Jock were shocked and frightened at the time of the intrusion but they were not injured and did not appear to be suffering any lasting effects. Lynda was pleased that she was able to put her karate skills to some practical use and Kate seemed to get an extra flood of requests for haircuts. I think people just wanted to talk about the event over and over again. The punishment may have been a bit severe but I hoped it would send the message, should any other group think that we were a soft touch, that we were not to be messed with in this way.

I received several letters of support for my methods from across the water: rowdyism was only too prevalent in some parts of the mainland. Several felt it was unjust that we should have been targeted at all. Most welcome of all and very much appreciated was that the local main-landers had arranged a collection, to which many had contributed, in order to provide us with a quantity of hay to replace part of what had been lost in the fire. It was a very good boost to further cement our good relationships with the mainland.

22

'This is the first full council meeting to be held on Ennis-kerry. I welcome you all here. A particularly warm welcome to you Miranda, as you join us today as the seventh member of the council. Miranda has been chosen by the popular vote of the islanders and will be representing the islanders directly. Her task will be to keep her ear to the ground and bring to us those general interests or concerns that may be missed by the rest of us here.

'Of course you have already met and know everybody here quite well, but for formality's sake, you will be aware that John, Gerry and Denise are our three Managers, Kate is our secretary and Philip is our treasurer. These five have been chosen for their specific tasks by me.

'I want to keep these meetings as informal as possible, which brings me to the first question. Should we have an agenda and keep minutes of each of these meetings? John?'

'I think we should begin by keeping a record of whatever we discuss and decide, but discard the idea if it doesn't seem necessary in the future.'

'OK, if you all agree, I will ask you, Kate, to take notes so that we do have a record. The next point that naturally follows is, should we have these printed and distributed to all islanders? Denise, what do you think?'

'I think it is imperative that the islanders are kept totally up to date with what we decide on their behalf and this cannot easily be done by word of mouth.'

'Fine, that means a copy to each homestead, Kate, and

perhaps you, Miranda, could visit each family during the intervening periods and ask if they have any points arising from those notes or any other matter that you can bring with you to our next meeting.'

'I do have one comment,' said Miranda. 'It crops up more and more frequently on the grapevine. Many feel that a shop on the island would have its benefits.'

'Yes, this has been mentioned before but it's more complicated than it sounds. It requires our islanders to have money. Some, I'm thinking of Nick, do not have any.'

'Doesn't he get any unemployment or social security money from the state?' Philip asked.

'I don't think he does. He had no fixed address before he came here and therefore seemed to have an impenetrable barrier to getting assistance. But, Philip, could you look into this for me and for him? It would allow us to go forward with our idea for a shop. I'd prefer if you would deal personally with him about this, I don't want his affairs to be distributed as part of the minutes of this meeting. Yes, Kate.

'Jim, I want to bring this next point up because Gerry here is directly involved and is reluctant to raise it with you, not wanting to get embroiled further in a situation that he feels is for the farmers to resolve. He is happy, however, that I should speak for him. There is bad feeling about that is not healthy for the well-being of the island. This is a problem that has been brewing for some time and it does not seem to dissipate. In fact the current dispute is becoming red hot. It seems that Charles has deemed one of Gerry's Highland cattle so unwell that he will have to put it down. The farmers are not happy with his diagnosis and generally do not have confidence in his methods. Also they do not understand his aggressive manner. It has been said that his experience in the main has been with domestic rather that farm animals, which may be true, They arranged for a second opinion from a vet from the mainland. This vet was with the animal earlier this morning and first reports are that in his opinion the problem can be cured with injections and medicine.

'Charles has never integrated well with the other islanders. You will remember there was an awkward situation when he insisted on testing our milk supply and almost closed the production down. As you may also know, he has already put down a number of pet animals. In Nick's words "'e's already put down one gerbil from the school, Sally's pet cat got the chop, five of the kids rabbits an' four sheep won't see the light of day again. I fink 'e's the Shipman of the veterinary world. Glad 'e's not our doctor, I wouldn't give much for our chances if 'e were."'

'Many of Nick's words can be quite amusing,' I said, 'but there is obviously a serious side to this matter. I know that islanders are favouring our doctor or one of the farmers to unofficially give an opinion of their pet's condition rather than go to Charles. This is, of course, undermining Charles in an already difficult situation. I may try and mediate shortly but although I fervently hope that the animal survives I fear that opinions will become all the more entrenched if it does.'

'Then, there is the on-going problem of the slaughtering,' Kate continued. 'Charles insisted quite rightly that an official, qualified slaughterman should carry this out. The farmers engaged the services of the roving slaughterman who visits the island on request. The farmers are content with the arrangement but Charles continues to make snide remarks around the island. Unfortunately Charles does complain rather a lot generally and his criticisms are often personally orientated, which naturally do not go down very well. In simple terms, he is not liked.'

160

'He seems to relate more easily to the women,' Miranda added. 'I've often seen him in conversation with them. But he is not liked by most of the men.'

'He was very rude to Lynda on one occasion,' Denise mentioned, 'and she vowed never to speak to him again.'

'Let's see how this develops, I think it is better left in the farmers' hands to reach the best arrangements for their animals. Gerry, are you sure you don't want to say anything?'

'I'll not comment on those problems at the moment, if you don't mind.'

'That's fine. Denise, your turn.'

'Jim, I think the time has come to put to you more forcibly than I have in the past, my view on the matter of these voluntary contributions paid to you from some islanders and not others, and your general support of us all during the past and present. I think we should signal more clearly that your period of generosity during this first year would terminate at the end of the year. I think I have the support of Philip when I say that we will be desperate in our need of income during the following year and beyond. Our present minimal income is derived from few sources. I know that the farms and tourism are set to start earning during the coming year but we do not know the extent or value of these ventures. My view is that it is essential for you to dispense with this idea you have given them of a money-free island. I would like to add to my previous comments about the need for islanders to contribute. I believe that it is essential for you to enter into binding contracts with each individual or family now, or at least set a fair rent for their accommodation. This will not only provide a regular and dependable income, it will cover the rather unsatisfactory matter of voluntary payments to you which do not show clearly in our profit and loss accounts. It would also be somewhat strange if we could not allow the introduction of a shop.'

'Philip?'

'Yes we certainly do need the income,' agreed Philip. 'Other sources will be slow to make an impact upon our viability as a business venture. I see nothing wrong with the principle but there may be difficulties in the method. A common rate for all properties would be the most simple, but it would not take into account people's ability to pay.'

'What do you think, John?'

'I noticed that you frowned at Philip's mention of a business venture, but I am sure he is right, we have to take heed of this. We are, in fact, operating a business concern here. If that aspect does not succeed, your island will not succeed – that is, unless you can plan on winning the lottery again.'

'I'm not a business type as you know,' declared Gerry, 'but the question is a simple one. If you look at what comes in and what goes out, if the former does not equal or exceed the latter, you have to do something about it.'

'You're certainly a hard-hitting lot, but that is why you are here and I appreciate your views. I can see that we will have to have a different policy after this first year and that I will have to scrap my idea of doing without money. But I'm worried about how to enforce this rental payment, I keep getting visions of how unpopular Maggie Thatcher's Poll Tax was. I would like to avoid anything that was unfair. Miranda, how do you think most would react to an enforced charge?'

'I think a lot would depend upon how you first introduced the scheme to each person at their interview and on their invitation to the island, whether you prepared them in any way for this eventuality. I can only remind you what happened in my case. I was only too pleased to come to the island and give of my best. At the interview we did not talk of any payment. As I understood it, your

162

advertisement stated clearly that the salary was nil and you did not mention that I should make any payment to you. I only have a small amount saved in the bank, which I would need if I had to go back. I could only afford to pay a rent if I was earning but not otherwise. I'm sure several are in a similar position to me.'

'Philip, do you want another word?'

'Yes, I think this has to be tackled on two fronts. First we must look into what grants and payments are available for work done here. For example, Miranda should be paid for her teaching from the local council or government. The building work should attract grants from different sources. Doctors and vets should get payments, and in return, you should pay people for their services on the island and then charge them appropriate rents. The Highlands and Islands Development Board may be a starting place, but there must be many other avenues open for investigation. I know it will strike a strange note with you, but I actually think we should apply for lottery funding.

'It stands to reason that people are happy to take advantage of a year of free lodging on a pleasant island with meals and all services paid for and, at the same time, keeping their options open by having savings in the bank or an alternative means of income on the mainland that they could possibly return to. I am sure that most of your choice of people living here now are honourable and many share your view of trust in each other as the way forward, but I see no reason why we shouldn't introduce a system of payment for work done by individuals and a proportion of those earnings being given back to the island for the housing and all other services provided.'

'It is true that I didn't address the matter of life beyond the first year at the interview stage. We are now nearly halfway through the first year and the time is perhaps right to inform everyone about the changes that will have to be made at the turn of the new year. As I see things, based upon Philip's provisional figures of income, we cannot hope to be profitable until late into next year. I think I can sustain the present level of expenditure until the end of next year but I do recognise that there will have to be change.

'How would you react if I announced shortly that from the first of January next, I will be paying the mainland minimum wage, or just above, to everyone who is working on the island's business, which would not include such things as their own improvement work on their existing crofts? I have been jotting down some simple arithmetic and I estimate that this wages bill could cost me about half a million pounds each year.

'If I also ask for a rental charge on each dwelling and make corresponding charges for electricity, gas bottles, telephone calls and other services such as canteen meals that I now provide, this could return, say, about two thirds of my expenditure. The rest would be offset by profits from the farms, tourism and other enterprises as they become established. I could also make an offer for some to buy outright their own or any other available property on the island. What do you think, Denise?'

'That is exactly what I had in mind. The island must not only be profitable, it must be seen to be profitable. You have made it possible by making the island available to us, you can subsidise things of your choice here and there if the money is available, but you cannot and should not be expected pay everybody's bills without some financial contribution from them.'

'I foresee a problem with Angus,' Kate commented. 'He could quite easily refuse to accept any wage at all, and there could be some others with similar views.'

'I'll have a word with Angus sometime before our next

meeting, and with anyone else who might feel the same way.'

To conclude, I asked Denise to look into what interest she could find for clubs and classes that could be held, mainly during the evenings. It turned out that she had already done so.

Lynda had already been instrumental in organising five-a-side football and five-a-side handball for the children at the school and considered that if there was sufficient interest this could be extended to evening sessions. Also, being proficient at karate, she would also be able teach this as an evening class. Several children had shown interest in both football and handball as well as the karate.

Basic computer lessons were already being given at the school by Robert, and he had also offered to give more advanced instruction in computer skills at different levels at evening classes.

The most likely person to encourage interest in various creative crafts seemed to be Susan. Five women had expressed interest in spinning, weaving, patchwork and tapestry. Additionally other interest groups have been suggested, which include cookery, keep fit, upholstery and basket work. Theresa had a natural talent for art and was convinced that she could form a class for painters.

Musical tuition at the school was enhanced with the help of Belinda, and she had agreed that this could also be extended to the evenings provided that we could rustle up enough instruments for a band or small orchestra. There was a lot of interest, even if some were only just starting to play an instrument. Belinda said that several of the children were quite talented, and the addition of the adults would give a great boost to their enthusiasm. Gwyneth said that she had done some singing in a choir when she was back in Wales and would happily join a singing group if one were formed.

As the foundations for most of these various activities were identified, Denise quickly managed to make further arrangements for them to start.

Following the meeting Philip, privately negotiated some financial help for Nick and James who were both unemployed before they came to the island. Their good fortune opened the door for me to look further into the idea of creating a shop on the island, now that they were not totally bereft of cash.

23

The summer months were with us and the school holidays were approaching. Throughout our time on the island Angus had been making trips to the mainland to collect building materials and other island and household needs. Often he would be called upon to take someone, more usually the wives, with him so that they could explore the 'rest of the world' – the expression quickly became a part of the island's vocabulary. The available time was used to go to the shops and chat with acquaintances previously made. He often went with every imaginable request which included newspapers, books, replacement parts for all sorts of domestic gadgets, equipment, alcohol, craft materials and, almost always, there were orders for hardy garden plants. Many were taking great pride in the gardens surrounding their crofts, and there was even a sense of competition developing between them. Sometimes Angus would bring an interested visitor back with him for a day visit, but the most eagerly awaited visits were from members of the islander's own families.

The school was organising an end of term sports day, which included all the usual running races, parents versus children races and a marathon hill running event. The day culminated with a bonfire and barbecue on the beach.

Two other big events during the summer were the completion of the school and canteen buildings. Each building had been initiated with my being asked to lay the foundation stones for both of them, and we now held opening ceremonies for each with a party and outdoor games for the children. It was decided that the school would not be fully used for schoolwork until the beginning of the following term, but it was available for various day and evening classes and other events. Robert was equipping a computer room in the school with a number of workstations for evening as well as day use. He was also offering evening classes at different levels of expertise and there was quite a lot of interest. All, particularly the staff who had worked under cramped conditions without complaint for so long, had anxiously awaited the new canteen. The old army tents were not redundant, however, because we still had a need for storage space. Another idea was that we should convert one of them to provide a badminton court, but further thought made us realise that the lighting might not be good enough.

A number of additional events were held for the children during the school holidays, including boat trips to see seals and birds with Angus. Several tug-of-war events were very popular with the children, particularly when they challenged and pulled against some of the parents. School teams competed against each other for five-a-side football, and handball continued throughout the holidays.

Both the school orchestra and a brass band had just been formed and were in the early stages of honing their varied skills. People passing the school during practice times varied in their comments from 'My God, what a row,' in the early stages, to, more recently, 'It's coming on slowly but I still walk on the other side of the track.' The orchestral group was supplemented in the evenings with adults of widely varied musical skills, which must have been very difficult to manage but Belinda seemed to take it all in her stride.

At the recent council meeting I had asked John to assess our current methods of waste disposal. It was all laboriously taken to our one and only landfill site at present. I had asked him to investigate and give direction as to how we should deal with our waste products in the future. I had tried to instill a greater awareness of the need to be ecologically conscious of our island situation. Both our magazine and minutes of meetings had been distributed with advice on how to deal with rubbish, explaining that we just had the one site that would become more and more under pressure as we increased our population. We should begin to separate our waste into those consisting of degradable materials and those that were not, and then deal with them in different but appropriate ways. It had not been possible to get our mechanical shovel digger to the site. As a result, John had recommended that we programme to make some improvements to the track leading to the site so that it would allow easier access and more regular attention could then be given to the appropriate distribution of the waste products.

The first person to get a visit from family at home was Kate, whose mother arrived unannounced. She made her own way, arranging a trip across to the island with Hamish, the same ferryman that I had used on my first visit. It was such a surprise, as it was intended to be, for Kate's birthday. She had been in regular contact with her daughter, but nevertheless had gathered a lot of information the previous evening at her hotel and on the crossing about how life seemed to be getting along with the new community. The people she met were full of praise for how the community were adapting to their new life. She was of course up to date with how Kate was getting along from regular letters and occasional telephone calls, but it was nice to hear these comments from others.

She walked up the slipway to the first crofts and met

Angus, who had spotted the ferryman arriving. He was surprised to see a stranger disembark and was even more surprised to be recognised by the lady.

'I think you must be Angus,' she said.

'Aye, that's right, but how did you guess?'

'Well, I've heard so much about you – I'm Mary, Kate's mum,' she admitted. 'She's told me all about the island and the boat trips, and her description of you was spot on.'

'Well I never. I'd better show you where she lives.'

They walked up to her croft and he left her at Kate's door.

'This is where Kate lives. Have a good time, she'll be pleased to see you and perhaps we'll meet again.'

'Thanks very much,' Mary said as they parted. 'I hope we do meet again.'

Kate appeared wearing a turbaned towel over her head, having just washed her hair. She was flabbergasted, having had no idea that her mother had harboured thoughts of a surprise of this nature. They locked into an embrace that seemed never to end.

'It's lovely to see you, Kate, and you're looking so fit and well.'

'I'm really enjoying it here, Mum, so many new experiences. Everyone is very friendly. But how are you, you're not looking so bad?'

'I'm quite well, Jack's keen on country walking and that keeps me fit.'

'When are you going to make it legal, Mum?'

'Oh, get away with you, you talk as if I'm in some sort of illicit relationship,' she laughed.

'He's a good man, Mum, it'll be good for you both.'

'I told you, you sort yourself out and then I'll consider it. I met your boyfriend on the way up here. What are you doing about that? I've a mind to put a good word in for you to speed things up.'

'Oh, don't do that, good words from mothers are sure to put an end to any relationship.'

'He seems to hope we may meet again here, he said so. You are good friends aren't you?'

'Yes, I help a bit on his boat and sometimes cook him a meal. I also help with the farmer's accounts, and I'm secretary on the island's island's council. It's a surprisingly busy life but I'm enjoying every minute. How long can you stay?' Kate said, changing the subject.

'I thought two or three days. How long do visitors usually stay?'

'There are no set rules and you are the first of the relations to visit anyway, but come with me to the canteen and we'll get something to eat. You can meet some of my friends there, we often gather about this time. Tomorrow we'll have a look round the island, it's so beautiful.'

Kate introduced her mother to the canteen staff and helpers and another half a dozen of those islanders who were present at the time. Her mother became very popular in a short time. A new face and a good humour made the time go very quickly. In the evening they called up to the Lodge to meet me and talked over several cups of coffee.

Mary stayed three nights and, during that time, had a boat trip with Angus and her daughter. They got along very well and I believe she went away convinced that she had been talking to her future son-in-law. Whether Angus saw things in the same way remained to be seen. Angus took her back to the mainland on the fourth morning and Kate said that it had been a wonderful reunion.

The visit of Belinda's parents turned out to be much more of a private affair. There was a lot of catching up for them to do as her father had been away at sea for the few months before she set off for the island. Her mother was quite tearful on the first day of their reunion but after attending an evening concert in which Belinda played a duet with Philip they all seemed much more relaxed and were able to integrate with the rest of the islanders. Her mother, having previously harboured fears that her daughter had abandoned a promising career in music, realised that Belinda was happy with her new life.

'Cheer up, Mum, I'm really enjoying my time here. Remember how you used to encourage me to do things when I was a bit reluctant? I'm glad I listened to what you said.'

'I know, I'm just being a bit silly having not seen you for such a long time. Dad keeps saying that you're doing what you wanted and that is what we both hoped for, but I wish we could see you more often.'

'There's no reason why you couldn't come more often in the future. We'll have some extra accommodation soon and, if it's available, there isn't much to stop you.'

We tried to accommodate visitors as often as possible, even though it had been difficult in the early stages with wintry weather, but, as the better weather came, many relations were happy to put up with rather overcrowded conditions to be together again. Their excitement was captured on film and became part of that week's story.

Although every family and islander, with the probable exception of Nick and Graham, had during their time on the island been in constant correspondence with their families either by telephone, post or e-mail, it transpired that it was from their personal visits that most was revealed about how we as islanders were viewed from 'abroad'.

I think many relations had, in spite of being constantly

reassured that life was quite civilised, had thoughts at the back of their minds that their 'black sheep' had in some way 'gone native'. They wondered if they really would stay the course, and several, I imagined, expected them back home after the first year, and having ended their affairs with nature, they would return to the fold and continue with their lives in a less unconventional way.

One exception to this view was Denise's family, who perhaps a little surprisingly, in view of the fact that she had given up a very promising career, held the opinion that it could only continue to be a great experience for her and that only good could come of it.

Denise's mother and father, Patricia and Harold, came with her brother Derek and stayed three nights. Her father was in publishing, her mother a freelance journalist and her brother worked for one of the aid agencies. I suppose inevitably, at the end of their stay her mother asked if I would mind if she wrote an article about her daughter and her decision to come and live on Enniskerry.

The next visitors were my mother and father. Of course I had kept them totally up to date on each element of progress and they had put in the odd suggestion from time to time on how they thought certain matters should be tackled. Their visit was effectively an extension to their regular annual holiday, which was normally spent near Braemar, a holiday retreat with a fantastic view of the Cairngorms that I knew well. They had invited Anne's parents Tony and Doreen, with whom they had kept up a fond relationship since Anne died, to join them in Braemar and then continue with a week on Enniskerry.

My father was a keen photographer, and it was not long before he passed a packet across to me which contained some photographs of landscapes and sea views that I flicked through. At first they did not mean anything to me.

'They're pictures of where you're living you daft so-and-so. Can't you see it's Enniskerry, although it's some years ago now?'

'Yes, of course, I can see now, that's the Lodge clear enough and the jetty hasn't changed at all.'

'There are a couple of the high street as it was. You'll be interested to see those,' he said, shuffling through to find them.

'It's wonderful. It's great to have them as a record. I think I'll have them blown up larger and get them framed. You didn't mention that you'd been here before.'

'To tell you the truth, I didn't know until recently that I still had the pictures. I took them when I was sailing round the Hebrides before I married your mum. It was populated then. There's a few photographs of the island's occupants included. Your Jock will probably know all of them.'

'Yes, I think that one actually is Jock. He'll be fascinated to see them.'

After these visits, relations and friends came in increasing numbers, limited only by the housing available to accommodate them. Progressively, those occupying rooms in my Lodge moved out to their completed houses, I was then able sometimes to help more of the visiting families by offering them rooms at the Lodge.

24

'I guess the whole population of the island is present here tonight, which is great. I thought I would open this first general meeting to be held on Enniskerry with an attempt to outline some of my proposals for the future for, as happy as we may be at present, it is how we prepare now which is of paramount importance.

'First, you may like to hear a few comparisons with the nearby island of Gigha, which was sold in 2001 as a result of a community buy-out when it was taken out of private ownership. Offers were originally requested for up to five million pounds.

'Gigha has about one hundred and ten islanders. It has a similar climate to Enniskerry, with a marked benefit from the Gulf Stream which gives it a relatively warm temperature throughout the year. It is frost-free and snow is unknown. There is a huge eight-bedroom mansion with staff accommodation, a twenty-six-bedroom hotel, five self-catering cottages, about six farms, twenty-eight tenanted houses, a nine-hole golf course and a boathouse that is used as a restaurant. There are three lochs and there is scope for shooting on the hills. They also have a shop and an airstrip and a well-surfaced road. In short, it has the potential of being a well-organised island with great opportunities for income.

'Our island of Enniskerry is further from the mainland but it also benefits from the Gulf Stream, so we also are frost-free and snow is most unlikely. Our island is much larger in area. It has many natural assets such as open moorland, three lochs, tree plantations, splendid cliffs, and several beautiful beaches. If we use Gigha as a comparison, Enniskerry, as you will know only too well, is not as yet anywhere near as profitable. In fact we hardly have any income at all, but I see the potential as greater if we manage it sensibly and build on the resources that we have. It will take time, and that is why we must always have our eyes to the future.

'You will know directly of the progress that has been achieved so far with our building construction programme and you will be aware of our ideas for the profitability of our livestock and arable farms, together with our fish farm, which are still in the early stages of setting up. Even with these ongoing projects in hand we must look at other aspects of our ability to produce, earn money and work efficiently.

'This brings me to one important matter that was discussed at our last council meeting. Basically it comes under the heading of tourism. The filming taking place here is now sufficiently well advanced for us to consider making it available to British television. You will know how Ken has been moving among you since we arrived, and more recently with Alice assisting. They have been able to capture many of the day-to-day events that have occurred on the island. Everyone has been remarkably co-operative. I have watched two of the early episodes and they make fascinating and entertaining viewing. There is, of course, a serious side to this. It is the first stage in making people aware of what we are doing here, in the hope that it will attract people to come and see us and pay for the privilege. I myself have to admit to certain regrets about this move towards commercialism, and I believe that there will be some among you who likewise will see this as an intrusion into our peaceful and contented way of life. However, it is essential that we move to explore all areas of possible income to ensure that we can sustain our lives here into the future. I ask you to continue to embrace the venture as you have done so far, being co-operative with the continuing filming even if you do have misgivings about the direction in which we are heading. We will have to build further accommodation and welcome new people into our way of life, but I am sure there are benefits apart from the obvious one of income. By opening our doors we avoid the danger of becoming insular and unreasonably introspective in our lives. We must look outward and embrace the wider world for the sake of our young people.

'I have one other important matter to put to you, but first I must eat humble pie and confess that I now think that my original idea of a money-free island is impractical for our future. I have been convinced that exchanging money would be a necessary requirement as we encourage people to the island. I think I can hear your thoughts of "We told you so!" Now I can only agree, "Yes you did, and I listened." This U turn allows us to consider how we should create a shop on the island, what it should stock and how we will finance it. It would for instance also provide an outlet for any arts or crafts that were created here.

'Next, I must mention that when we came to this island I did not give to any of you a clear indication of what may happen after the first year. The reason being that there were many things that I did not know myself at that time. I, and perhaps many of you, were all caught up in the novelty of the experiences of the new venture. Like me, perhaps you thought you would just see how things would develop and meet this point as it arrived. That time is with us now. You will be interested to hear that only one person questioned at interview what would happen after the first year.

'At our last committee meeting we talked at length about this matter of how the island will function after the first year and I would like to give you a clearer picture of what is proposed. The following is the result of much discussion and has the unanimous approval of your committee.

'One. As of the first of January, I will be paying a wage based on the minimum wage operating on the mainland, or just above, to everyone who is working on any task associated with the island's business. By this I mean it will exclude any improvement work carried out by people on their existing crofts or for personal benefit.

'Two. I will be levying a rental charge on each dwelling and making additional charges for electricity, gas bottles, telephone calls and other services such as canteen meals that I now provide free.

'Three. I will also make available some properties for sale, which may be purchased by negotiation at an agreed price. This could be the property in which you are residing or any other available property on the island which is not allocated for other use. You may like to comment on some of the matters I have mentioned. Giles, you have a point to raise?'

'Yes, I was interested in your comparisons between Gigha and ourselves. It would seem that Gigha is a much smaller island than Enniskerry and yet it has more than twice the number of people. In theory we could eventually support a much larger population here. Is it your intention to populate Enniskerry further?'

'The thought has been on my mind recently. I see two aspects, first a degree of natural evolvement in terms of the balance between our rate of construction of new properties, the flow of income to the island from different sources and the success of our attempt to advertise the island by the production, for instance, of our film, together with other advertising efforts in the press and on the web. Second, there is the further opportunity for me to advertise again for people with additional skills to those we already possess, or skills that we have now but will need reinforcing.

'I believe that simply to increase our numbers *ad lib* is not an option in itself. We must guard against providing a soft haven for anyone to come without being able to offer any significant benefit to the island as a whole. On the other hand, anyone who does offer something tangible should be welcomed.'

'Are we building new houses as part of the idea to house visitors?' Helen asked.

'The general principle is that when everyone is adequately housed, we would move to co-operate with those families who desire more spacious accommodation. When that accommodation is completed it will release their previous house for another use. Our aim will be to have an excess of housing over our need so that we can accommodate visitors.'

'I would like to know what sort of goods you envisage that the shop will stock and sell and how soon can we begin to set it up.' Alice asked.

'It can be anything according to our needs, but I see it as being a combined post office, newsagent and general store. Perhaps we could also incorporate a bakery. I hope it would have a good selection of books, games and other attractions for the kids, together with general needs for the home, such as gas bottles and a selection of more specialised foods. As I have said, I hope that it would also provide an outlet for art and crafts. As to when it will open, that will depend upon how soon we can allocate a suitable building.'

'How will you determine the amount of rent that we will have to pay?' James asked.

'I can't give you an actual figure at the moment. What I can tell you is that the income I receive for rents, which I envisage may be equal for all homes, together with the payments for services etc, will total about two thirds of the wages I will be paying out. I will endeavour to make it a fair arrangement so that no one will be worse off as a result.'

'Will I, as the island's vet, and the doctor and the farmers be included in the wages that you will pay, and can we make our own charges for medicines that we dispense from our practices in general?' Charles queried.

'Yes, you and Matthew will be included in the payments. No, you should not make any additional charges, all medical and veterinary services are to be free. I'm sure you remember that, in your case, the supply of medicine has been provided by me. The arrangements with our farmers will take a different form, in that a proportion of their profits will be allocated to the island.'

'How will you charge for electricity when we all use different amounts?'

'I have a choice, James. Either I install meters for accurate readings or I divide the cost on an equal basis. I propose to divide the cost initially because our usage at present is purely for lighting, which is a relatively small sum for each home.'

25

Just as things were, to my mind, falling neatly into place, we had the first of a series of several problems, such that the year did not end on the positive note that I had hoped for.

The continuing dispute about the welfare of our animals reached new heights of verbal abuse when I tried to mediate between the farmers and Charles, who had reached another deadlock over a never-ending series of minor disagreements. Almost before I had uttered my first words, Charles turned on me and issued a number of voluble threats along the lines that if I did not support him as the island's vet, who should have the final say in any matter relating to the animals under his jurisdiction, he would have to take these matters to a higher level and report the farmers for ill-treating their animals and restricting his movements so that he could not carry out his work effectively. When I said that I could not believe that they would ill-treat their cattle or any other animal, he then turned on me and issued another torrent of abuse. I tried to calm the situation, asking him to specify what he meant by ill-treatment. His reply in condensed form was that the problem was of a medical nature and I would not understand. He started flinging his arms around, his voice getting louder and louder, and referring to Gerry, Patrick and Ian as 'these idiots' having not the first idea about animals and their needs. I replied that we would not get very far if he kept shouting and insulting people. I was certainly getting nowhere. He then accused me of not having the intelligence to run the island's affairs efficiently, adding that he had no respect for me as the Laird and he had a mind to leave the island.

I could do nothing to repair this rift. I suggested we all went home to cool down and perhaps talk another time.

Within the next week the relationship between us had reached another low point with further accusations and some recrimination. Charles announced that he would be leaving the next morning. In the event weather and tides did not co-operate, so Angus was not able to ferry him to the mainland until the following day. His departure was a sad occasion, and there were some half-hearted attempts to get him to reconsider his decision, but it was to no avail. In the cold mist of a wintry morning a few stalwarts at the jetty wished him well for his journey and his future. He more or less ignored everyone and sat in the boat grumpily looking out to sea as Angus cast off and he and his boat disappeared into the gloom.

The poor weather that accompanied Charles' departure did not abate for several weeks. There were storms with a ferocity that we had not experienced before. The rain was relentlessly torrential and the wind reached such a force that at times one was unable to walk without a real risk of injury. Some were actually blown off their feet, usually to the amusement of all who witnessed these tumbles, but it was recognised to be actually quite dangerous to venture out. During the third week of these conditions our temporary army tents were almost swept away, leaving them badly torn and in a very sorry state, with a great deal of their previous contents now in the open and scattered to the elements. There was not much chance to take any remedial action until conditions improved but there continued to be unrelenting forecasts for even more bad weather. Structural damage was occurring to several temporary buildings, and a number of islanders were unlucky with cuts, bruises and sprained limbs. Matthew and his wife Ruth, our doctor and nurse, were kept exceptionally busy, their work hampered by the difficulty of actually getting around.

These accidents were bad enough but the most serious happened in Dafydd and Gwyneth's home when a high wind gusted, bursting open a previously closed door, which dislodged a table and caused a Tilley lamp to be knocked or blown over, spilling its contents over the floor and catching fire. Owing to the noise of the wind, Dafydd and Gwyneth, who were upstairs at the time, were unaware of any problem until they heard their daughter Alison screaming for help. Eight-year-old Alison had skidded on the paraffin-soaked floor and fallen into the flames, whereupon her clothing had caught fire. It took a while before her parents could smother out the flames. Their attempt to then cool her leg by applying cold water and not removing her jeans was probably the right thing to do, and their action undoubtedly reduced the burning effect to some degree, but her leg was painfully burnt. Doctor Matthew came to their house very soon after the accident and gave advice and medicines to reduce the discomfort. Alison was very brave but the pain must have been intense and some hours later there seemed little relief. Her main concern was that she would be scarred for life, and it certainly seemed that it would be so. Matthew had a dilemma. He thought that further hospital treatment would be desirable, but with the weather conditions outside that was an impossibility. He made her as comfortable as possible and tried to reassure her about the scars that would undoubtedly remain.

In subsequent weeks the weather improved a little, but our situation did not, for several islanders began complaining of flu-like symptoms, including chills, fever, headache, aches in the body and general weakness. All those affected said that they just felt so weak that they did not have the strength to go about their normal activities.

Matthew's fear was that his patients' resistance might be significantly lowered over the period of their illness, so that secondary infections, such as bacterial pneumonia, could follow the influenza. However, he was most concerned that his treatment should include dispensing medicine to combat any of the secondary infections, which could cause the most worrying effects, particularly in the elderly. He could control these infections, if they occurred, with antibiotics and other drugs, but he explained that most people recovered from influenza with continued rest in bed, together with the aspirin-type remedies that he was now administering, and he had more than sufficient of these in store for future needs.

His concern was justified, for as time went on, it was evident to those who visited Morag in her home that she was not responding as hoped to the treatment. Day after day the doctor emerged with the ever-increasing concern that her heath was slowly failing. Some three weeks later she had a bad bronchial attack and died suddenly in a fit of coughing.

A cloud of despondency covered the island. People had not imagined that illness and death would so quickly come and affect their lives. From the exuberance and excitement of the previous months of our occupation of the island, the enthusiastic activities of building work and the formation of new friendships, so many things were now going wrong. Basic confidences were being challenged.

Jock was immersed in his grief; hardly able to converse as he wandered about hardly believing that his loss of Morag had indeed occurred. Naturally he was unsure of his future alone. Jock and Morag were both God-fearing devotees of the truth of the Bible, together with a strong belief in the Almighty. Most of the rest of us were not well prepared or well equipped to deal with the practicalities of the death of one we regarded as our family. In a sense the whole island was in turmoil.

I decided that our first task should be to allocate a suitable place for the burial and then build some sort of monument or chapel in which people could pay their respects and worship if they wished. I turned to one person who I considered to be the most likely to be able to express the appropriate condolences for this bereavement, and Miranda immediately agreed to help.

There was an ancient graveyard beside some of the old crofts towards the site of the old village to the south-east of the island, which we had recently been referring to as Kerry. I went with Paddy to ask him to prepare a grave. While we were there we looked at the possibility of creating a small chapel. There was, Paddy decided, sufficient natural stone laying around for the construction. It would, of course, not be possible for the work to be completed for the funeral but we would give this priority over other building work.

The funeral was held on a cold wintry-like morning, rain and drizzle wafting in on a mist from sea. I said a few words to the gathering which, I was sure, included every member of the island. Miranda added an eloquent and moving speech, remarking on the deep faith that was held by Jock and Morag and feeling that Morag's life and short time with us was an example of the basic love and happiness that she had shared with us. Many had spent time weaving wild berries and grasses into colourful wreaths and bouquets. Philip was able to play a short lament on his flute and the congregation sang 'Abide with Me', followed by 'The Lord is my Shepherd', before the coffin was gently lowered into the ground.

*   *   *

As the year neared its close there was a general feeling that our run of bad luck should have, by now, run its course and we should look forward to ending the year with a Christmas party, not only for the sake of the children, which was most important, but also to enthuse us all and help lift us out of the doldrums.

Everyone did something to make it a grand party. Giles dressed up and looked a most convincing and amiable Father Christmas, who explained that as it was an island, it had been a rather difficult journey during the night to complete all his deliveries to the children before daybreak. That explained why he was still distributing them to us as lunch-time approached. Every adult also received a present, and among the most appreciative were Nick, who received a mountain bike, and Jock, who was given a splendid set of bagpipes.

The revelries continued through Christmas, and many saw the party atmosphere as a healing event. Nostalgic memories were exchanged, new friendships were formed and, generally, everyone was revived to eagerly greet the new year with optimism and determination.

26

A new year and new challenges. Although we were still in the midst of winter, the bad luck at the end of last year had now given way to renewed optimism, which I felt duty bound to encourage to the best of my ability. The one exception to feeling new optimism was Jock, who spent a difficult few months after Morag had died. He had lost any desire to care about his appearance or look after himself in general. He wandered aimlessly as a lost soul, as indeed he was without his soul mate. His demeanour seemed increasingly pitiful as his health declined. Rene could see what was happening and coaxed him into the canteen to get some reviving food into him. With Madge and Edith they gradually saturated him with their good spirits until he became a regular customer. Having seen him through the most difficult time, they saw the beginnings of animation in him and a slow return of his good humour.

Edith became a particularly good friend, and she could be seen to link arms with Jock to escort him back to his croft each evening. They would have to run the gauntlet of raucous wolf-whistles from Nick, who delighted in advertising it as the latest romance taking place on the island.

Jock made good progress and, one day, Edith heard a long, droning sound emanating from his croft. Discounting the possibility that Jock was having difficulty with his breathing, she came to the conclusion that he had picked up his Christmas present and decided that he could play a lament on the pipes which, no doubt, reflected his mood of the day. It was another landmark and good news to share at the canteen that day.

Our first Friday night ceilidh, held on New Year's Day, was an event that almost everybody attended and, although in its infancy, it was intended to be a gathering of traditional Scottish values. Angus had been only too pleased to take a turn with Jock and play his bagpipes as he introduced the evening's proceedings with a Scottish reel and a Highland fling. The accompanying dancing was, at the best, very amateur but at least the enthusiasm was there and no doubt proficiency would improve with time. Several of us had donned Highland costume, including sporrans and kilts. Traditionally the ceilidh is a winter evening's entertainment, with spontaneous singing, music, discussions and storytelling. We had tried to include all these things, with some encouragement to produce a degree of spontaneity. During the evening's gathering, Gwyneth suggested holding a similar event to their Eisteddfod in Wales. In Scotland this similar traditional event is known as a 'mod', and is held annually in the summer. It would also include competitions in Gaelic poetry, prose and music, but is held out of doors.

After a few weeks of the new year, most of the original members had made it known that they were now committed to stay for at least another year and had taken well to the introduction of receiving payment and paying rent. We had agreed that these payments should be on a monthly basis, with payment going out near the end of each month, and thereafter the rents being due on the first day of each month. Islanders had now started paying for their food at the canteen and purchasing some other essentials from the store, for which Jock had taken responsibility. All were looking forward to the opening of a shop but it was still not at the top of the priority list for construction.

I wanted to set new objectives and, with the agreement of the council, had already advertised in the press for new members for the island with a bias towards specific building and construction skills. This time the number of replies overwhelmed me. I decided to call another meeting of the council members to make this response known to them and float the proposal for the most radical reform to date, which was to double the population of the island.

'I'll get straight down to business,' I began 'We now have the replies to our advertisement and can select those people we want to join us. I want to create our own building company, incorporating new blood, to complete our programme of renovation and double the number of properties here. As we have repeated many times, nearly all the small islands around here have suffered steadily from depopulation. The movement of people through many years has been always away from, rather than to, any of these islands. Why is that so? My view is that it is because there is, in general, simply nowhere for any newcomers to live. Look at this number of applications I have for people who wish to come here,' I said, spreading out on the table some fifty or so letters. 'There is no shortage of enterprising families wanting to come. There is only one essential thing missing at present that will sustain life here in the future, and that is a new intake of people, thus increasing the permanent population. That obviously cannot happen unless there is somewhere for them to live. My suggestion therefore is that we aim to double the number of properties that we have at present. We cannot achieve that with our existing workforce over a short period of time. What better than to continue with the principle that some here have already started, that is, for each new family to build their own house? We can embrace this idea so that when I evaluate the new applicants I could, at first, give priority to those with building skills to help set us along this path.'

'Can you afford to pay these people for building their own houses?' Denise asked.

'This second-year contingent would live here on a somewhat different arrangement to those here now. Our existing arrangements could still apply. For example, at certain later stages, we could pay them for any work that they carry out for the island, but initially, they would be building their own house with their own money. John?'

'Is it possible that having built their house they would simply live here and not contribute anything at all to the island? I am also concerned that we would have this bias towards the one occupation. OK, for your initial idea, but we are then permanently biased into the future. Your cross-section of society policy may falter slightly.'

'There are dangers, but remember, they will still need certain things from us, and it follows that they will contribute by way of their need to first purchase their plot of land or pay ground rent to us. As we develop our services such as water and heating, appropriate charges will be made. If we open our shop, as we intend, all their day-to-day needs could be purchased on the island. Also, remember that we are engaged on a number of projects that will require additional labour into the future, for instance on both Gerry's and Ian's farms, the fish farm and any new ideas that develop in fishing or other areas.

'As for your point about bias, John, I can't agree with you there. Just because they all have the same job title of construction worker it doesn't mean they are no longer a

190

cross-section of society. They will all have a different outlook on the world and have varied talents. Building need not be their main occupation, people from many different walks of life may attempt a self-build approach, and there will be no shortage of good advice.'

'Quite right, Jim, it was not a valid point. I was just a little concerned that because the newcomers would operate on a different basis to those already here we could develop into a two-class society.'

'It's not a lot different in the sense that it reflects life on the mainland, where some own their property, others pay rent.'

'In which direction from the village would the new properties be built? I don't think it would be very popular to obstruct the sea views that many of us have at present,' Miranda asked.

'I'll get some plans drawn up so that everyone can comment on the proposals and make any suggestions. It will all be done as sympathetically as possible. I did have one idea: that some of the stone from the old crofts in Kerry could be used, but second thoughts suggested that we could actually site a new village there.'

'Would it be better to go for, say, half the increase in people and property that you suggest over a period of perhaps two years and not go headlong into such a drastic influx so soon?' Gerry suggested.

'I'd be prepared to compromise if the general view reflected that it would be a better option, but I was convinced that we must go in this direction as quickly as possible. Basically, the choice is whether we go for an increase of ten or twenty properties to be constructed over the first year, these being carried out by self-build and our own building company in a proportion yet to be decided. Perhaps we should have a vote on it?'

So we all voted and the result was a tie, three voting for

191

an increase of 10 and three voting for 20. I therefore had the casting vote but decided to compromise and settle for 15 new dwellings.

On the assumption that we had a similar balance of married couples, that meant we would attract in excess of 40 new islanders.

Ian joined us, having been invited into the meeting because he had gained further knowledge on the agricultural domes that we hoped to use. We all wanted him to share the information that he had obtained.

'The important news is that I have found a supplier who can provide exactly what we had anticipated we would need. They are known as "solar domes". Technically they are based upon the geodesic dome principle, as were those at the Eden Project in the West Country. Geodesic means that it is constructed of a number of triangles, hexagons or pentagons forming a grid in the shape of part of a sphere. They are normally supplied with glass within a supporting aluminium structure, although I suspect any other transparent material that was strong enough could be used instead of the glass. The whole structure is remarkably strong and stable. Glass four millimeters thick is recommended, and the great thing, from our point of view, is that the domes have been proved to have withstood winds of up to 120 m.p.h. As we predicted before, pressure from any horizontal wind force applies a downward pressure on a dome; any other vertical structure would be much more likely to be blown away. Apparently there is also an excellent airflow within, controlled by opening vents wherever required on the surface of the dome. I have been told that small units are proving to be popular on some of the Outer Hebridean islands, where they are used mainly as greenhouses. I thought this was an excellent advertisement to convince us that they were suitable on our somewhat windy island.'

'It seems these could be a good asset to extend the growing season for our vegetables, which I believe was your intention. Do you have any information about the costs involved?'

'Yes. It obviously depends on size. The largest I could find, available as a self-assembly structure from a moderate-sized manufacturer, was 9.5 metres in diameter. This gives a volume of 240 cubic metres and costs about £21,000. Of course, they offer several of smaller sizes.'

'I guess you would like to obtain one as soon as possible this year to get things planted in good time before the spring. If everyone on the council is agreed, then we'll give you the OK to get one ordered.'

Ian looked pleased for he had a burgeoning interest in providing vegetables for the island and had been checking through all the available catalogues.

It was a major and far-reaching decision to open up our island to a large influx of new people. Our requirement was based upon our need for 15 families. The interviews were similar to my earlier ones, but with the difference that this time there were many more rejections before the interview stage. We could be more selective as a direct result of the numerous applications we had. Only I, accompanied by Denise, actually carried out the interviews. This time, I was also able to take into account the views of all the council members.

John's earlier comment about bias resulting from our need for building skills did not come to the fore, for the simple reason that so many individuals appeared to be exceptionally confident about the task of constructing their own house, even though few were from the building trade.

In the event we were able to assure them that being part of our building company, where all the necessary skills were available, would ensure that information and advice could be exchanged and combined to progress their task. Consequentially we widened the scope of additional skills, abilities, nationalities and interests on the island markedly.

Past employment of those selected included industry, the social services, financial institutions, the media, leisure pursuits, the police and fire services, labouring, pig farming, public transport services, the oil industry and education.

Our final choice was not made just on the applicants' abilities which they brought to the island, we looked for the signs that they would relate to what we saw as the particular needs of island life.

Two of the families we chose were from Europe, one family from Holland, the other from Austria.

Not surprisingly, nearly all the applicants were from those who lived in or near the main conurbations. We detected that there was a great need to get away from the stress of city life, where work was less satisfying and did not give them time to enjoy the little free time that was available. Others just had a desire to be self-employed. Some simply had a more adventurous attitude and wanted to try to set their life in a new direction.

Immediate benefits to us following the selection, apart from the obvious one of additional labour, were the introduction of another teacher, more help in the kitchen and canteen and more artistic talent. In addition, several of the new wives were able to continue with their previous employment as a result of Internet communication.

The subject of lottery funding had cropped up during one of the council meetings that we held during the first year on Enniskerry. Then it was almost as a joke, but now I saw it as a possibility so wrote off for the necessary forms. My idea was that I could put up a reasonable case for our need to provide adequate accommodation for an increasing number of children requiring education in a school yet to be built. I emphasised the objective of sustaining and improving the standard of life on a vibrant new island community which was becoming successful against the trend of decreasing numbers on other small islands. I heard nothing for a long period other than an acknowledgement of the receipt of my submission.

It came almost unexpectedly. A letter from the lottery commission stating simply that my application for lottery funding for the school building had been approved and a cheque was enclosed, value £800,000.

I was galvanised into an excited frenzy of first telephoning Miranda to tell her the good news and then informing the rest of the council. There was something of an unreal quality about the two connecting events, strange in view of my original good luck with winning the lottery, now followed by a successful request for more money from the same source.

27

'Jim, I thought I would give you as much notice as possible because I have decided that I will have to return home soon. My solicitor partner in London is weighed under with work and it really is a two-man business. He was very kind to keep things afloat while I have been here, and I had hoped to be able to keep both the business and my time here going together. However, it won't be possible. I do hope you understand. I can offer to continue with any relevant work if you are prepared to operate by post or other means, but obviously I will lack the first-hand knowledge of everything that happens here.'

'We will all be sorry to lose you, Philip. We are not over all of the big challenges here, but if you would agree to be on call, that should suit our needs well. You have an unparalleled knowledge of our legal requirements and what has happened here so far. I don't want to intrude into a personal area, so don't answer if you regard it as none of my business, but we have all noticed that you and Belinda are seeing a lot of each other. Is she aware of your decision?'

'It's a difficult one for me. I am fond of her, but she's going too fast for me and I haven't been able to bring myself to tell her yet. She's going to be terribly upset, I know, but I don't know how to break it to her gently.'

'For goodness sake, don't leave it too long. I was with her this morning and I've never seen her so happy. You both have so much in common, particularly with the music.'

'I know, I'll break the news this evening but I'm not

looking forward to telling her. I'm not very good at this sort of thing.'

Sometime later that evening Philip walked along to Belinda's cottage and tapped on the door.

'Oh good, I'm so glad you're here, Philip. I was just getting ready for our rehearsal for the Schubert Trio. Miranda is going to be late as usual, but we can sort out those difficult bits in the first movement before she comes. To tell you the truth, I love these times we are together beforehand.'

'Belinda, I don't know how to say this but perhaps we shouldn't get too enthusiastic about this concert, we never know for sure about the future.'

'What do you mean, we don't know about the future? Of course we do. The concert will be in five weeks' time, and it's up to you and me to make sure it's a success.'

'Glyn is so overworked, he will have to have some help soon.'

Belinda looked bewildered. 'Who is Glyn?'

'Glyn is my partner in London. More than ninety per cent of my work comes from London and it's becoming more and more difficult to do it from here.'

'You mean you have to go back for a while?'

'Well, yes.'

'How long is a while, a few days or a week? Tell me, how long for?'

'I'll have to go for longer than that, I can't do my work satisfactorily from here.'

'You surely don't mean permanently, do you?'

'I will be back sometime, but it depends on how I can cope with the business side in London.'

'This is a big shock. I thought we had something going

197

here but now you abandon everything, just like that,' Belinda cried.

'Don't cry, please, I shall write, and who knows ...?'

'What do you mean, who knows?' she interrupted. 'It seems that you know but I am the one who doesn't know anything. Why didn't you tell me earlier?' she gasped, as she collapsed into a chair sobbing.

'I hadn't decided until recently. I didn't think you would be so upset.'

'I have come to love you, Philip,' she whimpered. 'We have been so happy. Now everything has changed and I am so sad.'

'Don't take it too badly. I'm really sorry for making you so miserable.'

'Well, I am taking it badly. You've misled me,' Belinda cried. 'I think you had better go and leave me alone to think things over.'

'Perhaps we can talk it over again sometime?'

'What is there to talk about? Either you're going back to London or you're not. Which is it? Tell me you're not going. Tell me.'

'I can't do that.'

'Then it's goodbye, isn't it? You don't need to speak to me again do you?' Belinda opened the door for Philip to leave.

Miranda arrived for the rehearsal just as he was going out. Surprised, as he brushed past without any recognition of her, she turned to go inside and found Belinda in tears. Belinda told her the whole story.

'Let's open a bottle of wine', suggested Miranda. 'We're not going to get any practising done tonight, unless you really feel you would like to.'

'No, not now. I suppose we'll have to make it a piano and cello duet for the concert. You're right, there's a bottle in the fridge. Would you mind pouring?'

*   *   *

And so Belinda's relationship with Philip ended. It was immediately obvious to all who subsequently came into Belinda's company that she was not herself. She tried very hard to make sure that her music tuition at the school did not suffer, and I don't think it did. The younger children would not have noticed any difference, but the older ones who were a little more perceptive would have realised that there was something missing in her personality, she was not her usual self. She drifted into spending more time in her own company and the previous happiness was lost. Lynda, who was as close to her as anyone, tried her hardest to coax her round but it was not an easy task. Lynda confided in me that Belinda showed all the signs of a real depression and said that she was not able to penetrate the outer shell surrounding her and her problem.

It was Robert who next realised that Belinda was not involving herself in island life when she failed to attend his computer evening class or any of the other social events on the calendar. He decided to go round to see her one evening and enquire why. He knocked on the door, but there was no answer. Instinctively he felt that she should be at home and walked in. He found her almost unconscious on the floor, with an empty bottle of wine on the table and tablets strewn beside her. Not knowing quite what he should do for the best, he quickly grabbed the phone and spoke to Matt, who raced round to be on the scene within minutes. He gave her something to drink that caused her immediately to be violently sick. It became evident that the tablets were a mixture of aspirin and codeine but, fortunately, Belinda had not taken a massive overdose so she was out of danger very quickly.

Doctor Matt and Robert both continued to visit

regularly to monitor her progress, trying to understand more about the root cause of her unhappiness. Gradually Robert became the sounding board for her to express her inner thoughts and fears. He was a sympathetic listener and he slowly gained her confidence. She admitted that she had been unreasonably besotted with Philip and could not bear the thought of him leaving the island. She told Robert of her perceived rejection, and gradually as they spent more and more time together, she became more dependent upon her regular meetings with him.

Some weeks later a few recognised a glimmer of the first positive reactions from Belinda and eventually the reason became evident. It was that Robert was spending time with her and it was his attention that now made the difference. Everyone regarded the friendship as beneficial for them both. There was no reason for anyone to question Robert's motives, but there was a complication. In fact there were three complications because Belinda, in repeating her trust in Robert, just as she had done previously with Philip, was totally unaware that Robert was also meeting Colleen.

James was not at all happy either with how things were developing.

When Robert first met Colleen, James was mending a pushchair for her that had been damaged on its journey from the mainland. James decided that he would have to go down to the store to see if he could find a couple of spare wheels to complete the job. Robert offered to stay on with Colleen and play with the baby for a while. Everything seemed perfectly reasonable, until James returned to find that Robert and Colleen were sitting rather too cosily together for his liking. James, disturbed by what he saw, bottled up any response at that time because he felt that anything he said might make the situation worse.

Not long after this event, James, although aware that Robert was seeing Belinda regularly – as he thought, with no more than just platonic intentions – heard on the grapevine that Belinda and Robert were in love. When he again walked into Colleen's croft one evening and saw her in what looked like a compromising cuddle with Robert, he yet again suppressed his anger. This time he resolved to have it out with Colleen the next day.

'Colleen, I thought we were friendly enough for you to not be two-timing me with Robert. I was very hurt when I saw you two last evening, I know you've been seeing him a lot recently but I didn't realise you were so close.'

'I'm not really seeing him like that James, it's just that he comes regularly and I don't like to say he can't come.'

'And kiss and cuddle?'

'He just put his arm round me and we didn't kiss.'

'It looked very much like it to me.'

'He just put his arm round me. Like you have.'

'I can't get used to the idea that you could see him in the same way.'

'Look James, I like you, I like Robert, I like you both. You both come round, we talk and you both help me in different ways. The baby is getting to know you both. It's OK.'

James left, but he wasn't sure about things being OK at all. Even knowing what he did about Robert and Belinda, it did not seem enough yet for him to start upsetting apple carts. He would wait. Perhaps something would turn up to help him resolve things.

Colleen had been disturbed by James's comment and she worried about how she had managed to bring about this tangle of emotions. It had not been her intention to cause any ill feeling. She had acted in all innocence, being a

201

generally homely and loving person. She had not realised before that James had more serious intentions in his relationship with her, and if Robert also had feelings for her that were of a more serious nature, then she would have to re-evaluate her own position. She would not want to mislead either of them. The trouble was that, having been deserted before at the time of her pregnancy, she did not know whether she really wanted a serious relationship at all with either of them.

Robert had not been honest with Belinda or Colleen. With what seemed to be a combination of an uncharacteristic lack of awareness and naivety, he imagined that Belinda would continue to welcome his attentions on a superficial scale as she came through her depression. He had no idea that, to Belinda, he had come to be her saviour after losing Philip and she was not easily going to let him go. He believed that even though he knew Colleen was a friend of James, he could have a good time with her without causing any conflicting feelings. In courting Colleen he was oblivious to the dangers that his dual role could create. He had not even considered that she would inevitably discover his other relationship and consequently was not aware that he, of all people, could now be the cause of a catastrophic downturn in Belinda's medical condition.

It was one of the children in the school orchestra who, during an interval, was overheard saying that Robert and Colleen had been seen kissing by the loch. Belinda, still trying to build confidence in herself and with the children was, not for the first time, devastated to become aware that once again she was in danger of losing a friendship. For a while she tried to contain the deep emotional feelings she felt, but that evening her pent-up agitation exploded and she decided to confront Colleen.

Meanwhile, James's mood moved between confusion, sadness and anger. He agonised over whether he should bring the matter to a head. When he did eventually decide that he would have to tell Colleen that she would have to choose between himself and Robert, he picked a bad time. Belinda had, just hours before, confronted her.

'What's up?' he said as he came into the room and found Colleen unusually quiet and tearful.

'Oh nothing ' she said at first, her face expressionless.

'Come on, there's obviously something wrong, I've never seen you so distraught.'

'I've messed things up, I've messed you up, and I think I've messed everyone up,' she sobbed, her tears flowing freely.

'Tell me,' he whispered gently as he sat beside her.

'It's Belinda, she's just been here and shouted at me. She went on and on, telling me off for taking Robert from her.'

'Didn't you know they were seeing each other?'

'Yes, but I thought it was because she was unwell. I didn't think, as she said, they were going steady.'

'And what else did Belinda say?'

'She said that I should leave him alone.'

'Belinda wants Robert very much, but I'm not sure that Robert wants Belinda in the same way. I really don't know what he wants but he's causing a lot of confusion. He's been good for her, but I've a feeling she's too clinging and he may not want any serious relationship with her, that's why he's looking elsewhere. To you, in fact.'

'I hadn't a clue.'

'Listen, I came here this evening to tell you that you have to choose between him and me, I don't think you should keep us both on a string. Perhaps you hadn't a clue that I love you too.'

Colleen looked contrite. 'Oh God, I've been a fool, I'm so sorry.'

'Just take it easy for a while. You may not have been aware of what's going on round here – mind you, you're not the only one – but I'm convinced that Belinda doesn't know him well enough. This is not her fault, he has misled her. He should decide between the two of you, and you may have to decide between Robert and me. I care for you a great deal, but you may have been a bit naive to think that Robert intends just a platonic relationship with you.'

'Do you mean you would stop seeing me if Robert still comes round?'

'Not entirely, but something like that. I love you and want to spend more time with you. It would be a bit crowded with the three of us and, of course, baby Jim.'

'I didn't think anyone would be interested in me in that way again now I have Jim.'

'Well, I am.'

'I don't want to lose you, James, I just need some more time to sort myself out. I don't know what to say to Robert, I can't lock him out and I can't bear it that Belinda thinks so badly of me.'

'I don't think you need to lock him out, but if you care for me then you can't be quite so intimate with him and expect me to close my eyes. Do you care for me?'

'Of course I do, I've always liked you since we first came here.'

'Do you care for Robert?'

'I do James, I mean I did, but I didn't know then that he and Belinda were so close. I thought he was just calling in to see her because she was unwell. I can't see him in the same way now that she was so aggressive to me, but give me more time. I'll have to talk to him, perhaps both of them. It's more difficult on a small island like this. Everyone is much more important to each other than they would be on the mainland.'

Colleen was not good in situations like this and did not know what she should do next. Her thought that she should see Robert and Belinda or even both was one thing, but what would she say to them? She did not know but she took the same action that had helped in a difficult situation before when she found that she was pregnant. She went to talk it over with her mother.

Rene was an unflappable mother and Colleen's troubles did not rate high on the disaster scale of family life, but she was wise enough to know that it required careful handling. Her first thoughts, when Colleen had explained things, was to find out what her daughter wanted from these relationships.

She asked her about James and what he was like, and how he treated her. Then she asked similar questions about Robert. Colleen liked them both.

'The problem seems to me that you have been honest in your friendships with both James and Robert, but maybe you have been giving inappropriate signals to both of them. If you have been kissing and cuddling both of them, what do you expect? I know things have moved on at a tremendous rate in recent years and sometimes anything goes with your generation but there are basic values that people of your age still go by. If I wanted to be your boyfriend, I would be put off if I knew you were seeing and kissing another lad regularly. It may be better if you choose one. Everything I've been told about James is favourable, but I hear conflicting stories about Robert. It may well have infuriated Belinda if he has been seeing you, but that depends on what sort of relationship he had with her. I think his arrangements with both of you are suspect, to say the least, but I don't think that absolves you completely.'

'What do you think I should do?'

'It starts with what you want. You can't continue giving the same messages to both boys. You must choose between them.'

'I met James first.'

'That's as may be, but if he is the one you would prefer for a more permanent relationship, then you will have to make it quite clear to Robert how you feel about James and not mislead either of them.'

'Then there's Belinda. I don't think she will ever forgive me.'

'Belinda has her own problems, but you could tell her what you have told Robert and try and mend things between you.'

'I think Robert will say that he never had anything going with Belinda.'

'Well, you know differently, don't you?'

'I suppose so, but I still don't like this sort of thing.'

'No, but you'll find that it will be best in the long run to be sure of what you want and then clear the air as well as you can.'

Another current cause for concern was that the Irish lad, Graham, from my earlier selection, was tending to be somewhat of a recluse. He had opted to vacate the small croft that had been allocated to him in favour of a disused barn that he had thoroughly cleared and equipped with some basic furniture. He was never seen at any of the social events or classes. Occasionally he would call in at the canteen for food, but he would take it away, hardly conversing with anyone for long.

The barn was situated on the far side of our furthest beach, well sheltered with a view out to sea. People venturing in that direction would say that they had seen him sitting and staring out to sea but when they spoke to him he seemed to be in another world. He had grown a full beard and was looking somewhat unkempt, giving him a rather wild appearance. Some were concerned about his health.

When I went out there to check for myself, I found, as I had been warned, that he was not very communicative and even depressed. I asked if there was a problem and if I could help, and he said that he had moved out to be able to think. He wanted to be closer to the elements and be part of nature.

'Have you been able to get down to some writing, some composition or poems perhaps?'

'I n-n-need to experience more f-f-first. I need t-t-time to c-c-contemplate.'

'Are you sure you're eating enough?' I enquired.

'I'm OK,' he said, turning his attention away from me and gazing out to sea. He was not ready for conversation or questions. I left him to his thoughts but I had an idea. I would ask Nick to have a word with him.

'Nick, you remember you helped me come to a decision about Graham. He's having difficulty in finding a role for himself here. I think he needs help and you may be the best person to give it. He's is becoming a recluse but I'm not sure that's good for him.'

''E's livin' in that old barn by the beach, ain't 'e?'

'Yes, but I don't think he is very happy or even eating enough.'

'I'll go 'an' 'av' a word wiv 'im tomorrow.'

'He may not want to talk to you but I think it's worth a try.'

* * *

Nick set off the next day, wondering if he would be able to help Graham. He didn't really know much about him as a person at all, but he felt proud to know that Jim thought he was the best person to try to help, and that increased his confidence no end.

Life had certainly changed for the better for Nick and he realised it all too well. He wanted to encourage Graham to feel that life could be quite good for him now on the island.

'Hi Graham. Remember me? We met in that grotty caff back 'ome jus before you met Jim.'

'Yes, I remember.'

'Never fort 'e would ask me to come,' Nick continued.

'Why not?'

'Well, weren't 'is sort, I s'pose. I lived rough on the streets, y'know.'

'He d-d-did want people of all s-s-sorts from d-d-different b-b-backgrounds. I s-s-suppose that's why I'm here.'

'We've got a lot in common, you an' me, we've both 'ad it rough, ain't we.'

'Seems so.'

'But there's one difference 'tween you an' me. I'm 'appy, you're not.'

'I keep thinking of my p-past in Ireland, I c-can't get it out of my m-mind.'

'What sort of fings do you fink about?'

'Everything t-t-t-that was h-h-h-horrible.'

'What was the worst?'

Graham bent forward and hesitated, his face completely enclosed by his hands.

'I was t-t-tarred and f-f-f-feathered, they g-g-got the wrong b-b-bloke.'

'Grief, that's terrible, 'ow did yer get away wiv it?'

'S-s-some p-p-people arrived just in t-t-time and took me home.'

'Grief.'

'On another occasion a g-g-gang at-t-tacked me and one of them threw p-p-petrol over me and then s-set me alight.

'Ow did you get out o' that?'

'Someone rolled me into a d-d-ditch to p-p-put out the flames, then they got me into h-h-h-hospital, I was in a bit of a s-s-state.'

'I bet you was. You was burnt?'

'Yes, you won't see m-m-me with my s-s-s-shirt off.'

'Tell you what I fink. I fink that's what you orter write about. It'll 'elp get it outer yer system.'

'I hadn't thought of that, I've always tried to forget it until now.'

'I fink you've turned a corner. Yer know why? That's the first sentence you've said wivout stutterin.'

Nick and Graham continued to see each other quite regularly and Graham steadily improved in health. He did not lose his stutter completely but it became less pronounced. He also moved back into his small croft but he would still often return to the old deserted barn. He became more amenable to visitors, who noted that he always had a pen and paper in front of him.

Philip's day for departure was nearly upon us and everyone gathered to give a rousing sending off party for him. Nominations were sought for his replacement on the council and Giles was elected to replace him as our treasurer.

As Philip left the island one morning, we all assembled to give him our good wishes. Loud cheers arose from the large accumulated group. As he stepped aboard the *Island*

Queen, Belinda was seen to hand him an envelope. It was an awkward moment for them both and neither seemed to know whether to kiss, shake hands or wave goodbye.

28

All of the houses for the original islanders' use were now completed, and one additional house was also available. We could therefore respond to the first applications that had been put on an extensive waiting list for holidays. This one croft had been prepared for self-catering with an adequately stocked larder, but the arrangement for visitors was that meals could be obtained at any time at the canteen. As we had agreed, the price for staying on the island had been set quite high, but there were no additional charges for any of the activities or services offered which, we thought, were quite considerable.

Theresa, who had volunteered to look after all the enquiries about holidays on the island, informed us that at the top of the waiting list were a man and his wife from Ohio, USA, who, as a surprise to us, because they had family in the UK, were unaware of the general publicity we had attracted here. We had regarded that as being the one attribute that would underpin the majority of our tourist applications. However, they had seen our advert on the Internet and responded immediately to the effect that they would be ready to take up the holiday as and when we were able to offer it. They wanted to combine their journey to Enniskerry with visiting their friends and relations in England.

Angus picked them up on a blustery day and found that they were a well-travelled couple, enthusiastic about this, their latest venture. They were shown into their croft, which had been cosily warmed by a peat fire, and then taken to our canteen. It now had a section partitioned off which was of a higher standard in terms of decor and suitable for a more intimate and relaxing meal. It was where we could also introduce visitors to what was available for them and give them an early opportunity to meet some of us.

I decided that I, accompanied by one other islander, would invite them to dinner on their first evening. I chose Denise, but I was not sure whether my idea to welcome them in this way would be a regular event and become a tradition for the future. We would see how things developed.

Ray and Vera were an enthusiastic couple, interested in all things British and now, naturally, the Scottish islands were paramount in their minds, in particular Enniskerry. We made a lot of the fact that they were our first visitors and they responded accordingly, quickly joining in the enthusiasm of being part of something so new. We also asked them to be critical if they found anything that was not to their liking or if they identified anything that could be improved.

We outlined the various activities and sights that we could offer and of course mentioned that they were free to explore any part of the island on their own if they wished.

They expressed interest in several things. Ray was eager to make his own creel and catch a lobster and to go sea fishing with Angus. He told us that last time he went fishing he didn't catch a thing and ended up eating the bait. Vera thought she would like to find out about spinning.

We told them that the canteen/restaurant was open to them at all times and we could provide a packed lunch if they wanted, to enable them to have a full day out. There was a concert on Wednesday and our usual ceilidh on Friday evenings. Ray was also keen to offer his time to

give a talk at the school, relaying some of the most interesting and exciting points of their travels over the years.
They had travelled widely in the Americas, the Far East
and Europe.

They decided that they would like a packed lunch for
the following day as they expected to walk over the island
to get the feel of it before they did anything else.

I did not see them again until late the following evening,
when they returned full of tales about their experiences of
the day and how friendly they had found every person
they met. They explained that although they started their
day very early in the morning, they did not get beyond
the village until after lunchtime because they stopped off
in conversation with so many people and were invited in
for so many teas, whiskies and snacks that they did not
need their own lunch pack until late in the afternoon, by
which time they had eventually made it up to the hills.

Angus, aware of the request to take the Americans on a
fishing expedition later in the week, asked Kate if she
would come and help. They met beforehand to work out
how they could deal with things.

'Angus, assuming that you and they are actually able to
catch some fish on the day of their outing, do you think
we could cook it and eat it on the boat?'

'I don't see why not, but it's not very comfortable on
board is it?'

'No, but perhaps you could rig up a table and four
chairs to start with. Then I would make it look pretty, you
know, bring plates, cutlery, napkins, wine, that sort of
thing.'

'How about some fresh bread and vegetables?'

'I'll make sure we have some on board.'

'Sounds a good idea. We'll have to provide a cooker for

the fish, of course, the gas cooker on board is not up to cooking for four.'

'That's OK, we'll use two of the double burner stoves that we have. It should work.'

'Better have a Plan B in case the fish aren't biting.'

'I'll pack a couple of lobsters in ice, just in case.'

'We'll be in trouble unless the weather is fair. There's hardly enough room in the wheel-house.'

'Couldn't you extend it in some way?'

'I suppose I could, but not before this week or next is out. And I'd have to be sure that there was justification for it. It's a fairly major modification.'

'Jim says we have tourists booked for nearly every week until the end of July. I'm sure that most would like to do some sea fishing and I guess we'll get more bookings to go right into the winter. I suppose we could also use it on bird or seal watching and round-the-island trips – nobody is going to refuse a snack whilst at sea. In any case, you'd want me to be comfortable when you take me out other times wouldn't you?'

'Yes of course,' Angus replied, smiling. 'I'll work something out.'

Angus and Kate met Ray and Vera at the jetty early in the morning, but immediately suggested that they returned for some warmer clothing. Waterproofs and life jackets were on board but extra jumpers were not, and it was as well to be prepared for the worst of weather. In the event, although there was a cold wind to start the day, it reduced to light gusts towards mid-morning.

Neither Ray, Vera nor Kate had ever been sea fishing so they were very attentive as Angus explained all about it.

'Most sea anglers fish from beaches, rocks or piers using rod and line, but they then may have to cast their baited hook a distance of up to about a hundred metres to ensure that it reaches water of a suitable depth. They use stronger tackle than those who fish in fresh water and, of course, in fishing from a boat need not cast their line in the same way. Different types of fish live in the deeper waters and include dogfish, shark and skate. As a rule, the autumn and winter months are the best for sea fishing. But anglers can take good catches of bass, mullet, and wrasse during the summer. The baits they use include lugworms, ragworms, mussels, soft crabs, and sand eels. They also use strips of fish such as herring and mackerel.'

'What are the chances of catching any flatfish?' Ray asked.

'Flatfish live on a smooth, sandy seabed. Therefore we are only likely to catch any number of these fish if we are in waters close to the shore,' Angus explained. 'Now I must let you know that this fishing business can be a rather messy, bloody and smelly occupation. This will be the first time I have ever fished for pleasure. We have to choose between fishing for quantity or finding a meal and having a pleasant day out.'

'We are doing this for pleasure,' said Kate. 'We can't expect Ray and Vera to literally work their fingers to the bone for us.'

'Don't do anything different for us,' Ray interjected 'We will go along with what you would normally do.'

'Perhaps a compromise,' suggested Kate. 'As soon as the first fish start coming aboard, I'll get cooking and then when it is ready, perhaps we can enjoy the meal without any loading, gutting and sorting going on.'

And that was how it worked. Fortunately, the weather stayed dry apart from the spray. Enough fish were caught to return with a good stock for the canteen freezers. They opened two bottles of wine to wash down a delicious fish lunch and after that and much conversation, the thought

215

of more work didn't have the same appeal. Ray, Vera and Kate returned exhausted but enthralled by their day out.

Ray kept his promise to give a talk at the school and although the 30-minute allocation overran, it was an interesting diversion. It was always Miranda's intention to be flexible with events to allow any chance for variety to enter the day's planned timetable. Ray talked about journeys in Europe and the Middle East that they had made using a Volkswagen camper van. He had a large map pinned to the wall indicating their route and the talk was generally laced with stories of their more humorous encounters. Questions at the end reflected the general interest and it was agreed that the talk had opened a few eyes about the cultures of other lands. Ray expanded the limits of his talk by relating an incident from his time with huskies in northern Canada when he was caught in a blizzard and huddled with the dogs for warmth at night.

His talk was filmed by Ken and shown to the adults during the following evening. Ray and Vera were given a video copy to take home with them on their departure, but they would have to wait some time to see the one encompassing their whole stay, which still had to be prepared for the TV production.

A family from Oxfordshire enjoyed the next week's holiday. They were a middle-aged couple with teenaged children, a boy and a girl. We continued with the same introductory meal and again told them what was on offer and asked what they would like to do with their time. Again they both wanted to go fishing with Angus as a first request. But they both had interests in bird-watching and photography, so they were out on several days walking as much of the island as they could. They mixed well with the islanders and said that they were offered so much to eat in their homes that when they made it to the canteen they were not hungry. Both their children, Jack and Lizzi, wanted to take part in the sporting activities. They were quickly found places in the five-a-side handball competitions and when Jack was introduced to Lynda for karate lessons, he said that he would like to do it all week. He was so keen that Lynda did indeed put in extra time whenever she could to give him additional lessons.

Lizzi had asked if she could go horse riding, but of course that was not possible as there were no horses on the island. However, it put the idea in Lynda's mind that one day it might be possible. She was determined to own a horse one day, and as she enjoyed island life she would definitely stay on. This was one place where she could own a horse and even offset the high cost when tourists arrived wanting lessons and rides.

At the first opportunity, she went to meet Jenny, remembering that she had once owned a horse, and asked her how she should go about getting one.

'It's strange that you should come and see me because only recently the person to whom I sold my horse Katy has contacted me. She's going abroad and wants to know if I could I suggest a suitable home for her. She also wondered if she could return her to me, and I've been turning over the possibilities in my mind. Originally I didn't think it would be suitable here, but now I see no reason why it shouldn't be possible.'

'I wouldn't want to take your horse from you. It would be great though if we could have one each and go riding together and you could tell me all about the tackle and looking after it.'

'It's an expensive hobby, you know, with the tack and

the feed. Do you know how much you want to spend on the horse?'

'I have some savings and I thought that I would have to pay between £1,000 and £2,000 for a horse. A friend told me I should allow another £500 or so for the bridle, saddle and blankets.'

'That's about right, but don't forget the day-to-day costs for feed, nuts and bedding etc. That could amount to another £20 per week perhaps more considering our extra transport costs here.'

'I could afford that and, eventually, it might be possible to recoup some of the costs with rides and riding lessons for some of our visitors here.'

'That sounds a good objective. If I do get my horse back, we could join forces on that. How about stabling, have you thought about that?'

'Yes, Bill has promised to build a stable for me and there's a suitable field just behind where I live.'

'If it works out for me and my horse, it might be advantageous to have them stabled jointly. We could share the workload and it would be more efficient to have them together. Perhaps Bill could double the size of the stable, if you don't mind?'

'As soon as you know what's happening and I can find my horse, I'll ask him. I'm sure he'll oblige.'

29

I was very surprised to receive a letter signed by a Lord Cameron, who was completely unknown to me. His letter was brief; stating that he would like to meet with me, having heard of my successful management of Enniskerry. He was now in a position to make me a profitable offer to purchase the island. I thought this was an extremely quick proposal, as we had only just completed one year of occupation.

I went directly round to see Giles and asked him if he knew of Lord Cameron or his organisation and whether he had any knowledge about why he should make an offer to buy the island.

'Yes, I know him. He is on the board of several companies, and was a financial director at Rio Tinto when I last met him in Brazil. He got wind of my living here and said if ever I wanted to sell, he would pay a good price. I told him that I was not the owner, you were.'

'Why would he want to buy?'

'Generally, it would purely be for investment but I have a sneaking feeling that he is moving to buy more real estate. Recently he has bought some prime shooting moorland from the Duke of Devonshire, which is somewhat out of character. He seems to believe that to own an island would be another feather in his cap.'

My immediate thought was that I must have been doing something right for the island if this person was prepared to buy it.

'Did you encourage him to contact me?' I asked.

'No, but I didn't discourage him either, I just told him that I would be very surprised if you would consider selling.'

'Well, that's absolutely right.' I was sure that I would never consider such a proposition but I thought that I would press Giles a little further.

'Do you think that I should consider his request?'

'I wouldn't have the temerity to advise you, Jim. I come from a world where money and possessions are paramount. This is what drives these people. You and I know that millions of pounds are paid for works of art, just paint on a small area of canvas, yet you can have something hanging on your wall aesthetically more pleasing to you for just a few pounds. For some people, it is the financial value and the actual possession, together with the anticipation that the value will increase to make them an even greater profit. You, I believe – and I hope what I say will not offend you – see it more like my grandmother. Before she died, she had a beloved trinket which she would not sell for whatever money she was offered. Therefore, my only advice is this; take an arbitrary figure that this man could offer you, let's say eight million pounds, which would be a huge profit for you made in a very short time. Ask yourself; what would you do with it? Then assuming that you would reject his offer because of your love for the island, ask yourself is there really a top figure that you just could not refuse? Would you, like my old grandmother, say no to eighty million pounds? I'm not saying he will offer anything near this amount but you have to look inside yourself to know whether you are a grandmother or not!'

I laughed at the way Giles looked at it. His comments were helpful. It was also ironical, for he had, in effect, asked the same question that my colleague Ron had asked us in that London pub before I told them the news of my lottery win. That was a time when I did know what I was going to do with the money.

'You may see me as a bit of a wimp, Giles, but if I sold I wouldn't know what to do with that sort of money whether it be eight or eighty million. This island has become my life and now I would feel lost without it.'

'I do understand. My situation is that, since being here, I have been able to evaluate and see both sides. I admire what is happening here, but I cannot completely sever myself from my upbringing and past history of successes. As I slowly recover I am beginning to live in two worlds, one here in simple tranquillity with you and new friends, the other where I still have a hankering to involve myself with some of the business affairs of my past.'

'Do you want to take a more active roll here?'

'No, I don't think so, but I may pass a few ideas to you from time to time. For instance, I was thinking we might benefit from a heliport or airstrip here one day soon.'

'Do we really need one?'

'I do, or rather I will, if I continue to live here and carry on with some interests I have beyond these shores. Also it would be very useful in times of any emergency. I have a vested interest in rapid and efficient access to hospital care.'

'It wouldn't cost very much for the helicopter pad if it becomes necessary, but I can't go to a helicopter' I said.

'No, I wouldn't dream of asking you to do that, I would be able to finance it, but since we are talking in this way, I would like to share with you some more of my thoughts about my future here. It's more a personal thing and not for a council discussion. Do you mind?'

'Of course not, Giles, carry on.'

'It really starts with my improving health, but first, I must convince you that I am more than happy to continue living here. Having said that, I have this urge and want

221

soon to operate in both worlds. Approaches have been made for me to reconsider directorships that I have in the past turned down, but now I am tempted to respond positively to them. I am also inclined to reinstate several of my previous business ventures. Obviously, in so doing, I have to consider the practicalities of operating this part of my life from this remote island, together with my desire to continue to live here.'

'Hence the helicopter?'

'Yes, but I am conscious that this would be progress in excess of what you had in mind for the island.'

'It certainly is quite early for me to consider expanding in this way. I would have to assess its impact upon our daily lives. It's not so much the helicopter, it's the direction of your ongoing requirements and the impact of different lifestyles. Would you not, in many ways, be remote in your way of life from the islanders and our interests here?'

'I can see your concern and I would try to continue to be part of the community. I value it tremendously.'

'I imagine that you would soon want your heliport to be expanded to an airstrip.'

'Jim, I can see your anxiety, and you're right. In fact, given the right circumstances, it could replace a helicopter and landing pad. Both would not be necessary. Let me put more of my cards on the table. If I go ahead with my idea, I would need fairly constant access to the mainland and abroad. This could only reasonably be achieved by aeroplane from here. I would need a personal assistant, with a pilot's licence, who would need to live on the island while I was here. I would like to have a larger house built to accommodate visitors and myself. These are in a way practicalities that can be paid for. What I really need is the understanding and co-operation of yourself and the islanders.'

'I don't feel that I can stand in your way any more than I would prevent anyone trying to improve their lot, even if it were on a smaller scale. What I have to do, and maybe what you will have to do also, is convince myself and then the council that your requirements will have some benefit to the islands economy and do not impinge unduly on our peaceful way of life here.'

'There would be some benefit in that I would ask your building company to construct my new house, but you may see that as a disadvantage if you are trying to build quickly for other purposes. I see the main advantages to the island as being financial, together with the opening up of the island to outside influences, much along similar lines to how I have heard Ken express his views on the future of the island.'

When it eventually came to presenting a request to the council for approval to go ahead with his requirements, Giles made it quite clear that unless every member of the council was in agreement and it was passed with a 100% vote to go ahead, he would not consider proceeding. It certainly concentrated the minds of most of us, each one being aware of the responsibility if their one vote was the one that would stop him and cancel out what could be a valuable investment for the island. It could also possibly lead to his departure

Miranda had spent all her spare time canvassing to measure what support existed for Giles and his idea, and come to the meeting with valuable information. All members of the council, apart from Giles, who abstained, voted in favour and no one expressed any doubts. It was a measure of the respect that Giles had already built up that he was trusted to have the best interests of the island at heart, whilst still pursuing his own.

*   *   *

223

Shortly after my talk with Giles, Lord Cameron made yet another approach, requesting a meeting with me about his offer to buy, but I again rejected it. He asked if I had any objection to him coming to the island to meet Giles, explaining that they were old friends. I had no reason to resist his coming but I wondered if his reason was to gain access to me by the back door.

When he arrived I was not surprised to get a call from Giles telling me of Cameron's presence and inviting me round for a drink with them.

I found Lord Cameron to be a remarkably well-advised and well-spoken man, very careful in his communication of words, and always ready to hear another view. He was tall with greying hair and immaculately dressed, giving no indication of that morning's windswept ferry crossing.

We talked of Scottish life and he asked many questions about the island, appearing to be genuinely interested in the way I was running it. The discussion then turned to hunting and shooting opportunities and I felt that he might well have considered the purchase of the island for this purpose. He was polite enough not to raise again the matter of the sale, but he did give one fleeting opportunity in a passing comment for me to open the subject if I wished. I suspected that Giles had painted the background quite clearly for him and so he would not have been surprised that I did not respond.

Eventually we did prepare a helicopter landing area. It was a relatively simple job, but it was a long while before we saw a helicopter land, as Giles did not have as easy a time organising a suitable pilot as he expected. No one, it seemed, was prepared to live full-time on the island to be at his beck and call. He did have a young man with a pilot's licence who had worked for him before as a chauf-

224

feur, but he did not or would not fly helicopters. Giles invited him over and found that he integrated very well with everybody over the few days he was there. Unfortunately for Giles, the man was unable to commit himself to life on the island. He could not envisage a life away from the city lights. I am sure Giles was disappointed at being unable to attract anyone for the job. His mind then extended to a more ambitious plan, aiming to introduce to us the benefits of a landing strip for small aeroplanes. Although this would be shelved for the time being, I had a feeling at the time that giving Giles the green light would be the catalyst for a whole series of events which would make us wonder about the wisdom of opening up the island in this way. It did promise to change its character, it was not clear at that stage whether the changes were generally beneficial or not.

Finding one person with the qualities of chauffeur, pilot and personal assistant continued to elude Giles for some time, so he turned his attention to obtaining agreement for the planning and construction of his new house. Yet again he was very persuasive, and before long it was agreed, its construction coinciding with the import of more families with men, and machinery capable of completing the task.

Then, in the course of a conversation on a completely unrelated matter at one of our council meetings, it emerged that John had progressed from his hobby of gliding to a certain level in his attempt to get a pilot's licence. Giles's eyes lit up like beacons and he asked John if he would like to revise his interest in flying. John nodded and said, 'Maybe, I've always been keen on flying.'

Although Giles had spoken with John on several occasions in the past when John's gliding interest had been mentioned, he was amazed that he had not been astute enough earlier to link John's abilities with his own current need. After the meeting Giles, as usual, came straight to the point with John when they met.

'Would you be interested in continuing your flying lessons at my expense and then flying my aeroplane for me?'

'Well, before I would be able to get that licence I would have to get to and from the mainland myself for the lessons. That could be difficult.'

'Yes, but it need not be individual daily lessons, it could be, if you'll pardon the pun, a crash course, in periods of a week or more at one time.'

'Some of my contribution here would suffer. I would have to agree the idea with Jim.'

'Certainly, but if you and he were willing, it would allow you to follow an interest that you enjoy and it would help me enormously. I'm also trying to convince Jim that some of these plans of mine will have positive benefits for everyone here.'

Giles asked me if he could employ a consultant to come over and look at the logistics of providing a landing strip on the island, and I agreed. Later he met up with John again, obviously anxious to get on with things in the quickest way possible.

'It's going to take ages to get this airstrip organised and completed,' he said. 'I'm thinking it would be easier to get the helicopter idea going first. Would you be happy to go for the helicopter pilot licence first?'

'Yes, I would be keen to do that, and it would be the quickest way to give you access to the mainland.'

'If you agree, I think it may be best for you to make all the arrangements for the training. All I know at present is that there is a course available near Glasgow. Get yourself enrolled for that as soon as you can. I will pay for it and then I would need you to find out what sort of helicopter would be recommended and how much it would cost.'

Within days John had the information about training and the cost of a small helicopter.

'As a general guide, pilot training to solo standard would cost about £10,000. The Robinson R44 is a small, popular, piston-engine helicopter which has a cruising speed of 130 m.p.h. It can be purchased new for about £250,000. I've asked for some brochures to be sent to give us both a better idea of what is available.'

Terry had worked very closely with John on several island projects and he was quite capable of standing in for him if required. We also agreed that John would try as far as possible to arrange his flying lessons around the council meetings. Within weeks John had been off to Glasgow and returned full of excitement at being able to re-kindle his love of flying.

30

Although we had agreed a total of 15 new properties, further consideration suggested that it might be somewhat too ambitious to tackle this all in one attempt. We therefore decided that the additional intake should be split into two groups. At first a total of eight new families with children, which included two single men, were selected to come in what we termed the second phase. A third phase was to be invited later. All of them were prepared to build their houses under the wing of our island's building company. Their agreement was that they would also lend their hand to work at times for the building and construction programme for the island. Having either purchased land or entered into a renting agreement with me, most decided to bring temporary accommodation in the form of static caravans.

This influx increased our population by 25 individuals to over 80 almost overnight. Additional strain was placed upon some of our existing resources, at the school and the canteen, but the extra numbers were absorbed without much of a problem, offset of course by additional hands to do the extra work. Without exception, everyone integrated very well.

Additional interests boosted our popular social activities, the new intake providing innovative ideas that were passed on to the council for consideration. The addition of more children boosted the sporting group events and the supplement of another teacher was invaluable in coping with the increased number of pupils.

Before long we were able to see the foundations being laid for the new properties at the recently designated second village of Kerry. It had been agreed that it would be more efficient to combine the building of all the new properties together, with all the labour shared. Giles, with a suitable cash input, had convinced us to give the building of his own new house some priority.

When spring had given way to summer we considered whether the time was right to introduce a further seven families to the island, thus completing the third phase of inhabiting Enniskerry.

Although this third contingent would be invited ostensibly to construct their own houses as the previous intake group had done, Giles saw it as an opportunity to convince the council that, as with the previous group, part of their time should be allocated to the island's building group. Now that his own house was nearing completion, priority should be given to the building of an hotel. He was convinced that a hotel was essential to supplement our croft-type housing for visitors, thereby offering a wider range of first-class accommodation for the future.

Much discussion followed in council, raising issues such as the desirable number of rooms, the degree of sophistication, who should manage and take responsibility for the project and whether we could staff the hotel from our existing and future residents.

It was generally thought that it would be possible and desirable to staff the hotel from our own resources, but Denise came up with the suggestion that we should seek a full-time chef in a separate advertisement, it being most unlikely that anyone would come with this skill as a result of our general enquiries. I confirmed that no such skill was available from our applicants so it was agreed that a more specific advert should be sent out to the appropriate catering publications. But we were running ahead of ourselves, first we must build the hotel!

Kevin, one of our second phase entrants, was an architect, so we asked him to draw up plans for a 15-bedroom hotel, and within a short time, he had some preliminary plans available for our perusal. Everything seemed just as we would wish – until he gave his estimate for the costs. It was not that it was too surprising, for Giles had volunteered the price he had paid for his house for our guidance. It was then that alarm bells began to ring regarding the several large expenditures we had recently incurred and the fact that our income was still relatively small. Giles, now our treasurer, had all the books and figures. I decided that we should have another session devoted purely to our financial status.

A detailed résumé revealed without any doubt, that there was a shortfall in the capital available. The stark choices narrowed down to just three. They were that we should abandon or curtail some of our plans for expansion, take out a bank loan to cover the costs, or wait until our income improved.

Expansion and the rate of our development were already ahead of what I had imagined would be possible in the time we had been here and I was very reluctant to take out a loan. My view was that we should wait.

Giles thought for a while and said that he could offer two other alternatives. He could put up half the cost of building for a half-interest in the profits, with the possibility of relinquishing his half-share when the island's finances were able to buy this back from him, or he could support the whole venture himself for complete ownership. It was for us, or me, to decide.

I recognised that this, in many ways, could be a turning point. Giles had always been totally honest and fair with me in all our dealings. I could see that his presence had already been of great value to the island. I could also see that he was the most influential of us all in terms of his activities on the island. Was there a danger that he would swamp our more modest progress through the years or would he, by virtue of his purchasing power, take us to an earlier stable success?

At first, I was torn between his two additional offers but eventually I made up my mind and decided to confront the other members of the council with my thoughts. I informed them of the options, then added, 'I am doubtful about the half-share option, so I have therefore come to the opinion that we should hand the project over to him. This is my view but I want to maintain a democratic approach to this and would now welcome your thoughts.'

'The first thing I would like to say,' said Denise, 'is that I hope you, Giles, can continue to wear two hats on this issue and give us your advice as our independent treasurer, even though you could be the prime mover in any alternative solution of this matter.'

'I can do that,' replied Giles, 'but I would like you all to express your views first.'

'As far as I'm concerned,' continued Denise, 'I think we would benefit greatly from having a hotel. It would give employment and income. Jim has given us a guide in this, the money is not directly available so I would have no objection to Giles running it.'

John added, 'I think a hotel will be good for us and we should go ahead with the recommendation.'

Gerry commented, 'I trust Giles to look at the issue from his knowledge of the island's accounts and give his independent view of what we should do.'

'I probably wouldn't go for a hotel so quickly,' said Kate, 'because I am rather careful and conservative by nature, but if Giles is prepared to finance it then there shouldn't be a problem for the island.'

Miranda added, 'I would prefer that the ownership should not be split between Giles and the island. It would be best under one wing, therefore Giles should have the option to proceed.'

'Jim has stated that he does not want to borrow money to finance this scheme,' Giles began, 'which has an element of basic common sense. My reading of the island's financial situation is that it would be inadvisable to incur even half the purchase price of this venture at this time. This leaves me with my view of the viability of funding this myself. I have a great love for this island and Jim's attitude towards it. I would do nothing that I believed would have an adverse effect upon him or his island. My time here, you may or may not know, has been almost literally a life-saving period for me and so, although I hope to revive my interests away from this island, my heart is here; I now regard Enniskerry as my home. Jim's far-seeing objective of sustaining life here by increasing the places for people to live and consequently the population as a whole is unrivalled anywhere in the Hebrides and possibly beyond. He deserves our full commendation. In financing the hotel I will utilise the plans drawn up by Kevin and I hope you will give me your support. I recommend that we pursue the building work as soon as possible and when we can see we are nearer completion I shall take up your idea to advertise for a chef to oversee a first-class restaurant within a first-class hotel.'

The council agreed unanimously to proceed and wished Giles success.

Hearing a few odd comments about the deteriorating state of the track between Ennis and the new village at Kerry, I could see that our continued progress and need for transport between the two places would soon lead to a request for road improvements. I set about getting agreement to some ground rules that I felt were necessary for the future.

I suggested that the time had come for us to upgrade the road between the jetty, Ennis, Kerry and the proposed site of the new hotel. However, I was adamant that other than the need for the current construction and farm work, I did not want to allow any petrol or diesel engine vehicles on the island. I was aware of one other island where motorised transport was banned. That was the policy of the Seigneur of the small Channel Island of Sark. Their only form of transport on a short road was by a tractor pulling a trailer, with the possible alternative of a horse and cart. The idea appealed to me, but I did see that we might have to approach the matter in a different way. I proposed that we should not allow any cars on the island but that we would have to provide transport for our visitors in the form of a bus service or something similar. I had in mind an electrically powered vehicle of the unpleasantly named 'people carrier' type. This would enable a group of six or so people to be taken to their rooms at the hotel and would also provide a service to and from the jetty, the two townships and the hotel.

31

It had been a wild night giving way to a bright windy morning. Bob and Susan started on one of their early morning walks to do some bird-watching. They trained their binoculars towards the seashore, noticing the heavy sea rollers, and thought that perhaps it would be better for them to move round to the lee side of the island, where not only might they see more prolific wildlife, but they would be better sheltered and generally more comfortable.

As they were about to turn away, Susan said, 'Look, there's a boat down there near the rocks.'

Bob focused the binoculars and agreed. 'I can see some figures. The boat will be taken against the rocks and soon break up in this wind. We'd better get some help.' They hurried back to the village and spread the news.

Paddy and his son Shaun were first to get to the vicinity with a few ropes. Soon several others arrived, but Paddy quickly decided that they needed additional heavier ropes, so he sent Shaun back with some help to collect them from the store. They were faced with a problem. The small craft was being swung backwards and forwards, powerless with the force of the wind and tide regularly crashing it onto the rocks, only for it to be swept out and back again. It seemed impossible to get anywhere near without risking their lives.

As usual Paddy took charge and decided that, given the severity of the storm, they would have to establish a safety line between where they stood and three outlying rocks before any sensible rescue attempt could be made. It would take time but they did not have long as, with each crash onto the rocks, the boat would progressively be reduced to splintered timbers. However, it was important to recognize the dangers. This had to be a calculated rescue attempt without any foolish actions.

The tide was rising and falling over several feet and. together with a strong onshore wind, this constituted the greatest danger for anyone in the deep water.

It was generally accepted that Bob, Bill and two of our newest arrivals, Bruce and Martin, were the strongest swimmers. These four, with Paddy, laboured long and hard making several abortive attempts before establishing the first safe line to the nearest rock. The procedure was to be one in which each person to enter the water had a lifeline back to the shore by way of the safety line and hand-over-hand movements from one rock to the other as each one was established. This was repeated twice more to extend the safety line to the two other rocks. It must have taken about two hours of exhausting effort, during which all five sustained cuts and bruises. Bruce was knocked unconscious on one occasion before he was hauled back through the turbulent water, but he was soon joining in again for the next thrust outward. Throughout this time the boat was repeatedly sent crashing into the rock. It was now rapidly breaking up and it could be seen that there were three very frightened occupants.

The last stage was the most difficult, with the added fear that the wind would change direction and the boat would be blown away from where the lines had been laid. It was decided that the only way to make a rescue would be for the people in the boat to make a leap from the boat to the rock, where they would be assisted back along the safety lines, but very early it was seen that it would not be that easy. It seemed that the boats' occupants were foreigners but it was not just the language barrier, it was that all three were so exhausted that they did not seem to have the ability to move to save themselves. Maybe they could not swim.

Bill, who was out on the last rock, called for one of the men to make the attempt. Gradually the man stood up and we could see that he was wearing a life jacket. At first it appeared that he was prepared to make an effort to take the leap, but when he attempted it, he did not jump, he more or less just flopped into the water. Instantly he was swept further out to sea. Bravely, Bill plunged in and swam out to rescue him, but it was not an easy task to reach him and when he did, the man clutched on to him so tightly that it was difficult to move them both back to the rock or the line. Fortunately, being still connected with his lifeline to the shore, his process was aided. but it was a painfully slow struggle. Having finally reached the rock, Bill found it impossible to get the man onto the slippery wet surface for any rest period, so he decided to make directly for the lifeline leading back to Martin on the second rock. At that point, Martin took over the responsibility for him and repeated the hand-over-hand back over the next stage. Bill returned out to sea in order to assess what he could do for the remaining two.

The first was a woman, who was being encouraged to make the next entry to the water by the remaining man. Bill, realising that it would not be safe or even possible for her to make the rock, decided to jump into the water to try and give her the confidence to jump straight at him. Eventually she found the courage to do so, but her timing was bad and both she and Bill found themselves dangerously placed between the boat and the rock. For a further three times the boat smashed to the rock and three times Bill and the woman narrowly missed being crushed between them. As with the first man, he made straight for the lifeline to Martin. As he did so, he heard a terrific crash behind him and a scream for help. The boat had been thrown yet again onto the rock, but this time it had been splintered severely, violently throwing the last man into the heaving water.

Bill was played out. He shouted for Bruce to try for the other man, who was now moving further out to sea. They changed places and Bruce struck out with a strong over-arm crawl, encountering much of the splintered woodwork from the now non-existent boat on the way. Finally he made it, guiding the man back to the shoreline via the fixed ropes. They all slumped onto the shingle beach, sucking in air and slowly recovering. Hot drinks and warm clothing had appeared and this helped all those involved to gradually get back to normal.

Their thoughts turned to the three survivors, who were huddled in blankets but shivering. They had only a few words of English – Paddy thought they were from Eastern Europe. It was decided that the first requirement was to get everybody back to the village for shelter, the questions could come later.

Bit by bit their story unfolded. They were illegal immigrants, as Paddy had surmised, from Eastern Europe. They, a group of 12, had stowed away on a vessel bound for the Clyde. They were discovered on board and told they would be arrested on docking in Scotland. Thinking they would jump ship, they imagined that they would have a better chance if they made for Ireland. They decided to steal a lifeboat in the middle of the night. This they achieved successfully, but in the chaos of lowering the vessel, nine of them had fallen into the water and could not be rescued. The remaining three, although in the lifeboat, were soon overcome by the bad weather and had no idea of direction. They had been afloat without power for several days when they were blown onto the rocks of Enniskerry. They did not know where they were and were in a poor and deteriorating state of health. It was decided to give them shelter for the night and consider what to do the next morning.

They woke feeling refreshed and considerably better. With more food they were able, with some difficulty and with a few words of English, to explain that the two men were brothers and the woman was wife to one of them. Soon there were some smiles and grateful thanks for saving their lives. An affinity developed between them and some of the islanders, whose initial thoughts were that we could invite them to stay on the island and become part of our community.

Overhearing this, I began to consider some of the ramifications of the presence of these three immigrants. I presumed that the captain of the vessel upon which they had stowed away would have reported their discovery and their subsequent jumping ship, as well as the loss of the lifeboat. The various coastguard services would have been alerted, but given the poor weather conditions prevailing, it may have been presumed that the small craft and its occupants had sunk.

As far as we were concerned, it would be possible for us to give them food and shelter without asking too many questions, and for a while I guessed problems would not arise. There were many things I could determine about how my island was run and who was invited, but it was clear to me that we were not above the law of the land. These three, pleasant as they were, were in fact illegal immigrants from a foreign country and there was a strict series of checks in the way that all immigrants were dealt with.

I reasoned that even if we offered them a safe haven, their presence could not stay a secret for ever – there were too many visitors and exchanges with the mainland. In general conversation, a few, aware of how unpleasant the immigration process could be for people seeking asylum and realising the degree of danger they had been prepared to put themselves in to gain entry, thought we should take them under our wing. We could not determine whether they were genuine or illegal immigrants, but their method of entry suggested without much doubt that they were illegal. By harbouring them there was even a risk that we would fall foul of the law ourselves. I called a council meeting to review our situation, the result of which was to agree unanimously that we had to report the matter to the authorities.

We told the three what we were about to do. They understood that we could not hide them indefinitely. They wanted to know what would happen to them but we genuinely did not know the answer to that. We tried to explain that if they were legitimately escaping from perse-cution from a place where their life was in danger, then our authorities would agree that they could stay; if not they would be deported.

I telephoned the police and the next morning a group of police and officials arrived and escorted the three to the mainland.

Several months later we learned that they had been refused entry to the UK and had been sent back to their country of origin in Eastern Europe. Several felt sad and tried unsuccessfully to make further contact with them.

32

Dafydd, our butcher, was able to set up a suitable place to work in one of his outhouses at the rear of his property. He equipped it with a number of benches, rails and one enormous refrigerated enclosure for the carcasses.

Following the dispute with Charles about the slaughtering of the island's animals, the farmers had continued to use the services of the roving slaughterman, Finton, who agreed to include Enniskerry on his round. Finton used a mechanical stunner to render the cattle unconscious, after which the animals were killed and passed over to Dafydd. Dafydd suspended the carcasses from his overhead rail for the dressing operation, in which the hide and internal organs were removed. He would normally cut the dressed carcasses into halves, wash them, and move them along the rail to his refrigerated room. It is well known that the tenderness and flavour of beef is improved by hanging. By following one common ageing method, the carcass is hung for about two weeks at approximately two degrees centigrade. This encourages physical changes in the muscle tissue that enhances the quality of the meat.

Dafydd could dress calves, pigs, and sheep in much the same way as cattle but, as yet, we did not have any pigs. Initially he supplied the meat just to the kitchen for the canteen but later progressed to supplying smaller amounts to the shop and to the residents. As the shop became established it became the main outlet to the islanders.

Both Gerry and Ian were talking with Dafydd, trying to get estimates of the amount of meat that would be required over the coming year. They concluded their discussion and then wandered up to the canteen for their regular follow-up lunch. As they started the walk Dafydd raised yet again his favourite subject with them. For some time he had been trying to convince the farmers to stock some pigs.

'It really would make a big difference to the variety I can offer to the island, you know. We're missing out on fresh ham and bacon, which would be an important addition for the shop.'

'We've got our work cut out as it is,' Gerry said 'I haven't really got any spare time and Ian here, as you know, has just got another solar dome to erect, equip and plant out.'

'Yes I know, but it is a pity.'

'Why don't you get some pigs and keep them yourself?' suggested Ian.

'I hadn't really thought of that,' he replied. 'I don't know much about their upkeep.'

'There's not much to it,' Ian said. 'There'll be plenty of scraps from the canteen, and they more or less look after themselves. We've both really got too much on our plates at the moment,' Ian laughingly continued, 'but if you get yourself a few pigs we'll point you in the right direction.'

'What are the main difficulties?' Dafydd enquired.

'There aren't many really,' Ian replied. 'Pigs are very suitable animals for small farms because so many can be kept on a small area of land. Decent housing is important, and nutritious feed, including maize.'

'I think you'll find it interesting,' said Gerry, 'and, as you say, there is a need for bacon. There is the question of supply to the shop and the island's need in general, of course, but you could also get a steady income from selling the piglets after they have begun to eat solid food. Look upon it as a business proposition with the

241

sale of fattened pigs to the mainland as you increase your stock.'

'Perhaps I'll have a go then, and possibly Gwyneth could help.'

Our shop had been built and opened for business. Ken's wife Jenny felt that she could volunteer to run it, as she did not have to consider who was to look after her two children after school hours. Helen, who had two very young children, provided additional help. She had an arrangement with two of the new group of wives who both had children aged under five themselves. For two days a week, each would take on the care of all six children to allow the other two mothers to work in the shop. This arrangement led directly to the formation of a crèche which others were able to use for their young children.

As far as provisions for the shop was concerned, it started with the transfer of some speciality pastries and other foodstuffs and drinks from the kitchen, followed by gas bottles and various small articles of electrical equipment, like batteries and bulbs, which were moved from the main store. Gerry ensured that milk was available for anyone to collect on a daily basis and Ian supplied fresh vegetables. Dafydd provided the meat. Angus and Pat maintained a regular supply of fish.

The only stumbling block, initially, was the provision of fresh bread, for those in the kitchen had far too much to do for them to bake it each day. Although a volunteer was soon found to do the baking, an oven of sufficient capacity was not available. Over 50 adults with their children, many of the men undertaking regular hard physical work would, if they were given an adequate supply, consume a huge amount of bread. We also had to bear in mind that we would undoubtedly have to supply bread to the hotel.

The matter was brought up at the next meeting and an order for the purchase of a suitable oven was issued straight away. It seemed sensible to install it in an area that was available adjacent to the kitchen and within two weeks we had it up and working.

Our volunteer, Julie, from the newest members to come to the island, soon recognised that she had underestimated the amount of work and was asking for help. Her friend Rosie stepped in to assist. With a six-day-a-week production, they were never out of work.

Everyone was very happy with the outcome, but it then dawned upon us that we did not have a post office. Our general stores would not be complete without us being able to post and receive letters and cover some of the other services that should be available from a post office. Our current arrangement was that Angus would pick up all our correspondence each time he visited the mainland. To date this had been very satisfactory because his journeys across were numerous. We imagined they would reduce in frequency as time went on. We didn't know if the Post Office had ever delivered to Enniskerry, so we asked Jock, who told us that there had been an intermittent weekly service that, of course, stopped when the ferry ceased. We contacted the Post Office headquarters and they agreed to the setting-up of an office on Enniskerry. Knowing that there was a good possibility of a ferry service being introduced in the future, we agreed a temporary solution that Angus would continue the delivery and collection as before. There would be a small salary for the postman or woman on the island and a small payment to Angus until the ferry service was reintroduced.

One day, soon after the post office section was opened, Jenny came running out of the shop as I was passing and called out, 'We've just been given the OK by Camelot to sell lottery tickets – we thought you should be the first to buy one!' I laughed and dutifully purchased one, marked it up at random and asked her to do the checking for me, thinking how unlikely it would be for lightning to strike again in the same place.

33

A résumé of our third year on the island showed that the third group of applicants, consisting of the final ten new families, had now been absorbed into the community, giving us a total population of just about a hundred people. A few of our second and third groups had experimented by installing private wind generators and batteries for their own use. Generally the power generated was about half a kilowatt, only just sufficient for lighting, TV, computers etc, but providing it by independent means gave extra satisfaction and Brownie points for self-sufficiency.

Pat had engaged the help of some of these second and third phase entries and had overseen the installation of two fish farms, one at our largest loch and the other offshore in a sheltered cove to the south-east of the island. Some important contracts to supply fish to the mainland and abroad were in hand and hopes were high that this enterprise would be successful and greatly assist with additional income for the island.

His sister, Theresa, had formed an art group which was in full swing, with artists using watercolour, oil and pastel to create some fine work. Theresa herself has turned her hand to creating sculptures and all their work has been shown on an island web site, resulting in the first sales. Theresa has also taken on responsibility for all matters concerning tourism on the island. It was becoming a significant occupation, keeping up to date with the advertising, organising the timetable and ensuring that our visitors were looked after when they arrived. She had computerised the work to offset the increasing paperwork, and found that tourism had flourished, with full bookings over the summer season and perhaps 30 per cent over an average winter. We were hoping the winter number would be higher now that Giles's hotel had fully opened.

Another evening class had been set up by Susan which was devoted to other creative crafts. About a dozen of the islanders were enjoying creating extensions to their homes.

The school had been built to an upgraded specification and was staffed by two teachers, with the help of two regular assistants. Pupil numbers had increased to 37. It was all running very smoothly with good standards of work being achieved at all levels. Throughout this and the previous two years Richard continued to show his hyper-active behaviour and this had caused Miranda to adapt her lessons so that he did not unduly affect the concentration of the other children. She found that he needed plenty to keep him busy, and fortunately she had one of the two assistants available to sometimes take him out of the class-room for personal tuition. In the current year Miranda had introduced a project on dinosaurs and Richard had caught on to this with a particular fascination for everything to do with these huge animals. The models that he had made were the largest and most colourful on show in the corri-dors between the classrooms. Richard's parents, Bill and Helen, were continually praising the efforts of the teachers in accommodating his boisterous ways.

Lynda had suggested that he might benefit by taking up an active sport and she encouraged him to learn and use karate to exert himself and channel his excess energy in this way. Doctor Matthew had also kept up with current research on the behavioural care of hyperactive children and medication, and he passed on to Bill and Helen what he thought appropriate.

Lynda and Jenny now each owned their own horse and were often seen riding together over the hills. They had started giving riding lessons to some of the children and were also offering lessons to interested visitors.

Bill had quickly constructed an adequate stable block but it was understood that the structure might have to be improved and extended if there were ever to be more horses. Lynda and Jenny had big ideas for a covered area in which they could broaden their venture to giving riding lessons in the winter months.

John had arranged for the installation of two generators, each large enough to supply the island's needs into the foreseeable future. At the present demand for power, one generator was more than adequate and therefore the other was able to act as a standby. The idea of a common wind generator was dropping down the priority list due to the high cost and the fact that we were operating quite well with the existing system.

He had also passed all the necessary examinations and practical experience to obtain his pilot's licence, enabling him to fly Giles's helicopter, which was called into service during most weeks. Occasionally it was used for the benefit of other islanders.

This method of transport to the mainland suited Giles very well. In fact he had abandoned his plans for the construction of an airstrip as not being appropriate or cost-effective at this stage and had asked the council to strike it off the agenda.

Giles had the building company complete further additions to his handsome house and was known to enter-tain, on a regular basis, many of his business colleagues. His hotel was situated on the higher slopes of a rise, showing a splendid silhouette against the sky. He had advertised for and appointed a professional chef who was due to be with us in the near future. The island's own population had been only too willing to be co-opted into service for tasks such as chambermaids, waitresses and gardeners.

With advice from Philip in London, Giles applied successfully to reinstate Miranda to paid employment. This was a relief to her and stabilised her commitment to stay on the island for a further extended period. The new teacher was also paid.

Philip had been able to act in his capacity as solicitor for certain other issues that had surfaced on the island while he was in London and these negotiations were successfully carried out via e-mail and fax. He did make one visit back to the island but only spent a few minutes with Belinda.

John and Alice's children, Jonathan and Trevor, had, with the help of their father, constructed from a kit their first Wayfarer yacht, which they had sailed on one of the lochs and at sea. This had given rise to others showing interest and deciding to make their own craft. It was thought that forming a sailing club to offer sailing lessons to our visitors was now a distinct possibility in the current year.

Both arable and stock farming had moved into profitable times, with scope for still more improvement. The solar domes had proved very efficient in terms of stability and were valuable for earlier planting. We had three of varying sizes and had recently introduced heating to them.

Graham eventually began to write prolifically and had articles and poems published, giving him the incentive to tackle larger compositions. He met with Edith from time to time to exchange ideas, as she had decided to write her life story. Nick's friendship with Graham had paid dividends of mutual benefit, and Nick himself went from strength to strength and was now our official bus driver, among many other tasks that fell into his sphere of work.

On several more occasions, after Nick had made that first approach at my suggestion, he and Graham had got together, once or twice at Nick's home but it was usually Nick who visited Graham.

"Allo, Graham, what'cher up to t'day?'

'Oh, I'm t-trying to write some more poetry.'

'It all 'as to rhyme don't it?'

'No it doesn't have to, it's all about g-getting the right words in the right p-places so that the reader g-gets a better sense of something without having to just write it in s-standard English.'

'Don't make much sense to me, wouldn't make much difference if it was written in gibberish. Got any drink in there, 'ave you?'

'Not much, but there will be a s-spare beer. Come and have a look in the back room, it's where I keep my writing.'

'Fanks. Christ, are all those boxes full of poems?'

'Not just poems, there are longer articles and even s-some b-books.'

'It's like a bloody library. Won't anyone ever see any of it?'

'Some of it has been p-published but not much really.'

'I fink you orter put more effort into getting' it out. 'ave you 'ad a word wiv Robert, 'e's got this Internet fing which goes all over the world. 'e might be able t'do somefink for yer about it.'

'Maybe.'

'Cheers, 'ere's to you gettin' some bloke to buy the lot.'

'Cheers,' Graham replied, knowing that would be totally impossible.

'What the 'ell would it all be for if you don't do somefink wiv it?'

' OK, OK I've got the message, I'll try.'

Jane was our only person to gain a place at university. Her special interest was medicine and during her time on the island, she had spent a lot of time studying at home in the evening and also with Doctor Matt, continually questioning him on numerous subjects. He was able to help her with many of the answers and was even able to give her some insight into the practical aspects of some simple surgical practices. He also gave her constant access to his library. Her parents were concerned that she was taking too much of the doctor's time but he was able to reassure them that it was a delight to be able to help her. Matt told me that she was one of the most satisfying pupils to teach. She had been quick to understand concepts, inquisitive, always totally absorbed with whatever subject they were discussing and she had an insatiable desire to improve her knowledge. It was, in fact, an opportunity that she readily agreed was very fortunate for her, and their time together had cemented her desire to continue to study medicine in the future. There was great jubilation and celebrations at the school when she obtained excellent A level results and again when she successfully gained a place at Sheffield University.

The problems surrounding Robert, Belinda, Colleen and James had settled down. Belinda was in good health and committed to her musical work at the school and for the now thriving orchestra and band. Robert had found another girlfriend from the new arrivals on the island and

James was seen to be almost continually in the company of Colleen.

'James, you know we wondered once whether we would still be on this island years on into the future?'

'Yes, I remember talking about it, why?'

'I was just pondering the question and thought that I was happy about being here and hoped you would feel the same.'

'I can't see any reason to move on yet, there's still lots to do and I'm enjoying everything about it at present.'

'I saw Doctor Matt this morning.'

'You mean you're unwell?'

'No. I, that is, we are expecting a baby.'

James was speechless. He sat on the nearest chair and stared long and hard at Colleen. She looked back into his eyes, smiling.

'Well, say something then. Are you pleased?'

'I,-I,-I'm delighted, I just can't believe it.'

'You should be able to, we haven't been as careful as we should have been perhaps. You know that.'

James felt a shadow pass. He hesitated but couldn't stop the words coming out.

'It is mine, isn't it?'

'No, James, it's ours.'

'Should we get married?'

'I don't know. Was that a proposal?'

'No, yes, I mean I don't know. I don't know what I'm saying.'

They both laughed and fell into each other's arms. James pulled himself together.

'I've decided, I do know what I'm saying after all. I love you and I want you to marry me. What do you say?'

'I say yes, but what comes first, the christening or the wedding?'

'I don't know, when is the baby due?'

'It must be in about six months' time.'

'So we could get married first and it would look almost legal. But I'm not even sure how we can get married here anyway, we may have to go over to the mainland.'

Colleen became momentarily very thoughtful.

'I don't want to do that, I want to be married on Enniskerry, it's where we live.'

'I agree. I'll have a word with Jim, he'll know how to sort it out. I'll tell him if it can't be done on the island we will make our own ceremony here. There doesn't have to be a church.'

'We do have one, there's the little chapel at Kerry.'

'Of course, I like the idea of being married there.'

'You're not really religious any more than I am are you?' Colleen enquired.

'No, I was christened but I don't think I have ever been in a church since, apart from when I went to my brother's funeral.'

'I think we could have a naming ceremony for our new child rather than any christening or baptism. There was nothing in church for little Jim, just a registration of the birth in my name, as the father wasn't present.'

'We could include little Jim in the event so that he doesn't feel in the future that he didn't have a ceremony.'

'What a good idea, how nice of you to think of him.'

The news about Colleen and James spread like wildfire. James approached me and asked what I could do about having the ceremony on the island and I had a word with my contacts on the mainland. It seemed that we could basically do whatever we wanted except with regard to the actual registration. That would have to be carried out at the registry office on the mainland. I made a request for the registrar to visit the island, and was told that it would have to be looked into. They would let me know. I had a similar response with regard to the registration of the anticipated birth.

James and Colleen were married with a simple ceremony at the chapel at which I was asked to say a few words. Naturally, Colleen's parents and brother were present, boosted by a dozen relatives from the mainland. Apart from the bride and groom, no more than six persons could fit into the small chapel at any one time so, given that all the islanders would be attending, Robert had foreseen the difficulty and rigged up a sound system so that people could hear the service from the outside. It would seem that, in family terms, James would be completely overshadowed by the numbers on the bride's side but, just before the occasion, his mother, to whom he had written from time to time without any response, telephoned to say she would like to come to the island to meet his new bride and wish them well on the day. James had not seen or heard from her for four years, so it was with mixed feelings that he awaited her arrival. I did not gather much about the reasons for her lack of contact with James since the break-up of her own marriage but they both seemed happy to have time with each other at their reunion.

We were all aware that Edith and Gary were in regular contact by e-mail. From time to time the canteen girls would enquire about him and push another suggestion that they would like to meet him one day. Edith was also thinking on the same lines and eventually invited him over.

Edith was at the harbourside awaiting Angus's return from the mainland. Her wave towards the *Island Queen* was returned with a two-handed wave by a tall grey-headed man, unrecognisable to Edith. Then within minutes they were reunited as he stepped off the boat onto the jetty. It had been some 40 years since their return from India and now Edith saw again some of the features that she had remembered from the past. His shock of blond hair was no longer, but his penetrating blue eyes remained the same. He said she had not changed very much and it was great to be in her company again, they had many things to discuss. She invited him back to her croft and they spent the rest of the day there talking over their past adventures.

As the canteen staff were aware, Gary had married and subsequently parted from his wife after their children had grown up. Actually she had left him for another man, but Gary admitted there had been faults on both sides.

Gary had continued with his interest in other cultures and spent much of his life working as a photo-journalist and travelling to different parts of the world, especially southern Africa. He admitted that his long periods of absence from the family home might well have contributed to his marriage eventually failing.

He was passionately interested in the African wildlife and the history and ethnology of the African tribespeople. His knowledge of the San, the early Bushmen from the Kalahari Desert, and the Herero and Himba from south-western Africa seemed unparalleled. Much of his time was now given to lecture tours at home and abroad. Edith was aware of all this by virtue of the photographs and long e-mails she regularly received on her laptop. What she had not received and was now handed to her as a colourful print was the photograph of her childhood home and garden in Lahore that Gary had taken at the beginning of their long journey back to England.

Momentarily she became nostalgic.

'You saved my life then you know.'

'No, you saved your own life, I just accompanied you on the journey home.'

'It was more than that, we became very close over that

year. You taught me many things that helped me re-establish myself in the West.'

'You told me you were writing an account of your life including those early times.'

'Yes, I am, I am writing it in my way, which I am happy with, but you may be able to give me some guidance with the presentation so that it could be suitable for publication.'

'Sure, any time. I'd be interested to read it and willing to help in any way I can.'

He stayed on the island for over a week. They had a lot in common and a great deal to catch up on. Gary was a popular visitor, giving a hand with island matters whenever he saw the need to assist, and people wondered if he was considering a more permanent life here. Edith would not be drawn to say anything to confirm his intentions. Perhaps they had misread the situation. Never-the-less he integrated extremely well and returned for a further two visits.

'You know, you should come to Africa with me sometime, I'm sure you would love it,' he suggested.

'Perhaps I could. It would be a wonderful experience and so much easier with you to show me around.'

'I'm off again in about two months time. You could come and miss the winter here.'

'I'll think it over and let you know soon. I feel I must talk it over with Jim first.'

'That's fine. Edith, how would you feel if I made Ennis-kerry my base for a while, if Jim would agree, of course? Do you think he would?'

'I don't really know. The usual arrangement is that everyone contributes to the island's affairs in some way, and you have been doing that already during your short times here. I'm fairly sure he would be pleased to have you here.'

Both Edith and Gary asked me for an opinion on their proposals and I could do nothing other than wish them well. Certainly there would be no difficulty in absorbing Gary into island living; he had wide experiences and those natural abilities that make a person adaptable to most circumstances. Edith with her different experiences of life came from similar stock. They would do well together.

Another memorable event occurred in our third year, following a contact I had with an equerry at St James's Palace. Prince Charles wished to take the opportunity of visiting Enniskerry while journeying in the Hebrides during the autumn.

I was aware that the Prince made fairly regular visits to one of the islands but was completely surprised that our island should now be of interest to him. I was asked directly if it would be possible to accommodate him. I could see no reason why not, but wondered for how long and what sort of accommodation would be required. I described how we could offer the simple but comfortable croft, or a more spacious suite in the hotel.

In due course a member of the palace staff came to visit and indicated that the Prince would favour staying in the croft. He seemed satisfied that it would satisfy the heir to the throne's needs. I asked whether there were any special requirements that we should make for his arrival, and was assured that it would be a most informal visit and that as far as he could see we should not do anything vastly different from what we offered any other visitor. It was explained that he was generally interested in how things were organised but would also like to mix among the islanders as he strolled around. He would stay for one or two nights.

Naturally this information caused a flurry of excitement and speculation among the islanders. It was a time when there had been much media coverage about his relationship with Camilla Parker-Bowles, and they wondered where would she sleep if she came as well. As I had not been informed that she would be coming at all, I assumed the question would not arise and did not join in on any discussion on the 'what ifs'.

I wondered what preparations, if any I should make for the visit. I normally met all our visitors personally and then invited them to our restaurant for an introductory meal. I would make up a foursome by inviting one or more of the islanders chosen arbitrarily, to join me on these occasions. If this was to occur with the Prince, I should be careful not to select who was to be chosen myself. I decided that the only way was to ask the islanders to vote for the two people they would most like to have the opportunity. Most had agreed before the vote was carried out that it should be two women who should join the Prince and me. The vote was counted and Edith and Denise achieved the highest scores.

Miranda quickly added the subject of royalty to her timetable and spent several lessons explaining the history of the kings and queens of England and Scotland and the members of the current royal family. Anticipation of the coming visit increased during the intervening weeks, with children and parents alike making colourful bunting to decorate their houses and Union Jacks for the children to wave.

When the day came, Prince Charles arrived, as we had been informed, by helicopter. Two helicopters on our pad! My, how things had advanced here! The noise from the rotor blades slowly spun to silence as I waited to greet him. He alighted alone. We shook hands and he asked what I normally did when visitors and holidaymakers first arrived on the island. I explained how I usually invited them for a meal with one or two of my fellow islanders so as to ease them into feeling at home and let them know what was available for them to enjoy during their stay. Would he like to do the same? He said it would be a most agreeable introduction. He was enthusiastic to learn more about what he believed was an exciting new venture.

Edith and Denise joined us at the table and the meal went smoothly and without the constraint that we had previously imagined. The Prince showed his interest in the part that Denise played as a council member and what had encouraged Edith to join the experiment. We then talked about the ups and downs of island life that we had experienced. I tried to get a feeling of how easily his official duties were compatible with his obvious liking of Scottish outdoor life. He described at length how necessary he found it to retreat to the peace and tranquillity of his garden, practise organic farming and enjoy the countryside in general. These relaxations enabled him to offset his otherwise continual association with official duties which, he said, he tried to associate wherever possible with worthy causes. The conversation flowed freely and we were all captivated. Edith, was overcome by his kindness and the ease with which they were able to converse.

The meal over, I asked whether he would care to walk around the village. He said he would be delighted to do so and meet whoever was about. Of course everybody was about, the children excited and cheering, the adults amazed at their proximity to him. Here he showed his ability for putting people at ease and withdrawing politely as the need arose. Nearly everybody had their share of a moment of glory and Ken had it all on film.

The Prince commented the following morning that he had slept well and would like me to accompany him on a walk over the hills. It was an enlightening experience. I had never had a particular interest in the matters of royalty, but this visit, and particularly this walk, had personalised it in a way that had not previously been possible. He helped me to see the wider picture of the relationship between the Crown and Parliament and his position with regard to the future and continuance of the royal family. He also made pertinent comments on my progress and the future development on the island and had a wide knowledge of some simple practical measures that could be applied in certain situations. I felt that he was in tune with my objectives.

My three friends from London, Ron, Graham and Nigel, visited. Although we had kept in touch over the period, they were anxious to see for themselves how I had fared. Only Graham had ever previously crossed the border into Scotland. They were staying for four nights and it was to prove as well that they did. They arrived on the island wet, windswept, cold and miserable as a result of the sea crossing. It was horrendous weather. Of course, I did not hear the last of it, even though I had welcomed them first into our comfortable visitor's croft and they had spent a restful first night, Nigel complained about the lack of central heating. So I suggested they reverted to the alternative of staying in Giles's recently opened hotel. Fortunately, as had happened with visitors before, the next morning dawned clear and bright and the sun shone from a cloudless sky for the remaining time that they were with me.

We often found, particularly with people from the cities, that it took some time for them to re-adjust from the hectic pace and the stresses to which they had been subjected. Only after the first day or so would they calm down to a slower way of life, the strained and lined faces giving way to contentment and a more pleasant attitude; it was as if the stress was at last removed from their shoulders.

So it was with my friends. First, I took them on a short tour of the village and they were overcome by the friendliness with which they were greeted, more than once being invited in for a dram or other refreshment.

'If I took a walk like this in my town, I'm sure no one would ever invite me in like this,' said Ron, 'let alone every other house along the way.'

'It's actually quite warm, isn't it?' Ron added.

'Yes, it's a pleasant day today but it's an island of extremes over the year. Come and have a look at the view from over this ridge.'

'That's fantastic,' said Graham, 'you can see islands all around for miles. What's that one in the far distance?'

'That's a very big island, it's Ireland,' I replied.

'Well I never,' he said.

I wondered what he really meant by that; what was going through his mind as he stared transfixed out to sea?

'Where do you live then?' asked Nigel. 'Take us to the millionaire's abode.'

'Don't forget I used most of the money to buy what you can see, so I'm not sure if you can call me that now.'

'I heard that you could sell it on for a pretty good profit,' added Nigel.

'Yes, I think I could, but then I would have to answer your question again as to what I would do with the money, wouldn't I?'

They all gave slightly amused grins and knowing looks, thinking back to that time in the London pub.

We walked back to my Lodge and they were suitably impressed by its size and full of advice as to how it could be improved.

'You don't own the hotel, then?' commented Graham.

'No, Giles our entrepreneur is the owner of that and he has also just had his house completed, the one you can see on the rise of the land over there.'

'What about the other properties, who owns them?'

'Some pay me rent, others have bought theirs outright and some have built their properties and naturally own them, but all pay me for the services I provide.'

The trio spent their other two days sampling other outdoor pursuits such as fishing at the loch and horse riding and during the evenings were happy to converse with anyone who happened to be in range. On the evening of a classical music concert they admitted they were thoroughly enjoying the whole experience. Observing that they were much more relaxed and looking much fitter due to their days out in the sun, I ventured my opinion.

'Not as bad as you thought, is it?'

'No, I've really enjoyed my time here,' said Graham. 'In fact I'd like to come again.'

'You're all welcome, any time you want some fresh air.'

'You really like it here, don't you?' Nigel observed.

'Yes, it's my life now, I was lucky.'

'It's been good meeting up with you again, but I've discovered that I'm no sailor, so I'm not looking forward to that sea crossing back tomorrow, good weather or not.'

'Don't worry, I'll get you all back by helicopter.'

'Really, how much does that cost?'

'Nothing, it's on the house.'

'Now that's what I call service,' Ron quipped. 'I'm changing my mind about you and your island!'

34

I waved my friends away on a calm afternoon, and after the helicopter had circled and headed off, I walked to one of my favourite places on the island. It was a spot where I could look across the sound in the direction of the mainland and it was there that I sat reminiscing on the differences that this stretch of water, dividing us from a land mass in the distance, made to all of us living here on Enniskerry. Attitudes to all things were so much different. My retrospective mood made me remember what we had achieved from the beginning to now, which was our third year on the island. I know that most, if not all of us, would sum up their time here as having been a most rewarding period and something that had become a major part of their life experience. Lying back on the soft grass and watching clouds float overhead, I recalled some of the advancements that had been made so far.

My mind wandered back to my first visit and the conversation with Hamish, the ferryman. We had met many times since then as he still ferried people across from time to time. We would share a drink when the opportunity occurred either on the island or on the mainland. He was a man of few words but genuine in his satisfaction that things were going well for us. Of course, as with all the local people, he was greatly saddened by the death of Morag but he indicated that one small thing had encouraged the locals to view me and my objective favourably; it was the knowledge that I refused to be known as the Laird of the island.

I mused over all the interviews I had carried out, chuckling to myself about my doubts concerning Nick and marvelling at his growing confidence in a range of activities that was almost unbelievable. There was Graham too, who seemed to have turned a corner thanks, in no small measure, to Nick's efforts. Miranda had become a stalwart headmistress at the school. I particularly remember her unfailing attention to Richard and his problems, and she was so proud that Jane had gained a place at university. Then there was Giles, how greatly he had affected and put his mark on the venture. Also Ken for his constructive ideas to take us positively into the future, and Angus for his generosity, plus of course all the others, each with important values to add to the sum total of experiences. But, I thought to myself, I must stop picking names like this; everyone was indeed part of a whole. Each and every one could take the credit for their own contribution.

I also looked back on the actual day of arrival and the raising of the flag on the Lodge, which became a moment to cherish, and the unfailing help given to me by the council throughout, which was indeed remarkable.

It would be misleading, though, to remind myself only of the successes. Young Alison had been badly burnt in a fire at their home, there had been the totally unexpected death of Morag and there had been the unpleasant exchanges between our vet Charles, the farmers and myself. I never heard anything more about him. I regretted not getting this one right at interview and felt sorry about the consequent unhappiness that he caused, but I did not regret his departure. That was the only major personality clash.

The visitation by vandals was also a particularly unpleasant event but was resolved satisfactorily. The fortunate saving of three lives at sea deserved bravery medals for those who had carried out the rescue even though it had an unfortunate outcome, as some saw it, in that they were not given sanctuary in this country.

In the overall picture these negative events were, by far, outweighed by the more pleasant exchanges. There were so many compensations as, for instance, the excitement when the children found the skeleton in the cave. Although they had searched long and hard, they were unable to find any treasure. However, they made the most of their experiences to tell long, scaring stories to the newest children on the island. And there was their unbounded joy when they successfully played an April Fool's joke on some of the fathers.

Jock had kept well and was playing his bagpipes on almost every social occasion. His whisky still was now in operation. The liquid it supplied was available and distributed to all of us on any visit in small quantities. He preferred the excitement of regarding the whole enterprise as illicit and secretive and we all joined in as part of the act.

Only last week Colleen had given birth to a six-pound baby boy, who they named Jason. As they had promised themselves they held a naming ceremony in the same chapel for Jim and Jason, and had asked me to carry out the formalities and become the modern equivalent of a godfather to them both. As with their wedding ceremony celebrations, we assembled for the reception in the main hall of the hotel.

I had seen this birth as another sign that things would thrive here in the future.

I watched as a group of oystercatchers winged over my head en route to the loch, the sound of their wing-beat the only disturbance to my wandering thoughts. I looked out towards the mainland and saw the *Island Queen* returning from a shopping expedition and realised how much Angus continued to get pleasure from shouldering the responsibility for all transportation between the island and the mainland, together with fishing and sailing trips for visitors with help from Kate. He finally, but reluctantly, accepted a wage for his work for the island, as every other person had done. Although he enjoyed all the work he did for the island, I hoped that some of his regular duties would soon reduce as talks were underway with Caledonian MacBrayne, who were considering reinstating their ferry service to the island. In addition to all this, the BBC had committed themselves to a complete TV series of *An Every Week Story of Island Folk*. Ten weeks of the series had been shown to date and there seemed to be an impressive following with ratings up there, rivalling *EastEnders* and *Coronation Street*, suggesting that one day it could do for TV, what *The Archers* did for radio.

My thoughts were broken by a cheerful voice calling, 'Hi there, Jim, don't forget that I'm cooking you a meal tonight.' I turned and watched Denise as she came walking towards me. Denise, who had been such a reliable ally in the whole venture, was often in my thoughts. She, with her good sense, had been able to turn many mountains into molehills. She smiled and gave me her hands. 'Come on,' she said, 'the sun's going down and it's getting cold. Have you been daydreaming long?'

'Yes, I suppose I have,' I replied, 'and I enjoyed every minute of it.'

Together we made our way back to the Lodge. Denise busied herself with the plates and within a short time the aroma of good food was in the air.

35

The following day Denise was again at the Lodge. She had come round to help me with the garden. We had worked hard to get some of the brambles under control and we were now relaxing after combining to make and then savour another delightful evening meal.

'Jim, you never told me about the accident, but don't go on if it still hurts too much.'

'It's about time I exorcised this memory,' I said. 'The dream still keeps coming back. It was my fault, you see. Anne and I hadn't been married more than six months. For a long time we had laughed and joked about her fear of water and swimming, though I suppose it was not really a laughing matter, but anyway I taught her to swim and although she was reluctant at first she soon became quite proficient – better than me, in fact. As we were not able to go on honeymoon directly after our wedding we treated ourselves to this holiday in Cornwall. It was a wonderful hot summer and we went for a swim from some rocks. In her exuberance, she challenged me to dive from an overhanging rock into a wonderfully clear pool below. It was not a particularly high dive, but perhaps a little higher than we had done previously. We had our usual banter about each being "chicken", and then she raced over to get there before me and dived. I heard her cry out. It was terrible. I could see the blood in the water. There was nobody else about; I carried her back to the track. There was a car, then the hospital, the rest became a blur, and she never regained consciousness.'

For once, I couldn't contain my emotions; Denise put her arm around me.

'Jim, you are a very sensible man, but you are wrong to blame yourself.'

'I know, you're right, but it seems there is a need for me to take some of the blame when there is nothing else I can do.'

'Yes, but not for ever. In any case, there are other things you can do and you are doing most of those things now, many things to help other people.'

'You've helped me to get it off my chest, I needed to do that. Let's talk about you, that always makes me happy.'

'You know, this island with all our friends really has been a wonderful success story, hasn't it? Did you ever have any doubts?'

'No, not serious ones, I only had one fleeting moment, it was when I was re-reading a book about Cyprus by Lawrence Durrell. At the beginning he has a quotation: *Journeys, like artists are born, and not made ... They flow spontaneously out of the demands of our natures ...* I have made a number of journeys to various parts of the world and I have always remembered those words. When the idea of the island formed, I took into account the same words and substituted "islands" for "journeys" and was happy with this. Then, as the plans progressed and I started to meet and select the people to come to "my" island, I substituted "islanders" for "journeys". For a while I worried, for these people were not islanders other than in the sense of probably being born in the British Isles. They would be, as they say in Yorkshire "Offcomedens" – people who come to live in the county but can never become true Yorkshire folk. But then, I was an "Offcomeden" myself before I returned to the south for business reasons, and it hasn't done me any harm. I

267

quickly came to terms with the fact that people would integrate and there was no reason to believe that it would be anything other than a success.'

Denise was now sitting curled up on my sofa enjoying a drink of her favourite red wine, as was becoming an increasingly regular event and dreamily, she said, 'Jim, I'd like you and me to make another islander.'

I could not believe my ears. I hesitated as I realised the full import of what she had said. I was overcome with emotion again.

'My dearest Denise, we have spent many happy hours together now, so many times I have thought what a wonderful girl you are, but pushed any further thoughts of a relationship behind me. I am so much older than you. You deserve to make your life with someone nearer your own age.'

She just smiled, a knowing smile it seemed.

'I have come to love you, that is all that matters to me. We get on so well and know each other's good and bad points as well as anybody.'

'You don't have any bad points. You are the most beautiful, caring and intelligent girl I know and you are everything I could wish for. I love you too, so very much.'

'We could get married with a great ceremony on the island, everyone would be so pleased.'

I leaned over and kissed her gently on the lips.

'Come upstairs and stay the night.' I whispered.

'I might, if you propose marriage to me.'

I walked over to a small drawer in my desk, took something out and quickly returned.

'A few minutes ago I wouldn't have dared to ask, but now as you can see I'm on both knees. Denise, my dear, will you marry me and spend your life with me? I will treasure you and make you as happy as I can. Please accept this curtain ring as a token of my love, it comes with a promise to get something prettier for your bramble-scratched but beautiful hand as soon as possible.'

She laughed. 'Yes, of course I will. I had no idea that you would have an engagement ring so ready for the occasion. You must have known. Now, what have you got for me upstairs?'

The First Interviewees

Angus: Experienced fisherman from west coast of Scotland, 40. Single. Offered his services complete with fishing boat.

Belinda: Musician, 25. Single. Inclined to be nervous. Initially friendly with Philip then Robert.

Bill & Helen: Bill, carpenter, 33. Partner Helen, 27. Two children: Richard 5, and Zoe 1. Bill spent one year in Australia where he met Helen. Helen was a shop assistant.

Bob & Susan: Bob, builder aged 43. Married to Susan, aged 40, artistically creative with furnishings etc. Three children: Jane 17, Sarah 15 and Paul 12. Jane eventually gained a place at Sheffield University to study medicine.

Brenda: Aged 18 wished to spend her 'Gap' year on the island before going to university but was not invited to join the group.

Dafydd & Gwyneth: Dafydd, butcher, aged 35. Married to Gwyneth, aged 32. Two children: Alison 8 and Mark 4.

Charles: Vet, 55. Divorced. Subsequently left the island after acrimonious dispute with the farmers.

Denise: Personal assistant, 28. Single, with a University education and great organisational abilities. Manager for Education, Food and Welfare etc. on the island.

Edith: Homemaker, 60. Single. Enterprising woman of dedication. Kitchen/canteen worker with Madge and Rene. Writing her autobiography.

Gerry & Doris: Gerry, farmer, 45. Married to Doris, 43. Two children: Patrick 22 and Theresa 19. Gerry, Manager for Agriculture Fisheries and Food. Doris, helper on the farm. Patrick, responsible for the fish farm. Theresa formerly worked in local tourist office, responsible for all of the island's tourism.

Giles: Company director, 46. Divorced. Offered £1 million with strings, then later as donation. Elected treasurer in second year. Built large house for himself.

Graham: Irish poet and author, 30. Nervous. Somewhat of a recluse and lived apart from everyone else on island for a while. Befriended by Nick.

Ian & Madge: Ian, self-employed farmer, 42. Robust, very fit and used to outdoor life. Inherited family farm in Scotland. Responsible for arable farming on the island, and sheep. Married to Madge, 39, kitchen/canteen worker.

James: Single, 21. Was unemployed. Kind-hearted and practical helper on island. Had child by Colleen.

Jock & Morag: Originally residents on island, both 55. Jock became storeman. Morag died having spent less than a year on the island.

John & Alice: John, engineer, 34. Manager of Engineering Services. Married to Alice, 32, former secretary; Ken's helper with filming on the island. Two children: Jonathan 12 and Trevor 10.

Kate: Secretary, 24. Single. Farm accountant and secretary on council. Friendly with Angus.

Ken: BBC TV producer, 41. Responsible for filming the islands' day-to-day affairs for TV series. Married to Jenny, 36, riding school co-manager with Lynda. Two children: Michael 13 and Kirsty 11.

Lynda: Model, 21. Single. Reliable. Assistant teacher in infants' school, organizer for all sport and evening classes, and the riding school with Jenny.

Matthew & Ruth: Matthew, doctor, 36. Married to Ruth, 30, trained nurse, Matthew's secretary and pharmacist. Two children: Andrew 6 and Nicola 4.

Miranda: Teacher, 32. Single. The island's first school teacher of 5–16-year-olds. Council member.

Nick: Unemployed, 22. Tearaway. Helpful in many areas and island's bus driver.

Nigel: City trader, 27. Single. Arrogant. No contact with him after interview – would not have asked him to the island.

Paddy & Rene: Old friends of Jim. Paddy, contractor, 42. Married to Rene, 38, kitchen/canteen worker. Two children: Colleen 17 and Shaun 14. Colleen came with her illegitimate baby Jim and had another boy by James, named Jason.

Philip: Solicitor, 44. Single. Musical. The island's first treasurer and friendly with Belinda. Departed after first year but continued to assist from London.

Robert: Worked in information technology, 25. Single. Responsible for all computer associated matters on the island. Friendly with Belinda, Colleen and others.

Terry & Kathy: Terry, 35, electrician. Assistant to John. Married to Kathy, 32, hairdresser. Three children: Allan 9, Sally 7 and Miranda 5.